PRAISE FOR LIZBETH LIPPERMAN

"It's a heart-pounding race right down to the end and a very satisfying ride."

— JONI SAUER-FOLGER, AUTHOR OF THE
RIVER BEND MYSTERY SERIES

"Brimming with intrigue and moral complexity, *Deadly Triangle* peels back the polished surface of wealth and power to reveal something far more dangerous underneath. A gripping mystery that keeps you guessing until the very end."

— KIT WITEK, AUTHOR OF *LITTLE GIRL X*

"*Deadly Triangle* is a chilling descent into corruption, betrayal, and deadly ambition. With mounting suspense and a truth that grows more dangerous by the page, Lipperman proves she knows exactly how to keep readers on edge."

— DANIELLA BLUE, AUTHOR OF *MATCH POINT*

"Explosive and razor-sharp, *Deadly Triangle* is a pulse-pounding mystery where every secret has a price—and someone is willing to kill to keep it buried. Lizbeth Lipperman masterfully blends high-stakes suspense with emotional depth and twists that hit like a gut punch."

— KARI LEE TOWNSEND, NATIONAL BESTSELLING AUTHOR OF *THE WISHVILLE MYSTERIES*.

DEADLY TRIANGLE

A **GARCIA GIRLS** MYSTERY

LIZBETH LIPPERMAN

OLIVERHEBERBOOKS

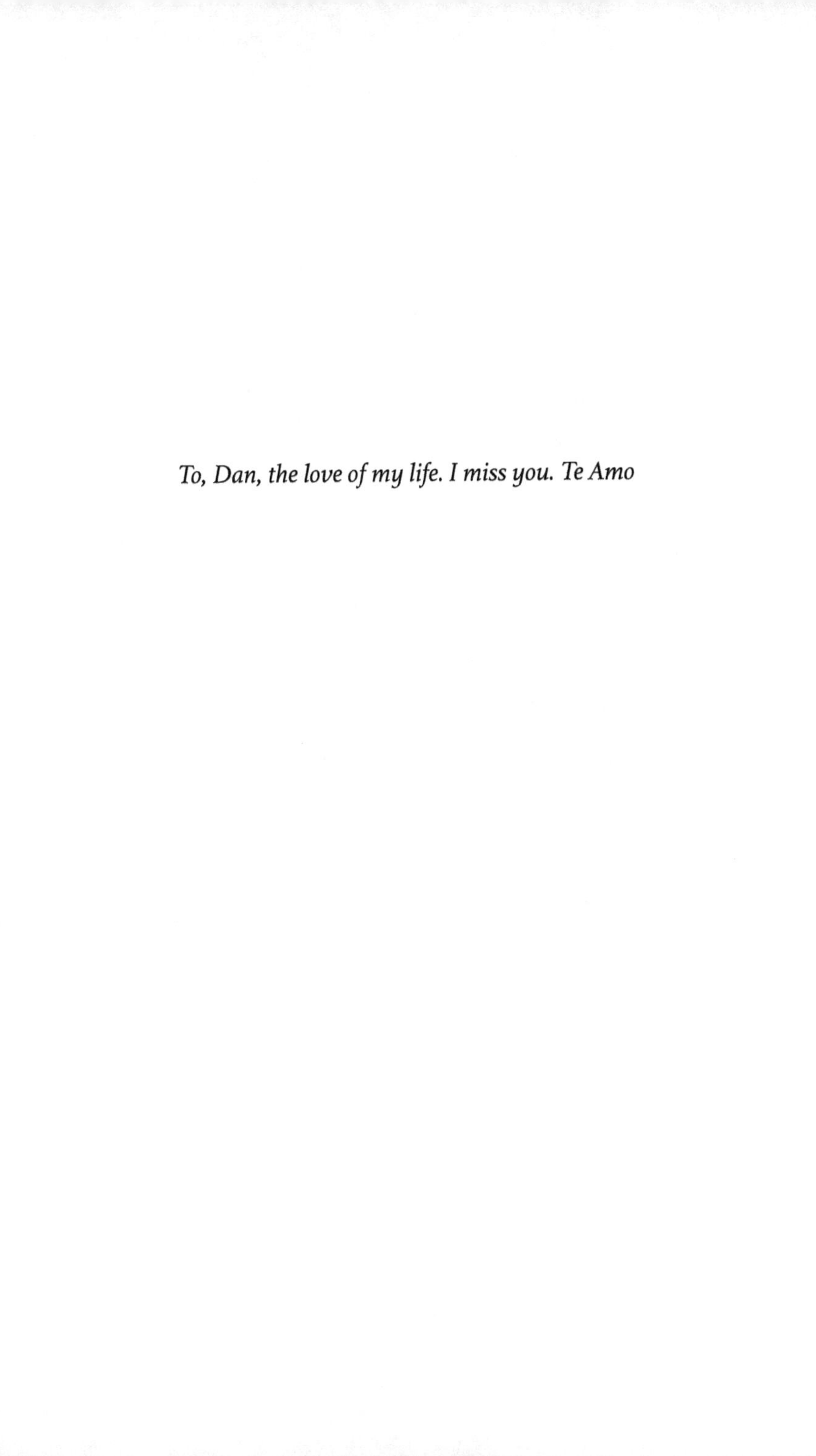

To, Dan, the love of my life. I miss you. Te Amo

1

———

"Put that down, or I swear to God, I'll drill you where you stand." Madelyn Garcia Castillo narrowed her eyes at her partner and touched the Glock strapped to her hip for emphasis. "I made a promise to Sara, and you and I both know how our lives will go if I break that promise and let you eat one of those."

Gary Mitchell kept his hand on the jelly donut while he stared her down. When she tightened her hand around the handle of the Glock, he dropped the pastry back into the box and glared at her. "You wouldn't really shoot me, would you?"

"Damn straight I would. It would be way more humane than watching you keel over from another heart attack. You keep forgetting how many needles they stuck you with in the ER last week." She took a step toward him, grabbed the box, and held it in the air. "These better be gone when we get back, or heads will roll," she bellowed to her fellow officers before dropping the box of pastries back on the desk and nudging Mitch toward the door. "Come on. We caught a case over on the east side. Looks like a murder/suicide."

"God, I hate those," he said, eyeing the donuts one last time as she pushed him toward the door. "And for the record, Maddy, it wasn't a heart attack. Doc said I had a bad case of 'post-burrito' syndrome. I don't know why Sara is making such a big deal about it."

"Oh, I don't know. Maybe because both your cholesterol and triglyceride levels are off the charts, big guy." She tsked. "And you could stand to lose that gut, too. Before long, people will be asking when the baby's due."

That brought a grin to his face. "Not if they want to live a long life," he deadpanned before getting serious. "So, let's try to make this a quickie. I promised Sara I'd take her to that new health food store that opened last week across town." He frowned. "Just what I need. The woman already has me eating like a damn rabbit."

Maddy smiled to herself. She and Gary Mitchell had become partners two years ago, right after she'd transitioned from the intake desk at the station to rookie cop. That was right around the time one of the older cops had dropped dead from a sudden heart attack, another reason why she was determined to keep her new partner healthy. She loved Mitch like the older brother she never had. He was a good cop who wasn't afraid of giving his all when he was on a case. Wasn't afraid of much, really, unless you counted his petite wife, who ruled the roost at home and kept him on his toes.

Vineyard had been extremely lucky to snag a guy like Mitch as he could have had his pick of any police station in the state. Since he'd been the head honcho at one of the largest police forces in Houston for so many years, he was a valuable commodity. Plus, Mitch had a stellar reputation for quickly putting the bad guys behind bars. The only reason he'd ended up in Vineyard was because of his wife. When Sara's oldest sister died of liver disease, her younger sister, Kelly, was unable to run the family real estate business by herself and begged Sara to come and help.

Apparently, it hadn't taken much to persuade her husband to pack up and move to the small town located north of DFW Airport. With no children or other family members in Houston, it had been an easy decision. Mitch even worked occasionally in the real estate office beside his wife and sister-in-law on his days off. Since he'd already had several episodes of stress-related chest pain that had sent him to the ER, his doctor had been trying for years to get him to take life slower. So, it had been a no-brainer for him. Impressed by his resume, Colt had offered him the job of Assistant Chief, but Mitch just wanted to be one of the guys, didn't want to feel compelled to take his job home. More importantly, he didn't want to be responsible for anyone but himself.

Ten years older than Maddy, Mitch could have pitched a fit when, as the newest employee of the Vineyard Police Department, he'd been partnered up with her on his first day on the job. The other cops at the station weren't too thrilled that the only female officer, who just happened to be the sister-in-law of their boss, Colt Winslow, had been given the coveted job of working under the guidance of a guy who had more experience under his belt than all of them combined. The fact that Maddy had been automatically upgraded from walking the beat and had passed her detective's exam after being tutored by Mitch had only caused the resentment toward her to rear its ugly head.

So, she'd worked hard those first few months after Mitch's arrival, drinking more beer than she should have and listening to seriously offensive jokes at the local cop watering hole in an all-out effort to be invited into their good-old–boys club. But it hadn't taken long for them to accept her, especially after Mitch made it crystal clear that he would kick their collective asses if they screwed with her. Now, two years later, her relationship with the young guys had developed into a sort of mutual admiration society.

Mitch had been patient with her, teaching her something new every day, and soon, her feelings for her new partner transformed into much more than just respect. Maddy considered both him and Sara as part of her family, especially since the only other family she had close by were her three sisters, who all lived in Vineyard. After their mother and stepdad had moved to Florida several years before, as the oldest daughter, she'd taken over the job of "mothering" to the Garcia girls, although it really wasn't a difficult job. They were all extremely close and had been best friends their entire lives. It hadn't taken long for a gruff, take-no-prisoners cop like Mitch to win them over as well. And now, he and Sara, along with Sara's sister Kelly, spent every holiday with the Garcia gang.

As Maddy climbed behind the wheel of the cruiser and waited for Mitch to slide into the passenger seat, her mind was already on her trip to Clayton the following week with her sisters. Clayton was a two-hour drive from Vineyard but well worth the trek as the entire city became one big flea market/craft show on the first weekend of every month. The last time Maddy had made the trip was over a year ago, and she was looking forward to spending time with her sisters, not to mention the great deals there. Although it was only the end of August, the Christmas stuff would already be on display, and she had every intention of blowing her budget and eating enough junk food to last a lifetime.

Turning on the cruiser's flashing lights, she headed toward the east side. Apparently, news of the murder had quickly spread around town, and most of the merchants on Main Street were lined up on the curb, waving as they passed. The last time Vineyard had seen anything this exciting was when old man Arnold had shot and killed his top two ranch hands after catching them stealing cows. Ordinarily, Texas law allowed for bodily force in such instances. However, before Arnold killed the two thieves, he'd held them captive in his house, torturing them until he got them to admit they'd sent his cattle to a slaughterhouse. Solving that one hadn't taken much effort since Arnold himself had announced to anyone in hearing distance, "I killed the sons-a-bitches, and I'd do it again if I had to." He'd worn his guilt like a purple heart up to the day they'd carted him off to Huntsville to serve a twenty-five to life sentence. Last Maddy had heard, he was still entertaining his cellmates with stories of how he'd killed the thieving "sons-a-bitches."

No, the people in Vineyard, population 20,900, were too busy with their own lives to bother with major crimes. Most of the men and three-fourths of the women made their living at Warner Chemicals—and had been there since graduating from high school. Warner Chemicals sat across the Red River in Rosemont, a small town just beyond the Texas/Oklahoma border and was the biggest supplier of fluoropolymers used to coat airplanes, water towers, and many other things nationwide. Although Warner Chemicals wasn't the only source of jobs in town, it was definitely the major one.

"Over there," Mitch said when they turned the corner onto Sheridan Road. "Crap! There's Sullivan," he added when they got closer to the two ambulances and three police cars lining the street.

"What's he doing here?" Maddy remarked. "This is Vineyard's jurisdiction, not Cordova's."

"I'm about to give that dickwad a geography lesson," Mitch said when Maddy parked the car across the street from the white one-story house, already cordoned off with yellow crime scene tape. There was bad blood between him and the Cordova cop, dating back to his first case on the border between the two cities. The situation had only gotten worse last year when Sullivan hit the winning home run off Mitch at the annual

Labor Day baseball game between cops and firemen of both cities.

Maddy opened the car door, got out, and started toward the row of police cars with Mitch right behind her. Walking up to Sergeant Larry Sullivan, she was about to ask why he was at their murder scene when Mitch stepped forward.

"Is it just me, or are you seriously directionally challenged?" Mitch got right in the other cop's face. "Since this is our side of the tracks, you and your boyfriend can take your fat asses and get back to your own house. My partner and I will take it from here."

Sullivan's face flared red before he gave a head nod to the younger cop beside him. "We got a call that one of the vics was from Cordova. Our mistake. But hey"—he threw his hands in the air in a gesture of surrender—"you can have this one. Working with a Navy cop isn't my idea of a good time. And by the way, hope you're pitching again this year." He turned and walked away before Mitch could think of a sarcastic comeback.

"Navy cop?" Maddy said out loud. "Thought this was a routine murder/suicide."

A young beat cop she recognized from the weekly Friday night happy hour crowd stepped forward and pulled out a notebook. "It was, but one of the vics has military ID in her purse, so we had to notify NCIS."

"Why the hell didn't you wait until we got here?" Mitch asked, taking out his anger over Sullivan's last remark on the patrolman. "You've probably just screwed up our case, kid."

Maddy gave him a disapproving glare before she patted the officer on the shoulder. "Don't mind him. He's got low blood sugar." She sent Mitch another hard look before turning her attention back to the young cop named Perez, according to his name tag. "So, do we know if they're sending someone?"

Perez frowned at Mitch before smiling at her. "An officer is already on the way from Fort Worth, and he says he has juris-diction."

"My ass!" Mitch bellowed. He nudged Maddy in the direction of the house. "Guess I have to dole out another geography lesson." He grabbed Maddy's arm. "Come on. Let's get in there before he shows up and contaminates our crime scene."

They walked up the steps, stopping only to grab shoe covers and latex gloves from the boxes left by the CSI technicians, already on the scene. After donning both, Maddy pushed the door open and was immediately hit by the smell of burnt toast. Wrinkling her nose, she walked into the hallway and glanced to her left, spotting the two bodies on the living room floor. Two crime scene techs were busy photographing and working the scene.

When they walked into the room, the tech bending over the female victim stood. "The housekeeper called 911 about 10:30 this morning. Looks like one shot to the middle of her forehead, probably from that .22 next to the deceased male."

"Are we still talking murder/suicide here?" Mitch asked, bending down to examine the woman's face.

"Hard to say. No defensive wounds on the hands, which tells me that First Lieutenant Linden probably knew her killer or was surprised. We'll know more when Lowell gets here and takes a better look at the rest of her body. Right now, it could go either way."

"First Lieutenant Linden?"

"According to the military ID we found in her purse."

"A .22 isn't normally the weapon of choice for a man this size," Maddy commented, pointing to the gun next to the male victim.

The tech shrugged. "Maybe it's hers."

Maddy inched closer to get a better look. The deceased female looked to be in her early thirties with short dark hair that was now clumped with blood and plastered to her olive-colored cheeks. Her right eye was swollen and almost completely closed from a large bruise above it. She turned her attention to her left where the body of the man lay sprawled. A river of blood beside his head made the blue rug appear purple. The back half of his head was blown away, and although Maddy had seen more than her fair share of suicides, her stomach still rolled when a gun to the mouth was used. The Beretta lay beside him. When the CSI tech turned the victim over, Maddy gasped. Both Mitch and the technician glanced at her.

"I know this man."

"Who is he?" Mitch asked.

Maddy shrugged. "Not sure of his name—David something or other—but he's some bigwig over at Warner Chemicals." She leaned in, and despite the damage done when he'd eaten his gun, she was positive her ID was correct.

Mitch looked up at the young cop standing in the doorway. "Do we have a name yet?"

Perez checked his notes. "The house belongs to a David Foster. Although we can't be one hundred percent sure until the medical examiner confirms, we've pulled the motor vehicle photo, and it looks like he's our vic."

Mitch turned back. "So, how do you know Mr. Foster?"

"If he's who I think he is, my sister Deena went out with him a few times. She introduced us one night a couple of weeks ago when I stopped by her apartment."

"So, why'd Mr. Foster kill a Naval officer and then turn the gun on himself?"

"That's what they pay you and me the big bucks to find out," Maddy said, noticing two tickets to a Dallas Mavericks game the coming weekend lying on the end table, along with confirmation for a suite at the Victory Park Hotel. "Looks like he had a big weekend planned," she said before motioning to the technician. "Bag these, Josh." She moved over to the female victim and bent down on the side opposite the CSI tech photographing the body.

She couldn't help noticing the wedding ring on the woman's finger and wondered if Foster and her sister were still an item, and if so, was he seeing a married woman on the side? "Where's her purse?"

Perez grabbed it from the countertop and brought it over. Other than the usual things women carried in their purses—lipstick, ibuprofen, tissues, breath mints, a tampon, etc.—the only other thing beside her wallet that stood out was a notepad. Maddy opened it to the first page where the words *David - 9 am* were written, along with the man's address. She opened the wallet. There were no pictures of kids or a husband, only one of her in a green flight suit standing next to a US Navy H3 Sea King helicopter and another of her with a man and a woman beside a different aircraft with CORDOVA HELICOPTERS in black letters on the side.

"What can you tell me so far about Lieutenant Linden, Maddy?" Mitch asked, standing over her.

"I know she worked for Cordova Helicopter Services and that she flew a Navy H3 Sea King once a month in the reserves."

"You got all that from two pictures?"

She cocked her head. "Even you can learn something from a woman, Mitch."

"Tell me something I don't already know. You've met my wife, right? I'm forever learning new stuff—especially that it's always a good move to smile and say 'yes, dear' to everything she says." He chuckled to himself. "So, what the hell is an H3?"

"Smart man with the 'yes dear' thing. To answer your question, the H3 is a twin engine, all-weather helicopter used by the Navy Reserves to track and destroy enemy submarines."

"Last I checked, there were no submarines in the area," he said with a grin.

She laughed. "You are such a dork. For your information, the H3 is also used for search and rescue missions."

"Since when did you become such an expert on Navy aircraft?"

"Since my dad started taking my sisters and me to the Naval station in Fort Worth when we were little."

"Forgot he was also in the reserves." Mitch looked down at the deceased woman. "How did you know what she did for a living?"

Maddy pointed to the picture of the victim with the two people and grinned. "She's in a flight suit. They're not, and the company name on the side of the helicopter is a pretty big giveaway."

"Let me see that." He grabbed the picture and held it close to his face. "If only I could read it."

Maddy bit back a grin. "Maybe it's time to get readers." Before he could respond, she held up the woman's driver's license. "I also know that she lived on the outskirts of Cordova and probably didn't have drinks with our suicide victim." She glanced at the two glasses on the coffee table. One was empty, but the other still had half a glass of what appeared to be white wine with a very distinctive red lipstick with shimmers of silver imprinted on the rim.

Maddy pointed first at the wine glasses, then back at the dead woman. She was no expert in the lipstick department, but any cop with half a brain could see that the light pink lipstick on the dead woman had not left the red imprint on the half-empty wineglass.

Mitch's eyes followed hers. "Someone else was here with Foster."

"Either that or these two had drinks, sex, and then she

changed her lipstick color afterwards." She reached for the woman's purse and pulled out the lone tube of lipstick. A quick check verified the pink color. "My guess—" Maddy stopped talking when she heard voices, followed by the front door closing.

After a moment, a man sauntered into the living room and glanced first at Mitch and then at her. Dressed in khaki slacks and a blue shirt, he stood over six feet tall, and although he was slender, there was no doubt that he knew his way around a gym.

"Special Agent Nicholas Ryan, NCIS," he announced before walking over to the female victim and bending down beside Maddy. "I'll take over with Lieutenant Linden now."

She almost didn't hear him as she was mesmerized by the blue-gray eyes accenting a chiseled face and dimpled cheeks that threatened to draw her in when he smiled at her. Reddish-brown hair contrasted perfectly with the creamy, ivory complexion, and she found herself thinking that he probably burned easily in the sun.

A second too late, she realized that he was now staring at her, waiting for her response. His gaze changed to a slight smile, as if her reaction was one that he was used to getting from every female who laid eyes on him for the first time.

She chastised herself for falling into that category and held out her hand. "I'm Detective Madelyn Castillo." She pointed to Mitch, who was glaring at the man by this time. "And this is my partner, Lieutenant Gary Mitchell. We'll be working lead on this case."

Although he still held the smile, his eyes turned dark. "You may be the lead on the deceased gentlemen over there, but I can assure you, the death of Lieutenant Pamela Linden falls on my shoulders."

Mitch moved closer to the Navy cop and took a few seconds to look him over. "While we appreciate the help, I'm afraid you've come all the way from Fort Worth for nothing, Mr. Ryan." He flicked his thumb toward the door. "This is Vineyard, and although we'll gladly keep your office updated on this case, both vics belong to us."

The other cop's expression never changed. "First of all, it's Special Agent Ryan, and secondly, I suggest you contact your chief." His voice remained calm. "And you might also want to catch up on the proper procedure for deaths involving military personnel." He turned his back on Mitch and leaned in to get a closer look at the female body.

When Mitch took a step toward Ryan, Maddy stopped him with her extended arm, motioning for him to move into the hall-way. After glaring at the back of the man's head for a few seconds, Mitch walked out of the room with her.

In the hallway, she leaned over and whispered in his ear. "Let's not get too bent out of shape here, Mitch. What's the harm in letting him have a look at the body? When we get back to the house, we'll find out if this guy's talking out of both sides of his mouth or if he really does have jurisdiction with the female vic. If he's wrong, I'll be the first to tell him to take his skinny ass back to Fort Worth. If he's not, we'll still work the case and let him believe we're sharing information with him."

Mitch narrowed his eyes and pondered that for a minute. "Unfortunately, I already know the answer, but it was worth a shot. You're probably right. At least he doesn't look like this is his first case, but if this military hack screws up one thing in this—"

"I'll keep my eye on him," Maddy interrupted, thinking to herself that it was a job she'd definitely enjoy, considering those gray-blue eyes and dimpled cheeks.

Ryan looked up when they walked back into the room. "Have you established who the other victim is?"

"David Foster," Maddy replied. "He's a bigshot at Warner Chemicals. It's possible he and Linden were lovers."

"I doubt that," Ryan replied. "Her lipstick doesn't match the red stain on the wine glass over there."

"Girls do change lipstick colors, you know," she said, more sarcastically than she'd intended. Since he was assigned to a low-profile base like Fort Worth, she'd pegged him as just a token investigator sent by the military. The fact that he'd noticed the difference in the lipsticks so quickly surprised her.

She moved closer to her partner, barely able to hear Ryan's low chuckle, and prayed to herself that her partner hadn't. Keeping the two men from going after each other over the next few days might prove to be more of a challenge than she could handle.

"This is true," he conceded. "And certainly, the sanctity of marriage never stopped some people from straying once in a while, but something to consider is that this woman was tied up at some point during her visit with Mr. Foster." He pointed to her wrists where ligature marks could be seen on both, faint but definitely there.

Mitch was intrigued by now and stood up before walking over, allowing the CSI techs to finish up with the male victim. "Kinky sex gone bad?"

Ryan shrugged. "Possibly, but if that were true, we'd undoubtedly see the same ligature marks on her legs." He reached down and shoved the bottom of the woman's black slacks up. "Clean."

Maddy waited until CSI finished with the deceased man before she bent down once again and checked his arms. Like Lieutenant Linden's, Foster's wrists showed the same faint marks. She glanced up at Mitch and nodded, then turned back to the body.

"He was tied up as well?" Ryan asked.

She inspected the dead man's ankles and was not surprised to find no evidence of ligatures. She didn't bother to respond to the Navy cop, and instead, addressed her partner. "Looks like things aren't what they seem." Turning back to the CSI tech, she said, "This is now the scene of a double homicide. I want everything bagged and tagged and taken back to the station." She glanced down at her watch. "Where's the ME?"

"On his way," one of the techs answered. "He was in Evansville pronouncing an elderly gentleman who died of an apparent stroke. Should be here in a few minutes."

Mitch was already checking out the rest of the living room, but nothing seemed out of the ordinary. Maddy followed him into the kitchen and immediately noticed the slice of burnt toast still in the toaster. "Obviously, he didn't have time for breakfast." She touched the cold coffee maker. "This hasn't even been turned on."

"There's an office off the main hallway with a laptop," Ryan said, coming up behind them unnoticed. "I'll need to have a look at that and everything you bag here today."

"After we get our hands on it," Mitch said, emphatically.

"I'm all right with that as long as you don't stall. I just spoke to my boss, and your chief has already contacted him. He's agreed to allow you to work alongside me in the investigation."

"Over my dead body," Mitch said. "As Maddy said, we're lead on this one, and we sure as hell don't need your help." He sent the Naval officer a look that would have brought a weaker man to his knees.

Ryan didn't even flinch. "Your Chief Winslow has set me up with a desk at the station. Whether I like it or not, we're partners."

Maddy couldn't resist making eye contact with him and was immediately sorry she had. The smoldering eyes were boring into her and now held the hint of mischief in them, like a young kid whose mother had just said he could tag along with an older brother.

"We'll have our own conversation with Chief Winslow," she said. "In the meantime, try not to get in our way, and we'll do the same with you. As long as you remember that all evidence comes to us first, we'll get along." She grabbed Mitch's arm and pulled him toward the hallway. "Come on. Let's check out the bedroom and see if Foster and the lady lieutenant partied last night."

On the way there, Mitch stopped her. "So, how are we going to do this? You play good cop, and I'll be the bad one to keep him off-balance?"

"Didn't we just try that?" She laughed. "We must be losing our touch, partner, letting a Navy cop find those ligature marks before we did."

"He caught us off guard," Mitch replied. "Another few seconds, and we would've picked up on that ourselves."

He opened the door to the bedroom and allowed Maddy to go in ahead of him. The first thing she noticed was that the room was immaculate. No man she knew ever made his bed or picked up his clothes before that first cup of coffee. Most of them lived with rumpled sheets until the next visit by the housekeeper. Either David Foster was a neatnik, or he hadn't slept in his bed the night before—or longer.

She walked over and opened the nightstand on the side where the alarm clock glared 11:31 in bright red. There was a flashlight, several unopened condom packets, and a bottle of prescription muscle relaxers she herself had taken a few years ago after an on-the-job back injury. On a hunch, she yanked the drawer out further and spied a 9-millimeter handgun in the back.

With a gloved hand, she pulled it out and held it up for Mitch to see. "If this is Foster's gun, whose .22 is next to his body?"

2

———

Before her partner could answer about the gun, Maddy's cell phone rang. She glanced at caller ID, ready to ignore it. But after seeing who it was, she immediately answered. "Madelyn Castillo."

"Ms. Castillo, this is Martin Warner." He paused before adding. "I'm the CEO at Warner Chemicals. I commissioned your sister Deena to upgrade our lobby and all the executive offices at the compound. She's already completed the lobby—a fantastic job, by the way—and she was supposed to be coming in this morning to give the executives some ideas for their offices. I've been trying to locate her all morning to no avail. We have an important meeting with the board members this afternoon at two, and she's got the entire power point presentation on her laptop. I need to go over a couple of things with her before then."

"What makes you think I'd know where she is?"

"She's listed you as her emergency contact. We were hoping—"

"Look, Mr. Warner, I have no idea where my sister is. I'd suggest you keep trying." She walked into the hallway for more privacy. "Sometimes, she forgets to charge her phone. I'm sure she's on her way in if she has a meeting scheduled." She wondered if news of the death of one of their employees had reached him yet. In a city as small as Vineyard, it was hard to keep anything secret for long.

"I'm sorry to bother you, but I am getting a little worried. She mentioned she needed a few hours this morning for something personal, but she assured me she'd be in around 11 or 11:30. If you talk to her, could you ask her to give me a call? I hate to sound desperate, but this is an important meeting."

"I will, and if you talk to her first, tell her to call me right away as well." Maddy hung up and stood there for a few seconds as a current of anxiety pulsed through her. She took a few deep breaths to calm herself.

But she knew something wasn't right. Although Deena wasn't a party animal, she'd been known to frequent Wild Stallion Saloon, a popular honky-tonk on the west side of town. The club had a reputation for serving the best damn ribs in the county and a dance floor that could hold half the people in the town two-stepping the night away—and usually did.

But Deena had worked hard after her husband's death, gone back to school to get her designing credentials, and quickly made her way up to being the go-to-girl if you needed classy upgrades. She'd been so excited when she'd landed the Warner Chemicals job, seeing it as one of the best advertisements she could get without forking out advertising dollars. No way she'd risk putting it in jeopardy for any reason.

Maddy quickly dialed her number only to be sent to voice mail on the first ring. She left a short message and walked back into the bedroom where Mitch was directing the CSI tech to the garbage can where he pointed to a used condom.

He looked up at Maddy and grinned. "So, Foster clearly got it on at some point with someone."

She tried to smile back but her mind was on her sister. Where was she, and why wasn't she answering her phone?

Dear God, Maddy. What have you gone and done now?

Maddy whirled around and came face to face with her sister Tessa who was standing behind Mitch and glaring at her.

Her *dead* sister Tessa.

The look on her face caused her partner to rush over and ask. "Maddy? Are you all right?"

She took a few seconds to compose herself as Tessa leaned against the wall and grinned.

Go ahead. Tell him about me. Watch how fast he drags your butt off to the funny farm.

Maddy took a deep breath and exhaled slowly. "Got a little dizzy, Only had a bite of a muffin this morning before hitting the ground running. Barely got Jessie out the door for her band camp trip. Guess my blood sugar is as low as yours," she said with a grin.

No way would she tell him the story about how Tessa had been murdered four years before and had reappeared from the other side to beg Maddy and her other sisters to solve her murder. Eventually, they had, despite the fact that the entire community of Vineyard had probable cause to see the woman dead. Of the five sisters, Tessa was smack-dab in the middle. With Maddy and Deena growing up as best friends and Lainey and Kate also best friends, Tessa had always been the loner and had fought with all of them their entire lives. Although she was the most attractive and ambitious of all the Garcia sisters, Tessa had only been nice to anyone she could use or manipulate. The only really good thing she'd ever done was to give birth to her beautiful daughter, Gracie, who was now being raised by the child's father, her boss at the police station, and her stepmother, Maddy's sister Lainey.

When Mitch turned away from her, Maddy shot her dead

sister a squinted eye look and shrugged her shoulders. From experience, she knew that Tessa only showed up when one of her siblings was in trouble and was only seen and heard by the one in danger.

So, why was she here now? Maddy's life was going great, despite the fact that her long-distance, two-year relationship with Jake Matthews was on hold at the present time.

"Find anything else in the drawer?" Mitch asked, still eyeballing her with concern.

"No, let's move on to the dresser."

Maddy started toward the dresser with Mitch alongside her. Tessa had to press herself against the wall to let him get by.

This one's a chunker, she said, wrinkling her nose at Mitch. **Not sure how much help he'd be keeping up with you on a foot race with a perp.**

Maddy ignored her and began rummaging through the drawers, wondering if they'd find blood spatter anywhere. But they didn't. And other than the wrinkled clothes and an expensive watch hidden behind one of the books on Foster's bookshelf, nothing gave them even the slightest clue as to why someone would want both the man and his possible lover dead. After an hour of searching with very little to show for it, the CSI techs had everything that could possibly be a clue in evidence bags, and the bodies were enroute to the morgue. Unfortunately, they were no closer to finding answers than when they'd first arrived on the scene.

Nothing looked out of place. No overturned furniture or anything to indicate the victims had put up a fight. There was a sixty-two-inch flat screen TV nestled in a mahogany entertainment center in the living room along with several pieces of sophisticated surround sound equipment. Foster's wallet was found in a drawer in the bedroom containing a little over two hundred in cash and several credit cards. Although Linden only had sixty dollars in hers, she was wearing a diamond necklace that had to be worth a few bucks. They felt comfortable ruling out robbery as a motive for now, and with no signs of forced entry, the working theory was that at least one of the victims knew the killer or killers.

With very little physical evidence, Maddy contemplated if this could have been a professional hit. But why?

After spending the better part of the day at Foster's house, Maddy glanced down at her watch, thinking about the earlier call from the CEO at Warner Chemicals. It was after four. Surely, the presentation was over by now.

After excusing herself, she walked toward the front of the house, out of hearing distance. Quickly, she dialed her sister's number, but again, there was no answer. Finding Martin Warner's number on her phone, she called him, only to find out that Deena had missed the meeting and still hadn't checked in. He wasn't real happy about it, either.

What was that all about? Why did you call him about Deena?

Maddy lowered her eyes, trying to decide whether or not to tell Tessa. In the end, she realized that there was no point withholding that information. Deena was just as much her sister as she was Maddy's.

"Deena's missing."

Missing as in she took a weekend trip or missing like... Oh God, I've been sent back for her, not for you, unless you're in trouble as well.

Hearing her dead sister verbalize what had already popped into her mind was like a blow to Maddy's chest. The powers that be up above only sent Tessa when there was real trouble, and in the past, trouble always meant imminent danger to the sister in trouble.

"I..." Maddy looked away. "I honestly don't know. I think

everything in my life is going good, but I also thought that the last time you showed up for me, and then I was accused of murdering that man in his jail cell." She blew out a noisy breath and turned around. "I have to get back to my partner, or he'll be suspicious."

Walking back into the bedroom, she turned to him. "You got a handle on things here, Mitch?" When he looked confused, she added, "I want to run by Deena's house for a minute. I'll catch up with you back at the station to start the paperwork."

He eyed her suspiciously. "What's up with your sister?"

She knew it was useless to pretend it was nothing. Mitch knew her almost better than she knew herself and would see right through her lie. "That was the head honcho at Warner Chemicals on the phone earlier. Apparently, Deena was in charge of some big presentation this afternoon and didn't show up. I called him back a few minutes ago. Not only did she miss the meeting, but he still hasn't heard from her to find out why."

"That doesn't sound like Deena." He stepped closer and lowered his voice when Special Agent Ryan walked into the room. "You talk to her about it?"

Maddy shook her head. "My calls go straight to voicemail. I'm trying not to worry, knowing how OCD my sister is, but lately, she'd been hanging around with a couple of single women at the apartment complex where she lives. From what she's told me, those girls know how to party, and I wouldn't be surprised if we find out she shacked up with some cowboy after she left the bar last night and never made it to her workplace." As soon as the words left her mouth, she was immediately sorry and wished she could take them back. She knew it was just her frustration talking, and her sister deserved better. She took a deep breath and met Mitch's intense stare. "I'm worried. Why isn't she returning my calls?"

He patted her shoulder. "Your sister may be a little reckless sometimes, but she's built out of the same stuff you are. Wherever she is, she's okay."

She knew he was trying to convince himself as much as her. "I know you're right, but I'll feel better when I can talk to her myself. Can you catch a ride back to the station with Perez or one of the other uniforms?"

He nodded. "Call me if you need me."

She tried to smile. "I've probably seen too many cop shows. This is Vineyard, for God sakes, not Dallas."

Somewhere between walking to her car and sliding into the driver's seat, Tessa must have disappeared as there was no sign of her. Maddy waved out the window at Mitch who was still eyeing her up, trying to figure out if she was telling him the entire truth. She thought about turning on the siren but decided that was a little dramatic since her sister only lived five miles away. Still, she couldn't stop the uneasy feeling that consumed her. Halfway there, she reached for her phone and called her mom in case Deena had talked with her that morning. Waiting for her to pick up, she tapped her fingers nervously on the steering wheel. When she was directed to voicemail, she hung up without leaving a message. No sense worrying her mom right now.

The churning in her gut intensified as she pulled up in front of Vineyard Gardens, an upscale apartment complex in the better part of town. Deena had sweet-talked the owner into giving her a discounted rate for a two-bedroom apartment if she'd spruce up the place for him. The front of the building, the lobby, and the greenery and flowers around the front that Deena had chosen with the yard guy probably brought in a much higher rent from any new tenants.

For sure, the owner had gotten his money's worth.

On the elevator up to the eighth floor, images of what she might find raced through her mind before she was able to stop them. Was it just coincidence or did her sister's sudden disappearance have anything to do with her sometimes-lover and a US Navy pilot, both of whom would soon be on their way to the county morgue after being shot execution style?

She chased those thoughts away. She was here as a sister checking up on her sibling, not as a cop. When she found her asleep in her bed still groggy from a night of partying, there would be hell to pay for causing all the anxiety.

Getting off the elevator, she headed to her sister's apartment and was surprised to find a man lurking outside. The minute he spied her, he turned and hightailed it down the hall before disappearing down the stairwell. Her first instinct was to chase him and find out what he was doing there, but she was too concerned for her sister right now to waste time on something that might have only been coincidental.

"Where in God's name are you?" she mumbled to herself as she used the key her sister had given her. "Deena?" When there was no response, she hesitated momentarily. Something about the eerie silence compelled her to touch the service weapon strapped to her hip before she walked in—more out of habit than anything else.

A quick check of the apartment confirmed it was empty. She relaxed her grip on her weapon and walked from room to room looking for anything that might help her figure out where her sister had gone. Deena had always been a little OCD about neatness, and her apartment was no different. It looked like the housekeeper had blown through the place that morning, but Maddy knew that wasn't the case. No cleaning service out there would ever meet Deena's standards, and because of that, her sister did all her own housework.

Maddy smiled to herself, thinking how Deena would react if she walked into her own house across town. The unmade bed, last night's dishes in the sink, and the Pizza Hut box still on the living room table with a couple of empty beer bottles would have freaked Deena out. She'd once called Maddy a slob when they were forced to share a room temporarily as teenagers after their aunt came for an extended visit. Maddy was pretty sure her perfect sister would use a stronger word to describe her now.

After a search for Deena's laptop turned up empty, Maddy couldn't decide if this was a big deal or not. Who took their laptop on a hot date? Then again, Deena was somewhat of an odd duck. She rarely left the device out of her sight. If she'd planned on hooking up with Foster the night before as she suspected, it made perfect sense that she would have taken her computer with her to the bar, knowing that she had the presentation in the morning.

She found a phone number scribbled on a notepad on the hall table. Pulling her cell phone out of her pocket, she dialed with the hope that whoever answered would be able to shed some light on Deena's whereabouts. When it went to a generic voicemail, she hung up. She'd run a check on the number when she got back to the station. Ripping off the top page from the pad, she grabbed a pen from the drawer and left a note for her sister to call the minute she walked in the door.

On the way back to the station, she phoned Mitch and asked him to ping Deena's cellphone to see if they could pinpoint a location. As an afterthought, she requested an APB on her sister's Jeep Cherokee, knowing it would scare the bejesus out of her when a cop pulled her over and questioned her. But right now, Maddy didn't care.

She thought about calling her mother again to let her know what was going on but decided to wait a little longer. Carolyn Garcia had gone through a rough period after their dad passed away from injuries sustained in a car accident several years before. She'd withdrawn from life and rarely left the house until her kids talked her into volunteering at the local no-kill animal shelter across town three years ago. There, she'd met Charles Andrews and fought hard not to fall for him when he'd relentlessly pursued her. But Andrews, the vet at the shelter, eventually wore her down until she agreed to go on a date with him. It hadn't taken long for her to realize that there was still a lot of life to live, and a year later, she agreed to be his wife. The smile on her face on her wedding day had brought tears to Maddy and her sisters as they could see how happy she was. It didn't hurt that they all adored Chuck.

Shortly after the wedding, the couple agreed that life was indeed too short. Chuck closed down shop, and he and his bride moved to a retirement community in Florida where they were having the time of their lives. Unless she absolutely had to, there was no way Maddy was going to worry her about her daughter's possible disappearance. It was probably nothing, anyway.

As that thought ran through her head, she said a quick prayer that Deena would show up soon, excited about some new romantic interest she'd met the night before. Of course, Maddy was going to kill her—right after she hugged her.

3

The moment Maddy walked into the precinct, she could tell by the way her coworkers stared at her that something was up.

Mitch met her when she was halfway across the room. "That Navy hack is going to be a major pain in my ass," he said, cocking his head in the direction of her desk.

She followed his eyes and spotted Special Agent Nicholas Ryan sitting at the desk directly across from hers, concentrating on the computer screen in front of him.

"Oh, hell no," she said loud enough for everyone in the room to hear. "Where's Landers?"

"Seems your brother-in-law moved him to the desk by the wall," Mitch said before nodding his head in the direction of the chief's office.

"No way. Is Colt in there now?"

Mitch pointed to Chief Winslow's office. "Nothing you say will matter, partner. Trust me when I tell you that I've tried it all. Apparently, the boss is acting on specific orders from NCIS headquarters."

"I don't care whose orders he's acting on. I'm not sitting

across from that man." She glanced toward Ryan. Even though she knew everyone in the room had heard the conversation between her and her partner, the NCIS agent continued to scroll through what looked like legal documents as if he were deaf.

"I'm not crazy about this arrangement, either, Castillo," Ryan said, finally looking up at her. "Unfortunately, since I'm not a hundred percent convinced that you and Mitch here will be forthcoming about what you discover in the investigation, it seems to be necessary. With me so close to both of you, it'll be that much harder to withhold evidence—like I heard you mention to him in the hallway back at the crime scene."

"You were eavesdropping?" She glared at him now.

His eyes twinkled with mischief. "What can I say? I'm a good cop."

She slammed the keys to the cruiser onto the desk and flopped down into her chair. "Yeah, a legend in your own mind. So, tell me, Mister Good Cop, what have you found out so far?"

He bit his lip, obviously holding back a grin. "Did you know that even though Lieutenant Linden was wearing a wedding band, she'd recently divorced her husband?"

Maddy huffed and cursed herself for letting him see that he'd pushed her buttons. "Some women do that to keep obnoxious men from hitting on them. But you probably already know this from personal experience."

She heard Mitch snicker behind her, but Ryan's facial expression never changed. "If women only realized that most of the obnoxious men hitting on them consider a wedding ring as good as a winning lottery ticket, they might not be so anxious to keep those gold bands on their fingers. Think about it. No pressure to spend quality time with them outside the bedroom, no whining about walking down the aisle, and no begging for babies. Just afternoon sex with no strings attached. It's a win-win." He met her gaze head on. "That being said, it might interest you to know that Carl Linden fought hard to keep his marriage intact. At one point, Pamela even had to get a restraining order on him."

She tried not to look impressed that he'd dug up that much information so quickly. "And do we have an address on Mr. Linden?"

He stood up. "We do. If you and your partner want to tag along, I was just about to pay the man a visit."

Before she could fire back a sarcastic remark, he was halfway to the door. She glanced toward Mitch, but he was already heading that way himself. Grabbing the keys off her desk, she had to hightail it to catch up to them.

Slow down, Maddy, Tessa said as she suddenly appeared and began running behind her sister. **No way in hell I'm missing out on this one with Chunky Monkey here, and to coin a phrase from Gray's Anatomy, Agent McDreamy. Please tell me you're hitting that Irish dreamboat.**

NICK FORCED himself not to look back to see if Maddy was behind him. He would've loved to keep the banter going, but he had a job to do—and that was to get justice for one of his own. Pamela Linden deserved that much. And even though the back and forth with the feisty Hispanic cop was more enjoyable than he wanted to admit, he had no intention of taking it any further than the precinct.

Settled in his unmarked police car, he programmed Carl Linden's address into his GPS. Linden lived in the neighboring town of Cordova, and according to the directions on his dashboard screen, fifteen miles to the south. As he drove through downtown Cordova, he was reminded of the small East Texas town where he grew up. He missed Leroy, Texas, missed the way the people seemed more like family than neighbors, looking after each other in times of trouble. Even missed the way everyone knew your name, where you went to church, and most of what went on in your private life. Although, that part could get a little annoying at times.

Pain gripped his heart like a vise as he remembered how the entire town had rallied around him at the funeral. Not too long after that, he'd requested a transfer to Fort Worth, unable to handle the grief he felt every time something reminded him of her—and almost everything did.

Sharon. He still couldn't say her name out loud without choking up, even though it had been almost two years since life as he'd known it had taken a radical downward spiral. He remembered that day like it was yesterday. She'd waited until they were doing the dishes before telling him she'd found a lump in her right breast. Days later when the doctor walked into the examination room, his face awash with empathy, Nick had known immediately that the news wouldn't be good.

But neither of them were prepared for the Stage IV breast cancer diagnosis that left them in shock for over a week. Even worse was finding out that Sharon had known about the lump months before she told him but let herself believe if she ignored it, it would go away.

How could she have been so naïve? With her type of aggressive cancer, maybe that extra time could have made a difference. Maybe he wouldn't have had to bury her just six months to the day after her first chemotherapy treatment.

And maybe he would still be able to lie in her arms at night after a particularly hard day on the job and listen to her assurances that the next day would be better. They'd just begun to talk about starting a family as well. Maybe if...

He slammed his hand on the steering wheel, then recoiled as the pain shot up to his elbow. *Dammit!* He had to quit wondering about all the maybes and what-ifs. There was no going back in time to make things right. He couldn't resurrect his high school sweetheart, and the sooner he got that through his thick skull and moved on, the better.

He was jarred from his devastating walk down memory lane by the melodic voice coming from his dashboard telling him to turn right in half a mile. After rounding the corner, Lola, as he called his GPS voice, announced that the address was on the right. Even before he saw the small gray house halfway up the street lined with huge oak trees, he noticed the cruiser parked out front. As a courtesy, he'd called ahead to the Cordova Police Department to let them know he was on his way to interview a person of interest in their jurisdiction. He'd requested that one of their officers meet him at Carl Linden's house.

Hopefully, the Cordova cop had been smart enough to wait for them to arrive before approaching Linden. If he hadn't, that meant the man would have had time to come up with well-thought-out responses. There was so much information to be had from a person's face when you caught them off guard. It would be a shame to lose that valuable interrogation tool.

He pulled up behind the other cruiser and waited for Castillo and Mitchell to follow suit.

The Cordova cop got out of his vehicle just as they approached.

Nick held out his hand. "NCIS Special Agent Nicholas Ryan." He hooked his thumb toward the others. "And these are detectives Castillo and—"

"I know who they are," the cop interrupted, extending his hand only to Nick. "Sergeant Larry Sullivan. I took the liberty of running a background check on Linden. Just a couple of drunk and disorderly arrests, none of which were prosecuted. He sobered up in jail on both occasions and paid a fine. There was, however, a domestic abuse allegation by his ex-wife, but that one never went to trial, either. It seems he'd had a little too much to drink one night and pushed her around. She refused to press charges, though."

"That the one that led to her taking out a restraining order?" Mitch asked, stepping forward.

Sullivan ignored him and spoke only to Nick. "I was about to mention that before I was interrupted. The man's not allowed within a hundred yards of her or her house." He paused. "There was no mention of her being in the Navy."

"Reserves," Nick corrected, before turning to walk up the steps. His own sheet on Carl Linden was on his desk back at the station. He'd had to bite his tongue to keep from mentioning to Sullivan that they were all cops with most of the same resources. However, he'd noticed the animosity between the Cordova cop and his two "new" partners right off the bat. Good sense told him not to antagonize the man himself if he wanted him to cooperate. Let the guy believe he'd done them a favor. "Let's see what Mr. Linden has to say about all of this."

The house was in desperate need of a coat of paint, and the steps to the porch were loose. He reached back to grab Castillo's hand when she stumbled but retracted it quickly when she gave him a look that said, "Don't even think about it."

After opening the screen door, he knocked several times before someone finally came to the door. Nick nearly had a heart attack when they were greeted by a big, ugly dog, who barked loud enough to be heard back at the precinct. He closed the screen door without a second to spare as the mutt jumped up against it and it bowed alarmingly.

"Luke! Dammit, boy. Go lay down." The big canine stopped barking immediately and wandered out of sight.

That's when they got their first look at Carl Linden. About five-eleven, the overweight man with a prominent gut looked like he'd just crawled out of bed, even though it was already close to six in the evening. With dull brown hair that probably hadn't seen a comb in days and puffy eyes to match, he filled the entrance. "What do you want?"

After making introductions all around, Nick said, "We need a few minutes of your time to ask you a couple of questions about your ex-wife."

Linden looked annoyed. "I swear I wasn't anywhere near her last night," he snapped.

"Can we come in?"

The man hesitated momentarily, and for an instant Nick thought he would refuse. Then he swung the door wider and allowed them to enter.

"Don't let my dog get past you. A couple of snot-nosed teenagers think this street is a racetrack. I have to be careful about letting him out front."

When they were seated in the living room on a faded brown couch, Linden sat down in the matching chair and scrubbed his hands down his face. "Okay, maybe I was in my car outside her house last night, but I never got closer than a hundred yards."

"She know you were there?" Maddy asked, staring intently at Linden's face as if the answer would magically appear on his cheeks.

He nodded. "I saw her in the window before she closed the shades."

"Why were you outside her house, Mr. Linden?" she continued.

He lowered his head briefly before meeting her gaze. "Why was I always there? To try to get her to listen to me. I said a few things after our divorce that I wanted to take back, but she wouldn't even give me ten lousy minutes of her time."

Maddy leaned forward and glared at him. "And when she wouldn't talk to you, did that piss you off?"

"Damn right it did. It wasn't my fault even though she always claimed it was. I needed her to know that."

"What wasn't your fault?" Nick asked, making eye contact with Maddy and nodding. She'd just managed to get him to open up with only a few direct questions. He was impressed.

"The miscarriages. She blamed them on my drinking, and for a long time I carried that guilt around with me. But I've been researching it on the Internet. I wanted her to know that once she lost the first baby, her chances of losing another increased with each pregnancy. I needed to talk to her about trying something called a surrogate pregnancy." He shook his head. "She wouldn't even hear me out. All I wanted was a few minutes of her time."

"What time did you leave?" Nick asked, deciding to get right to the chase.

His head popped up. "Why?"

"Just answer the question," Mitchell instructed.

He glanced first at Maddy and then back to Ryan. "I don't know. When she wouldn't talk to me, I drove home and might've had a few too many."

"Might've had?" Nick leaned in, then backed away when the sickening smell of old alcohol, mixed with a bad case of halitosis, hit him full force. The man had clearly picked up where he'd left off the night before. "Can anyone verify that you were here all night?"

"Only Luke over there." He pointed at the mutt who was asleep in the corner. "Why is that important?"

"And what about this morning? Have your seen your ex or talked to her?"

He shook his head. "I woke up with a migraine and took one of the strong pills the doctor gave me a few months back. Must've fallen asleep."

"Do you own a .22?" Mitchell asked.

Linden nodded. "A Baretta. Bought it for Pammie a few years back for protection, but she preferred her own gun."

"And what gun was that?"

He sniffed. "Some kind of shotgun."

"Can we see that .22?"

Linden got up from the chair and walked over to the cabinet against the wall with Nick right behind him. He pulled out the center drawer, and after fumbling around for a minute, he shrugged. "I'm sure I put it here before she moved out."

"When's the last time you saw it?"

"Hell, I haven't actually seen it since I cleaned it about a year ago." He turned to Nick. "You're going to have to tell me why you're asking all these questions, Officer, before I say anything else."

"So, you haven't spoken to your ex-wife at all today?"

"I already told you that. What the hell is going on? Did she say I violated the protection order? Because if she did, she's lying right through her teeth."

Nick looked toward Mitchell and Castillo, then turned back to Linden. "I'm sorry to have to tell you this, but Pamela Linden was murdered this morning." He watched as Linden's face registered disbelief before his eyes filled with tears.

"You must be mistaken. Who would want to kill Pammie? Everyone loved her," he choked out between sobs.

"I'm sorry for your loss," Castillo said right before her cell phone buzzed. She stood and walked over to the front door. "Excuse me for a minute." She opened the door and stepped out onto the porch.

"There is no mistake, Carl. And I have to tell you that she and another man were killed with a .22 Beretta, just like the one that's conveniently missing from your drawer." Nick pulled out his cell phone and called the precinct to start the ball rolling on getting a search warrant.

Linden scowled and pointed a finger at Nick. "Now wait just a damn minute. I loved that woman, and I know she loved me, too. She even left me her old computer so that I could have a copy of our wedding pictures, but she forgot to tell me how to turn the damn thing on." He stood up and pointed to the laptop on the table. When Mitchell pushed him back down in the chair, he took a deep breath. "Who was the man she was with?"

"David Foster," Nick responded. "Do you recognize the name?"

He shook his head, grabbed a tissue from the coffee table, and dabbed at his nose. "Never heard of him, but then my Pammie hasn't shared any details of her personal life with me in a while. Probably someone she met on the job or at the cowboy bar where she likes to drink every weekend." His reddened eyes narrowed. "And she calls me the alcoholic."

Nick eyed him. "I don't think I have to tell you not to leave town, do I, Mr. Linden? I'm sure we'll need to have another conversation after the police are through searching your house."

"Do you want me to stay with him until we get that warrant since it will be our guys executing it?" Sullivan asked.

Nick nodded. "I'd appreciate that. And if you could let us know if you find anything that might help our investigation, I'd appreciate that as well."

Outside, he walked to his car, his mind on the case when he noticed Mitchell and Castillo huddled close to their cruiser, whispering. Worried that they were discussing evidence with no intention of sharing with him, he approached them. "So what'd you think about Linden?"

Castillo looked surprised by the question. "My gut tells me he's just a guy still in love with his ex and trying to figure out a way to get her back." She looked away, but not before he noticed the concern in her eyes.

"Everything okay, Castillo?"

"Fine," she said, way too quickly.

He saw the look that passed between her and her partner. "I thought we'd agreed there'd be no secrets in this investigation. It hasn't even been a full day, and I can already tell that you're holding out on me."

She looked away for a second before facing him. "The phone call I got a few minutes ago was from Chief Winslow. He wanted to let me know that my sister's car was found on the outskirts of town."

"Why would he call you personally to tell you that? Was her car stolen?"

She glanced up at her partner, and when he nodded, she continued. "My sister Deena has been missing since this morning—or at least that's the first time anyone noticed."

Nick's voice softened. "I'm sorry. If there's anything I can do to help, let—"

"Colt also said the fingerprints lifted from the wineglass with the red lipstick stain came back, and they're not Pamela Linden's." She paused and bit her lip, again looking toward her partner. "They're a perfect match to my sister."

And that's why I was sent back here, Tessa said, suddenly appearing at her side. **Hope I'm not too late.**

4

"Why are her prints on file?" Ryan asked just as Sergeant Sullivan approached them. He turned and gave the man a disapproving look. "I thought I made myself clear in there. I need you to stay close to Linden until the officers arrive with a search warrant. You can't let him out of your sight."

"Any rookie cop knows that, Sullivan," Mitch said with a smirk. "Linden's probably hiding evidence as we speak."

Sullivan's face turned the color of a rare steak before he spun around and sprinted back to the house.

"That idiot would forget his head if it wasn't attached," Mitch said, a half-grin on his face as he watched the Cordova cop charging up the steps two at a time to get back to Linden.

"Guess you don't see many homicides around here," Ryan commented without changing his expression.

"Nope. You gotta love small towns. You don't need a search warrant when someone complains about the neighbor's dog killing the chickens." Mitch turned to face Maddy. "Before you go getting all upset over Deena's prints on the wineglass, keep in mind that she had a thing with Foster. You told me that yourself, remember?"

"Your sister knew the victim?" Ryan's expression turned serious. "Shouldn't you have divulged that information back at the crime scene, and at the very least, excused yourself from this investigation?"

Maddy stared at him, unsure of how to respond, when Mitch got in his face. "Look, Ryan, this is not Fort Worth. Everyone knows everybody. Geez, if we had to excuse ourselves every time we came up against a familiar face, nothing would ever get solved around here." He stepped closer to Maddy and squeezed her shoulder. "Besides, she told us the minute she recognized Foster as a friend of her sister's. It's not her fault you were late getting to the party."

She shot her partner a look of gratitude, before focusing back on Ryan. "As to your earlier question about why my sister's fingerprints are on file, she's an interior decorator. When she was hired to renovate the downtown courthouse, one of the requirements for anyone who works in the building is to get printed the first day on the job."

Ryan's facial expression turned pensive, as if allowing that to sink in. "So, your sister's a decorator? Does she have a gun that you know of?"

Maddy shot him a look designed to kill. "No, she does not have a gun. My sister has a hard time killing spiders. Scoops them up in a paper towel and lets them loose in the front yard of her apartment." She paused to send him another go-to-hell look. "Right now, she's missing, and her prints are all over the wineglass at her dead friend's house. So, if you'll excuse me, I have to meet a couple of the guys at her apartment while they execute a search warrant there, too." Not waiting to hear his response, she swung around and headed to the cruiser.

"Wait up, Maddy. I'll go with you," Mitch said, the beads of sweat already forming on his brow from rushing to catch up to her.

"You, my friend, need to come with me to the gym sometimes," she said before nodding. "I appreciate the offer, but I know you promised Sara you'd go with her to that health food store tonight."

He rolled his eyes. "You're kidding me, right? I'd rather walk on a bed of nails than spend even a minute in that place while my wife comments on every stupid label. It's bad enough that she's got me eating pickled okra from the regular grocery store. I don't think I can stomach looking at all the gross stuff she'll make me check out at that healthy place." He groaned. "Holy hell, this is Texas. It should be a sin to eat okra any other way than battered and fried with ranch dip on the side."

Maddy couldn't help herself and smiled. "Thank you. It's going to be weird watching the guys go through Deena's things. I could use you there, big guy."

"Then it's settled." He grabbed her arm and led her to the police car. Once inside, he wiggled his eyebrows. "I do have an ulterior motive. Hopefully, your sister will have a cookie jar full of Oreos. My stomach has been screaming at me ever since I ate that tofu crap that Sara packed in my lunch today."

Just what you need, Chubbs, but since my sister seems to want you there with her, I'll give you this one, Tessa said from the backseat.

"Ordinarily, I'd kick your butt for even thinking about eating cookies after what you went through last week at the ER with that chest pain, but tonight, I'm feeling a little beholden to you." Maddy turned down the street to Deena's apartment before adding, "But only one."

"Two. Don't forget how beholden you are to me."

She tried to keep her voice stern. "Okay, but no more. And for goodness' sake, don't tell Sara."

When they arrived at Deena's apartment, Officers Sean

Flanagan and Danny Landers were already out of their police car and waiting at the door with a search warrant in hand.

When she and Mitch joined them, Flanagan keyed in on Maddy, his facial expression solemn. "We'll try to make this as quick and painless for you as we can."

She smiled with appreciation. "Thanks, Sean. I have no doubt you'll go out of your way to accomplish that." Then to lighten the mood, she pointed to the other cop. "Now, Landers here is another story."

The youngest cop on the force grinned like he'd just been handed a compliment. "You got that right. I've seen your sister in jeans and skimpy tops. I'm going to have fun rooting around in her undies drawer."

Maddy slapped him on the shoulder playfully. "Which is why you're going to be in the kitchen, Danny. It might get a little uncomfortable for both you and Deena the next time you come over for Sunday dinner with my sister Kate if you get a sneak peek at her personal stuff. So, no, happily married Sean here gets to go through her personal things."

"Oh, baloney!" Danny faked disappointment, but he didn't have to try very hard.

The guy had a point. At thirty-two, after losing thirty pounds several years ago, Deena Garcia Rodriguez was still in her prime and could rock a pair of skinny jeans with the best of them. Although her signature long dark hair had been cropped close to frame her face, it still emphasized those dark, sultry eyes— eyes that usually conjured up bedroom fantasies in most of the men who knew her.

"Okay. Let's get this over with," Maddy said, making her way to the elevator with the three cops right behind her.

Once inside Deena's apartment, a sudden feeling of failure washed over her. She was a cop—a pretty good one—and yet, she was totally helpless trying to find her sister. Her gut told her that Deena was probably okay, but she couldn't rid herself of the nagging feeling that she might be in trouble somewhere. She prayed that if something bad had happened, it wouldn't be life-changing.

Come on, Deena. Call me, for heaven sakes, she thought as she grabbed the warrant out of Danny's hand.

Remembering Ryan's reaction when he'd learned that the fingerprints on the wineglass belonged to her sister, she walked into the living room and sat down on the couch. "It's probably best if I just supervise from here."

Mitch studied her face for a minute. "Good idea. You just take it easy while we do our thing." He turned to the younger cops. "We're looking specifically for a red tube of lipstick with silver glittery things and a laptop."

"The computer's missing, too. I checked when I was here earlier," Maddy said just as Mitch's phone rang. He got up and walked to the kitchen leaving her alone in the room with Danny.

"You were already here?" the young officer asked.

She nodded. "My sister's working a job at Warner Chemicals over in Rosemont. Earlier, the CEO called me to ask if I knew where Deena was. Seems they had an important meeting sched-uled, and when he couldn't reach her, he called me since I was listed as her emergency contact. Apparently, she didn't make it to work today, nor did she call in." Maddy paused to take a slow breath. It seemed worse when she actually verbalized it. "It's not like Deena to be that irresponsible, so I made a quick trip over here about two hours ago to check things out."

Before she could explain further, Mitch walked back into the room, and from the look on his face, Maddy knew he was about to tell her something she wouldn't like. "We got a hit on her cell phone from when I pinged it earlier." He sat down next to her on the couch, and his voice softened. "They found it on a deserted road in the boonies outside Cordova city limits, totally destroyed like it had been run over a few times." He tried to hide his doom-and-gloom look, but he never did have a great poker face, and he certainly would never be considered for an Academy Award.

"What do you think that means?" Maddy asked, even though she'd already reached her own conclusions. Deena pinched pennies and would never throw away an expensive cell phone unless she was in some sort of trouble or...

Her imagination shut down before she'd let it finish that thought, and she bit her lower lip to keep her emotions in check.

"It could be as simple as the darn thing dropping calls, and in her frustration, Deena flung it out the window," Mitch offered.

She knew that was a longshot, but for now, it was all she had to cling to. "Maybe."

She was about to say something else when Flanagan hollered from the bathroom. "Found a red lipstick."

Both Maddy and Mitch jumped up and sprinted to the bathroom where Sean was holding a tube of lipstick in his right hand. He held it in the air for a closer look, before placing it in an evidence bag. "Does this look like what we're after?"

Maddy studied the red strip on the outside of the tube. She couldn't be certain, but it looked a lot like the color on the wine glass at the crime scene. She'd have to wait until the crime lab confirmed it, but with a sinking feeling in the pit of her stomach, she nodded.

"If it is a match, it only means Deena shared a drink with Foster at some point, Maddy. Nothing more. Until we can talk to your sister, let's not jump to conclusions," Mitch advised.

But it was too late for that. Her mind was already past that stage, as she remembered the way they'd found Foster's bedroom that morning, how pristine it had been. The first thought she'd had was that he was not your usual male slob, but that wasn't it at all. She should've put two and two together, especially after they'd walked the rest of his house, which more closely resembled the apartment of a messy, single man with no kids.

No, it was Deena's unmistakable fingerprint. Her sister could never have that first cup of coffee in the morning unless her bedroom was spotless and the bed made. Maddy wasn't a betting woman, but if she were, she'd put money on the fact that they'd find Deena's DNA on the used condom from the trash in Foster's bedroom.

She blew out a slow breath before speaking. "Chances are Deena was with Foster last night or this morning. What I can't figure out is why she's disappeared."

Although no one said a word, she could see the same question in the eyes of the two younger cops.

Finally, Sean asked, "Are you thinking love triangle?"

"That would go against everything my sister believed in, but I'm not ready to rule out anything, yet." Maddy shook her head. "I do know that Deena could never have been involved in the homicides, though," she said, more for herself than the others.

"Oh, hell no," Mitch said, stepping closer to her. "We'll find her. I promise. And when we do, this will all get cleared up."

"You know this apartment," Flanagan said when he finished his assessment of Deena's bedroom. "Is there anything missing or out of place that you can tell?"

She looked around, but she already knew the answer. Nothing had jumped out at her earlier and right now was no different. Then she remembered the phone number she'd taken from the hall table when she'd been at the apartment before. Grabbing it from her shirt pocket, she handed it to Mitch. "I found this number earlier. I tried calling it, but it went to a generic voicemail message. I meant to look it up in as soon as I got back to the station but forgot when Ryan told us about Carl Linden."

Mitch dialed the number on his own phone. After a minute, he shrugged. "Same as you—a generic voicemail." After hanging up, he called the precinct and requested that they run the number and call him right back.

"That was Ryan," he explained when he disconnected. "He's on it now."

It didn't take long for Mitch's phone to ring. Whatever Ryan told him apparently didn't sit well with him, and a worried look covered his face. "You're sure?"

When he hung up, then glanced down at her with a fake smile, she braced herself for bad news.

"What'd you find out?" Danny asked.

Mitch's eyes bored into hers. "The number you found on Deena's table belongs to Pamela Linden."

You could've heard a pin drop in the room as all three contemplated what that could mean. Maddy was sure she knew what the younger cops were thinking and felt compelled to defend her sister. "There's no way she had anything to do with the murders," she emphasized once again.

"Like I said before, let's not jump to conclusions. So, Deena and the dead woman may have known each other. Maybe she was going to give your sister a helicopter ride or something." As soon as the words left his mouth, Mitch shrugged, as if he knew how ridiculous they sounded. "All I'm saying is that this isn't a smoking gun."

"I wish Deena were here and could give us her version," Maddy said. "This speculation is killing me. I can't—"

"Oh, I forgot to tell you," Mitch interrupted. "Ryan's on his way home now but said he'll be in late tomorrow because he's got to make a stop in Fort Worth before heading our way."

"For what?"

Mitch smiled for the first time since talking to the NCIS officer. "He's been checking Foster's financials. Seems the man had a serious gambling problem and refinanced his house a year ago, probably to pay off the goons. Ryan said that when the techie checked out his company computer, he discovered that Foster apparently hadn't learned his lesson." He paused to allow them to take that in. "The man was in over his head once again to a fantasy football gambling site. Geez, football season hasn't even officially started yet."

"Do they know how much he owes?" Flanagan asked, coming out of the bedroom.

Mitch nodded. "Over a hundred grand to an outfit based in Fort Worth called The Sporting Place."

"Is that where Ryan's going in the morning?" Maddy allowed herself to be hopeful for the first time. If the dead guy was up to his eyeballs in debt to some really bad guys, maybe there was a logical reason for the murders that didn't involve her sister.

"Yeah. He asked if we wanted to meet him there, but I declined. It could be a dead end, or it could yield a very unhappy business owner who used aggressive enforcers to collect debts. Either way, I figured we all didn't need to be there." He turned to Danny. "Are we finished here?" When the young cop nodded, he grabbed Maddy's arm. "Let's go, partner. Try not to worry too much tonight. Tomorrow is another day."

"Did you call Sara to tell her you'd be late?" Maddy asked as they walked to the cruiser.

"Yep. Told her that you and I might have to pull an all-nighter."

"An all-nighter?"

He gave her a mischievous grin. "That way I get a reprieve from tofu. My dinner tonight will be take-out." He smacked his lips. "Oh my God! I think I'm having a cheeseburger orgasm just thinking about it."

Maddy couldn't help it and laughed out loud. "Oh, if it were only that easy."

"It is for guys," he said with another grin. "Hey, you're my alibi for the night. Want to join me?"

Guys only have one purpose when they're having sex and trust me when I say it isn't to satisfy the woman. Heard Renault and Ford were working on building a smaller car for women. They're trying to come up with a version that uses the Renault Clio and the Ford Taurus and call it Clitaurus. The idea is to make it so that it can't get stolen since the average male thief won't be able to find it even if someone tells him where it is. Tessa, who'd been sitting in the easy chair, unusually quiet for some reason, shrugged as she stood up and walked over to stand behind Mitch. **Pretty ingenious, don't you think?**

Maddy couldn't help herself and grinned. Tessa had always had a warped sense of humor and came up with the most ridiculous, funny things sometimes. When Mitch looked at her with squinted eyes, probably wondering what was so funny, she quickly recovered and said, "Actually, do you want to ride over to Cordova with me for a look at Pamela Linden's residence? Now that we know Deena might have known her, I'd like to check the place out myself." She lowered her eyes. "See if maybe Sean was right. See if we can find evidence of a possible love triangle between the two women and Foster."

"Even if that were true, it doesn't mean your sister had anything to do with the murders." He patted her shoulder. "Okay, I'll go with you, but keep in mind that I'm starving. And remember what you told that rookie cop this morning? I can get ugly when my blood sugar's low."

"Oh, please." She smirked. "You're the biggest pussy cat I know." She started the engine and headed toward the neighboring city. "And I'm way too easy. After we check out Pamela

Linden's house, I'll personally take you to Sorrento's and buy you the biggest steak and baked potato on the menu. I might even throw in their world-famous chocolate volcano cake if you're good."

"Oh, good Lord! You have no idea how much I love you right now."

She shook her head and tsked before calling Colt to request a warrant for Pamela Linden's residence and to ask him to fax it to the Cordova Police Department. Next, she called the Cordova station to see if one of their officers could meet them at Pamela's residence with the warrant. Located on the far outskirts of the city, the house was set on at least several hundred acres with no neighbors as far as the eye could see.

Mitch whistled when he got a good look at it. "Helicopter pilots must make a helluva lot more than I thought. This is a huge ranch."

She stared at the two-story white ranch house. "I read somewhere that the latest thing with the big ranches around here is herding cattle from the air. Apparently, it saves a lot of time and manpower, but it's not cheap. If she was getting a cut of that lucrative business, she probably had no problem making the payments on this place."

The Cordova cop was waiting on the porch when they arrived and handed Mitch the warrant. When they were ready, he positioned his battering ram and prepared to power through the front door before Mitch stopped him.

"No sense destroying this nice door." He pulled out his wallet, took the small pick hidden in a side pocket, and within minutes had the door open. He smiled at the young officer. "Live and learn, kid," he said as he drew his gun and entered cautiously.

Maddy followed close behind with her gun in her hand just

in case they might encounter danger. When they entered the living room she tightened her grip on her weapon.

A quick glance around the room told Maddy that it wasn't what she'd expected. She figured the dead woman would have rustic furniture with lots of aircraft paintings on the walls. Or maybe just the opposite with hardly any furniture or decorations since, according to the report on her, she'd only moved to the house three months before when her divorce to Carl had been finalized. But whatever she'd expected, there was no way Maddy could have anticipated the actual scene when she stepped into the foyer.

The entire room was torn apart—couch cushions ripped open, lamps knocked over, and pictures torn from the wall and slashed.

Mitch moved up behind her, nearly scaring her to death. "Looks like someone was seriously looking for something here. Wonder if they found it?"

5

Mitch surveyed the mess in Lieutenant Linden's living room and slowly shook his head. "Do you suppose that whatever they were looking for warranted killing her?" Turning to the young officer standing alertly by the door, looking like he would bolt and run if Mitch said boo, he asked, "What's your name, son?"

"Jenkins, sir."

"Tell me, Jenkins, do you know if your guys checked out this place after the body was found this morning?"

The young cop shook his head. "Not for sure, but I don't think so. I heard Sergeant Sullivan talking about how the case belongs to you guys and the military cops."

"So, we don't know when the house was ransacked," Mitch mumbled to himself. Facing the cop again, he asked, "Is there a camera outside? A Ring, maybe?"

"I'll check." Jenkins opened the door and stepped out onto the porch. A few minutes later, he came back into the house and shook his head. "There's one out there, but it looks like someone used it for target practice."

"Crap! I was hoping it would tell us the answer to my question. Was her house torn apart before or after she was shot?"

"Maybe she was here and when she heard the intruder breaking in, she ran out the back door before they discovered her," Maddy offered. "They could have followed her to Foster's house, tied her up, and then killed her. That makes me think they might have been trying to get information out of her. She did have that nasty bruise above her eye that we assumed was from falling to the floor with her hands tied behind her. If this is true, then maybe Foster was just collateral damage—in the wrong place at the wrong time."

"Could be. The question is why." Mitch walked into the kitchen before looking back over his shoulder. "What is it about this Linden woman that we're not seeing?"

"I don't know," Maddy said when she joined him in the kitchen. "Hopefully, we'll find something in the house to give us a little insight, because right now we have zilch."

"Criminals always slip up and leave something behind or get drunk and brag about the crime to the guy on the next bar stool." With his gloved hand, Mitch rifled through the cabinets and the drawers, and other than a coffee can containing $500, he found nothing out of the ordinary.

"Mad money," Maddy explained. "Most mothers tell their daughters to sock away a little for emergencies."

"Why just daughters?"

"Before I answer that, let me ask you a question. Do you have a coffee can with money in it?"

"No," he said defiantly. "What does that prove?"

"My point. Most men don't plan further ahead than the next year at best." Maddy grinned. "Bet Sara has a coffee can."

Mitch hitched his eyebrows. "Put your money where your mouth is, Castillo. How much?"

"Fifty bucks."

"You're on." He chuckled to himself. "Easiest fifty bucks I'll ever make. I know my wife like a book."

"We'll see." She gave him a nod toward the back rooms. "Now that it's settled, let's move on to the bedroom."

It took about two hours to finish up with the walk-through while Jenkins waited by the door, glancing down at his watch every few minutes. In the master bedroom they'd found a computer desk but no computer.

"Lieutenant Linden may have had her computer with her when she went to Foster's house," Maddy said. "If it had been here, it would have been in plain sight and there would have been no need to tear the place up."

"You're probably right. If that's the case, then whoever killed her apparently absconded with it, along with her cell phone, after they killed her. That would explain why neither was at Foster's house or in her car." Mitch walked over to the nightstand beside the bed and opened the drawer. "No gun," he reported before smirking. "Well, lookee here." He held up several packages of condoms. "Our lieutenant may have been a party girl."

"Don't be sexist," Maddy scolded. "Just because a girl has protection doesn't mean she's a party girl."

"Do you have condoms in your nightstand?"

"Number one, that's none of your business, and number two, even if I did, it wouldn't make me a slut puppy."

He stared at her for a minute. "Of course, you don't have condoms by your bed. You haven't had a date since last year when lover boy moved to California. Truth be told, one might conclude that you're a man hater."

Maddy laughed out loud. "You know me too well." She walked over to Jenkins. "Since this is Ryan's case, we'll let him know what we found and get him to send the CSI team to check for fingerprints, blood splatter, or anything out of the ordinary. Also, we'll have them check out that camera on the porch and the surrounding areas. Maybe we'll get lucky and find a gun casing or the actual bullet used to destroy it. It would be a big help if we could pinpoint the caliber of the gun used. Right now, we know absolutely nothing about Linden except that she was in the Reserves and was a commercial helicopter pilot."

Mitch turned to Maddy, a little sprinkle of hope spreading on his face. "Where do those door cams record?"

"Usually on a computer and/or smartphone, both of which are missing." She blew out a frustrated breath. "That brings us back to square one with no idea if Linden was here or not when her house was ransacked."

She walked to the door. "I think we're done here. You did good, Jenkins," she said and was rewarded with a huge smile. Knowing how sarcastic Sullivan was, the young cop probably never got compliments from his lieutenant.

Once they were outside, she turned to her partner. "I do believe I owe you a steak for coming here with me on your time off."

"Damn right you do, and don't forget the volcano cake."

Maddy closed her eyes. "Sara is so going to kill me if she finds out."

THE NEXT MORNING Maddy stopped by Deena's apartment to see if maybe her sister had come home to crash after a wild night. Hopefully, she was fast asleep in her bedroom, oblivious to the fact that the police were looking for her as a possible witness to the murder of her boyfriend and another woman...or worse, as a scorned woman who had confronted her lover and his new squeeze and killed them both in a fit of rage.

Maddy would give her the biggest hug ever—right before chastising her for making them all worry.

She stood outside Deena's apartment for a few seconds, making sure there were no suspicious characters in the hallway like the last time she was here. Using her key, she slowly pushed the door open. Pulling her weapon from her holster, she walked in, getting more nervous by the minute about what she might find.

It felt weird being there under the circumstances, as if she was spying on her sister. Taking a deep breath, she walked the entire apartment twice, searching for something—anything that might give her a clue about where her sister was.

Same as yesterday. Nothing.

Ready to give up on finding anything useful for the investigation, she walked past the front window and glanced out, as if somehow Deena would magically appear like nothing was wrong. Where could she be? Her mind wouldn't let her go to the worst-case scenario about why she hadn't called if she was in trouble.

This was so unlike her sister.

Even though the apartment was about a forty-five-minute drive to Warner Chemicals, Maddy would bet money that her sister was the first one there every morning when they opened the doors. Her gut was now screaming at her that there were no more rational excuses. Something was definitely wrong.

She decided it was time to call her mother and siblings to tell them what was going on. Deena had always been the responsible one and the most level-headed of the Garcia sisters. But she felt guilty about withholding the disturbing news from them. It was time to set up a pow-wow with her sisters. They were Deena's family as well and deserved to know what was going on.

So did her mother.

But she couldn't stop clinging to the slim chance that Deena would show up in the next few hours with some logical reason for being MIA. Then she would have upset her family for nothing, and now that her mom was beginning to enjoy her new life in Florida, it seemed almost cruel to burden her with this.

She decided to call her sisters that night and bring them up to speed about Deena. As much as she wanted to believe that nothing sinister had happened, all the signs pointed to that not being the case.

Still standing by the window, she detected a slight movement in the black luxury SUV parked outside the front door of the apartment. She'd noticed the vehicle when she'd walked past it on her way in but hadn't given it much thought—thinking that someone might be waiting on one of the other residents. Glancing down at her watch, she realized she'd been in Deena's apartment for over twenty minutes.

A long time for someone to wait in a car.

Her cop instincts kicked in, and she focused on the black SUV, catching a glimpse of the driver staring up at her. Before she could react, he backed out and drove off in a hurry.

She tried to think of all the reasons why someone would sit in front of the apartment for so long. Maybe the guy was simply casing the joint with the intention of burglarizing it later. Or maybe he was there to pick up someone and just got tired of waiting. Maybe it had nothing to do with Deena or the case.

Then she remembered that she'd seen a man at Deena's door the night before after she'd exited the elevator. Although she hadn't gotten a good look at him before he rushed to the nearest exit, she'd seen enough to know that he was about six-two with dark hair, thinning at the back of his head.

The guy in the SUV also had dark hair.

She took a deep breath, mentally scolding herself for not noticing the man when she'd first walked past him. The smart thing would have been to at least talk to him to see why he was there. But her mind was on one thing and one thing only—her sister.

With nothing more that she could do, she locked the apartment and walked to her car.

On the ride to the station, she couldn't get the man out of her mind. Her instincts were usually spot on about anything suspicious, but today, not so much. Maybe she *was* too close to the investigation, as the NCIS agent had implied. Maybe she should step down and let one of the younger cops work with Mitch. Sean Flanagan was the nephew of Jeff Flanagan, who had retired from the force the year before, and both Flanagan and Landers had only been out of the academy for a few years. Although neither had any experience with a homicide investigation, they would probably do an okay job under Mitch's guidance.

Probably better than she was doing. Missing something like a man possibly surveilling the apartment building was something even a rookie cop would follow up on.

That thought lasted until she arrived at the police station and saw the two young cops by their squad car, laughing about something. She had to smile. She loved those two, but both were still green, and still had that boyish immaturity thing going on. Even though they might do a good job with Mitch's help, this case was so important—and too personal to pass on to them.

The minute she walked into the squad room, Mitch ran up to her and gave her a bear hug.

"What's that for?"

"The steak you bought me last night. I slept like a baby for the first time in a week."

"Did Sara ask you what you had for dinner?"

"You know she did. And trust me when I say that woman can spot a lie from a mile away. I had to improvise."

"So, did you lie and tell her you had tofu?" Maddy narrowed her eyes. "Hope you left me out of that conversation."

"Quit worrying. I didn't mention you, and if I had lied, that woman would have sniffed it out like a drug dog hot on the trail of a suitcase full of cocaine." When Maddy continued to glare at him, he continued. "I told her I had a dry baked potato and a salad with Ranch on the side."

"You did not tell her that! Even I wouldn't believe you, and I'm not nearly the bloodhound that Sara is." Maddy blew out a breath. "Can't believe you lied to her face."

"Technically, it wasn't a lie. I did have a baked potato that started out dry, and Ranch was on the side." He grinned. "It's what the Catholics call a sin of omission."

Maddy laughed out loud. "First of all, you're Methodist. And I'll bet you didn't mention that your so-called-dry potato had oodles of butter, cheese, sour cream and bacon on it when the waitress placed it in front of you." She settled in her chair before nailing Mitch with a glare. "And for the record, if I remember correctly, you asked for extra Ranch dressing on the salad itself and an extra ramekin of it on the side."

"You just made my point. Technically, I did have salad dressing on the side. And the potato did start out dry." He gave her a mischievous grin before pulling up his chair close to hers. "Enough about my fabulous dinner last night, we should probably talk about what we found at Lieutenant Linden's house before the NCIS guy gets here."

"Mitch, you know we promised transparency. How can we expect him to share his findings with us if we don't share ours?" She looked across at Ryan's empty desk. "Where is he, anyway?"

"Not sure. Colt said he called in to say he would be late—that he was checking out a lead. Remember I told you that before he left yesterday, he discovered that Foster had some interesting transactions on his bank statements. He mentioned that he was going to check it out. Not sure exactly what he'll find."

"Hmm." Maddy opened the case file. "What's your gut telling you? Was Foster or Linden the intended victim?"

Mitch rubbed his cheek, as if contemplating whether to answer truthfully. "This isn't going to make your day, but I'm leaning toward either Linden or your sister."

She struggled not to react to hearing that there was a good possibility that her sister might have been the target. "Why would anybody want to kill Linden? Or Deena, for that matter?"

Mitch shrugged. "A wise woman told me not too long ago that it's what you and I get the big bucks to find out. And remember, that's just my gut talking. I have nothing to back it up. Right now, there's so much we're missing that might point us in a different direction. But the fact that nothing was out of the ordinary at Foster's house, yet Linden's was ransacked, and your sister's gone missing makes me think the two women might be the key to solving these murders."

Maddy turned away so Mitch wouldn't see the tears welling up in her eyes. She had to quit acting like a sister and think like a homicide detective. She was a decorated cop, for God's sake. Plus, it was highly possible that her sister's life depended on her bringing her A game to the investigation.

When she composed herself, she lowered her voice so that only Mitch could hear her. "Forgot to tell you. I went by Deena's apartment before I came to work this morning."

"Anything different from yesterday?"

Maddy shook her head. "I did notice a man in a black luxury SUV parked out front when I walked from my car to the apartment. It was still there twenty minutes later."

Mitch's eyes lit up. She had his attention now. "Did you get a good look at the driver? Or the license plate?"

"No, I was so caught up with praying that I would find Deena in her bed, I totally blew past the vehicle without even glancing at the driver." She slapped her forehead. "Good Lord, what's the matter with me? Other than the back of his head and the color of his hair, I have nothing. Thought he was probably waiting for someone, but when I saw his SUV there after twenty minutes, I moved closer to the window for a better look. He must have seen me because he took off like a bat outta hell." She sighed. "Ryan was right. Maybe I'm not the best cop to be investigating my sister. Obviously, I'm not on my game."

Mitch patted her shoulder. "I'd take you a little off your game any day before anyone else right now, partner."

She smiled her appreciation. "Here's the thing. I think he might be the same man I saw in front of Deena's door when I got off the elevator yesterday."

Mitch stood up. "You saw a man outside your sister's apartment yesterday and didn't think it was something I should know?"

Maddy caressed her forehead as if to rub away a migraine. "I didn't get a good look at him, and he walked away from me and took the stairs when he saw me. I figured he was at the wrong apartment."

He stared at her and for a minute, and Maddy thought he might take back the compliment he had just given her. "Probably is nothing, but I'll still get Sean to check the security cameras from the hallway again. We only concentrated on footage from the night before and the early morning hours after we got the call about the murders." He looked over at Danny Landers. "Can you compile a list of all the black luxury SUVs in Vineyard and the neighboring cities?"

Danny shrugged. "Luxury SUVs?"

"Yeah. Lincoln Town Cars and Cadillac Escalades to start with. Maybe even Lexus or Mercedes. Might be a dead end, but then again, it might not be."

Danny got up from his desk and walked over to them. "Almost forgot. Ballistics came back on the gun found at the scene of the crime. The .22 was the murder weapon. And get this —it was registered to Carl Linden and his fingerprints were all over it."

Before Maddy could react to the news, Nick Ryan walked into the squad room, grinning like he'd just won the lottery.

"Someone must've gotten laid last night," Mitch whispered to Maddy loud enough for Nick to hear.

To his credit, the NCIS officer never flinched. "Wouldn't you like to know?" He walked to the breakroom and poured himself a cup of coffee. By the time he sat back down at his desk, both Maddy and Mitch were staring impatiently at him.

"Well, are you going to tell us what's got you so jolly this morning, or is the whole 'we'll be transparent with each other' out the window?" Mitch walked over to Ryan's desk and plopped down on the edge, still glaring. "Oh, by the way, we got a warrant late last night to search Lieutenant Linden's residence, and Maddy and I drove over there to check out the place. It's a freakin' ranch house with a lot of acres."

Ryan glared at Mitch. "You couldn't wait until I got here this morning?"

"Sorry. We were going to dinner, and it was on our way. We found the place ransacked." Maddy looked away from him, hoping that he wouldn't catch her in the lie.

"Hmm. I was thinking that maybe she was just collateral damage after what I found out last night." Nick shook his head. "Find out anything else at Linden's house?"

"Only that whoever ransacked the place didn't want to be identified and used her Ring camera for target practice." Mitch said.

"I appreciate you telling me. Now back to what I found out." Nick took a long sip of his coffee before leaning toward Maddy, totally ignoring Mitch. "As you already know, before I left yesterday, I got a look at Foster's financials and stumbled across multiple big money payouts to a company called The Sporting Place. It's an online high-end sports betting facility with the corporate office on the outskirts of Fort Worth. Since it was only a thirty-minute drive from my apartment, I decided to check it out." He picked up a manila folder on his desk and opened it before addressing both Maddy and Mitch. "Not only did Foster refinance his house last year to pay off his apparent losses, but there was also another fifty grand withdrawn from his bank account and paid to the gambling site."

"That doesn't surprise me. Players like him usually go for high-risk ventures," Mitch said, before flashing a grin. He pointed to the manila folder Nick was holding. "And in the spirit of our agreed-upon transparency, I also got a look at his financials this morning."

Even Nick couldn't hide his amusement. "If you read through all the man's financial records, you probably already know that a few months ago he received a one-hundred-thousand-dollar payment from Warner Chemicals. When I called to ask about it, I was told that Foster took out a loan against his 401K."

"Was that to pay off more gambling debts?" Maddy asked.

"If it was, he never learned his lesson." Nick leaned back in his chair and put his hands behind his head and his feet on the desk. "Apparently, he had a bad run the past few months and owes another hundred grand to the sports betting place."

"Wow! Sounds like the guy could have used a twelve-step program, but I still don't know how this relates to our case," Maddy said.

"Nick nailed her with a grin. "Maybe it does. Maybe it doesn't. Although I couldn't get anything out of the head honcho, I got chatty with one of the secretaries. She mentioned that she'd overheard her boss say he'd spoken to Foster this week about coughing up the money–or else."

"Or else? Could that be our motive? I'm thinking maybe they sent an enforcer to Foster's house to scare the man into coming up with the money, and the dude went a little too far and killed him instead. Because Linden had seen his face, he killed her, as well," Mitch said, his face scrunched in deep thought.

Nick flashed a huge smile, and Maddy struggled to not get lost in his dimples. "That would definitely be a motive, but unfortunately, it didn't happen like that."

"What makes you so sure?" Maddy asked.

"I haven't told you the best part yet."

"You're enjoying keeping us on the edge of our seats, aren't you?" Mitch said with a growl. "This better be good."

"Oh, it is," Nick said, stopping to take another sip of his coffee. "The man at the sports betting place must have figured he would appear less like a suspect if he told me what he knows after I mentioned what the woman said."

Mitch moved closer. "And?"

"And, apparently, Foster called yesterday morning and told him that he was about to come into a large amount of money and would be able to pay off his entire debt after the weekend."

"Way to bury the lead, Sherlock," Mitch said, but even Maddy could tell he was impressed.

For the first time since this investigation began, they had their first real lead.

6

___

"Are you thinking that maybe Foster was blackmailing Linden to get the money he owed to the sports betting place? That maybe she pulled the gun on him and shot him before Deena tried to get it away from her? That somehow, in the ensuing fight over the weapon, the gun went off and hit Linden?" Mitch shook his head. "Nice explanation, but it doesn't take into account the fact that both Linden and Foster were restrained."

"I thought of that, too, and concluded that it couldn't have happened that way." Ryan glanced toward Maddy before continuing, "But if Foster was blackmailing Linden, what could possibly be the reason?"

"Maybe he was playing house with both women and maybe Linden, after a couple bottles of wine, told him a secret under the sheets that he immediately saw as a path to paying off his gambling debts," Maddy said.

"All speculation with no way to prove any of that right now unless we can find out what kind of secrets Linden may have shared." Mitch smiled. "Hell, we couldn't even get a search warrant based on that."

She sighed. "I was hoping it might be easy. I feel like we're missing something really important."

"I know. We'll have to dig deeper," Ryan said.

Mitch glanced toward Maddy. "Something you need to know about my partner in the interest of full disclosure. She went by Deena's apartment and noticed a guy sitting in a black luxury SUV outside. When he saw her staring, he left in a hurry before she could get a better look at the make of the car or the plates. But she remembered seeing a guy about the same build and the same dark hair outside her sister's apartment several hours after we discovered the bodies. He headed for the exit as soon as he saw her, and again, she didn't get a good look at him. Her concern at that point was to make sure that her sister wasn't in any danger or possibly inside fighting for her life."

He paused to blow out a breath. "At first, the team concentrated on the security camera footage in the hallway at Deena's apartment on the night before and right after the bodies were discovered. Now, they're going back over footage from several days before as well as the last two days. Hopefully, we'll get a look at our mystery man, and with a little luck, pinpoint him with facial recognition."

Ryan stared at Maddy, and she wondered if he was about to give her another lecture on why he felt she was too close to the investigation or perhaps admonish her for thinking the two incidents weren't important enough to relate to them until now. The sad part of it all was that it would be a lecture well-deserved. Her silence may have given the prime witness—or possibly the killer himself—a jump on them, enough so that he might easily be on his way to Mexico and out of their reach.

Instead, Ryan shook his head. "I can't imagine how hard this must be for you to investigate your own sister, not even knowing if she's okay."

Maddy met his gaze. "While I appreciate that, it's no excuse. I know better."

"Don't beat yourself up, kiddo," Mitch said. "Neither of us know how we'd react in the same situation. Let's just concentrate on going forward and find out what we're missing."

Just then Maddy's phone rang, and after glancing down at the caller ID, she said, "It's my sister Kate. I have to take this call." She brought her hand up to her mouth. "Oh God, I haven't told my sisters that Deena is missing." She stood up and walked into the breakroom before answering, and in as cheery of a voice as she could muster, she said, "Hey, Katie, what's up?"

"I was about to ask you the same question," her youngest sister said. "Nobody's heard from you in a couple of days."

Maddy sighed. There was really no easy way to say it but straight out. "That's because I was working a murder case." She sucked in a deep breath and then went on. "And it looks like Deena might be missing. I've been working hard to find out why."

"Wait. What? How can she be missing?"

"That's my thought. I can't talk about it now. I need you to call Lainey to set up a meeting for tonight. Text me the time and place, and I'll explain everything to both of you then."

"I've got a bad feeling."

Maddy hesitated. "Well, about that, Tessa showed up—"

"Oh, no! Is everything all right with *you*?" Kate interrupted.

"As far as I know, yes. Tessa thinks she was sent back for Deena."

"That's weird. She usually only appears to the one in trouble. Are you sure there's nothing going on in your life that you're not telling me?" Kate probed.

"If there is, I don't know about it." Maddy glanced up as Danny Landers walked into the breakroom and handed her a piece of paper. "Gotta run. I'll fill you in tonight." She hung up and glanced at the official DNA report from the condom found in Foster's bedroom. Proof that Deena had been there and had sex with the dead man. She blew out a breath.

"Sorry to be the one to bring you this," Danny said, looking sheepish. "But all it means is that at some point your sister and Foster were intimate."

"I know. I'm trying not to make too much of it." She smiled at him. "That was Kate on the phone. If she calls you and asks about Deena, tell her you don't know anything about it. Especially not that she may be a suspect in a murder case."

"Why? She's *her* sister, too, you know."

"I do know, which is why I want to tell her and Lainey in person tonight. And if I hear that you went and blabbed to her, there will be hell to pay."

"You know I can't keep anything from your sister," he argued. "She has a way of forcing it out of me."

Maddy narrowed her eyes. "Don't make me ask Mitch to impress upon you how important zipped lips are in this case."

Landers laughed. "Good one, Maddy. He's the only person I'm more afraid of than my girlfriend."

"Katie does keep you on a short leash."

He frowned. "That's what I let her think. The truth is the older I get, the better I get."

Unless you're a banana. Tessa said, plopping down in one of the chairs before looking up at Maddy. **What time are we meeting our sisters?**

MADDY DROVE to Kate's house with Tessa right beside her in the passenger seat. "Why am I seeing you if Deena is the one in trouble?" Hearing Kate ask that very same question earlier bothered her. What if she was the one in trouble? Or what if Tessa had come back because it was Jessie? She made a mental note to call the band camp in the morning to make sure that it wasn't her daughter.

Beats me. I go where they send me, the ghost quipped. **And by the way, why are we meeting at Kate's? Of all my sisters, her house is the smallest. Not that she needs a big house. She's always at the hospital or on call, waiting for someone's water to break. She should have been a dermatologist and not an obstetrician.**

"She loves her job. And you're right, she's rarely home, so why pay for a big house?" Maddy turned the corner at the intersection. "And to answer your question, my house looks like a CAT 5 hurricane blew through with all Jessie's things strewn about every room." When Tessa squinted at that, Maddy explained. "She left for a two-week long band camp this morning. You'd have thought she was going away for a year or so."

Jess is more like me than Gracie, my own flesh and blood.

Maddy shook her head. "No way. Jessie has never said a cuss word in her life or chased after boys the way you did."

Ouch. That stings. I only meant we were alike in the way we dealt with our wardrobes. I always overpacked when I was going on a trip.

Maddy softened. "Sorry. You know I love you. I'm just really all freaked out by Deena's disappearance."

No apology necessary. I get it. So why not Lainey's house?

"You're kidding, right? The last thing we need is for Colt to catch wind of all this. Right now, he doesn't know about our little secret sister powwow. You know how he hates it when he thinks the Garcia girls are interfering with his investigations. I'll sit down with him tomorrow and be straight about all this." She paused. "Well, not about everything. No sense making him suspicious and watching my every move—or Lainey's, for that matter."

Good point. My ex always did overreact when it came to family matters. He would have a big internal conflict dealing with his sister-in-law as a criminal.

"Deena's not a criminal," Maddy argued. "Right now, she's just a person of interest and might be in trouble."

I hope you're right. Of all my sisters, she's the least likely to break any laws.

"I know. That's what's so baffling about all this. There's got to be some kind of explanation other than her being a criminal."

She pulled into the driveway and slipped out of the car. Halfway to Kate's front porch, she turned to see if Tessa was behind her.

She wasn't.

"Oh great. You're going to disappear on me and make me face our sisters alone with the bad news." She waited for a response, but none came. She finally gave up, threw her arms in the air and rang the doorbell.

Almost immediately, Kate flung the door open and pulled her inside "Lainey's already here, and we're about to explode with questions."

Maddy kissed her sister on the cheek, waved at her other sister on the couch, and walked into the living room. "I'm afraid I've got some bad news."

Both Kate and Lainey gasped.

"Geez, I haven't even told you yet," Maddy said, wondering how they would react when they found out what that bad news really was.

"Tessa, why are you here?" Kate asked, her eyes as big as saucers now.

Maddy turned around to see the ghost standing right behind her, then faced her two sisters once again. "You can see her, Kate?"

"I can see her, too," Lainey said. "Oh Lord, this must be really bad if we can all see her." She glanced up at Tessa. "Answer Kate's question. Why are you here? Are we all in trouble?"

Your guess is as good as mine. How's my daughter, by the way?

"Gracie's awesome," Lainey said. "She's barrel racing in the local rodeos and already has a cabinet full of trophies."

That made Tessa smile. **She's the only good thing I ever did in my prior life.**

"Enough about that," Kate interrupted, turning toward Maddy "Start talking. Where's Deena?"

"I wish I knew," Maddy said. "Kate, can we have something to drink before we get into all the details? The sausage biscuit that I had for breakfast is making me thirsty."

Kate jumped up. "Almost forgot. I made sangria." She walked into the kitchen and returned with four glasses of the wine.

Honestly, Katie. You really think a ghost can drink with you?

"Oh, sorry. Forgot." She set the drinks on the coffee table and plopped down beside Lainey on the couch.

After taking a long sip from hers, Maddy put the glass down, knowing her sisters would gang up on her if she waited any longer to explain. "Deena was at the scene of a double homicide and went missing before the cops could question her."

"What?" Lainey asked. "Does Colt think she's the killer? I talked to him earlier, and he never mentioned it to me."

"Anyone who knows Deena knows she's not a killer. But until we get her version of the story, she remains a person of interest and quite possibly, a witness."

"What makes you think she was even there?" Kate asked.

Her lipstick was on a wine glass, and her DNA was on a used condom, Tessa answered.

"How do you know?" Lainey asked.

Seriously, Lainey. Tessa rolled her eyes and sighed. **That's a dumb question.**

"Not really when you think about it. Remember, you didn't even know who killed you a few years back?"

Tessa grinned. **You have a point. To answer your question, I've been following Maddy around since yesterday.**

Both Kate and Lainey shot Maddy a look.

"And you're just now telling us about her showing up on your proverbial doorstep?" Kate frowned. "Are you sure you're not the one in trouble?"

"No, I'm not sure. I guess we'll just have to find Deena and ask her about all this. Now back to my story before I was interrupted," Maddy said, sending her sister a warning glance.

The entire time she was talking, you could have heard a pin drop, which was so unlike any of the many sister sessions where all of them usually talked and interrupted each other constantly. When she had updated them about everything she knew so far, she leaned back on the sofa and took another long drink of the sangria. "This is excellent, Kate. Is this Mom's recipe?"

Kate nodded. "I called her early this morning before I talked to you. She never even mentioned anything about Deena."

Maddy lowered her eyes. "She doesn't know. I didn't want to worry her until I was sure there was something to worry about."

"You have enough on your plate," Lainey said, standing up and putting her arm around her older sister. "I'll call Mom on the way home. I'll try to keep it light, telling her only that we are waiting to hear back from Deena. I'll try not to let my own fears come across in my voice."

"Calling her from your car away from Colt is a great idea, Lainey," Maddy said, munching on the chips and salsa that Kate had brought out. It suddenly dawned on her that she hadn't had lunch—or dinner. "Anyone think of anything that Deena might have mentioned over the past few days? Sometimes things that seem irrelevant might end up being a clue."

Lainey shook her head.

Kate's eyes lit up. "Were either of the murdered people named Roger?"

"Why would you ask that? Who's Roger?"

"It might not be anything, but a few weeks ago Deena told me that she'd met a cowboy at the Wild Stallion. Said he'd been eying her up and wanted to buy her drinks all the time. Since he was a hottie, she accepted, and it wasn't until she'd two-stepped a couple of times with him that she noticed the tan line around his ring finger."

"Deena hates married men who prey on single women at bars. She'd had her fill of them after dealing with her own womanizing scum of a husband before he was killed. How many times has she told us that?" Lainey asked, before turning to Maddy. "Tell me she didn't have sex with this Roger guy who ended up dead afterwards? That is totally not something our Deena would do, knowing how she hated cheaters."

"She said she tried to discourage said cheater after she saw the ringless finger, but he was persistent. She finally had to get Josh, the bouncer, to get the guy to lay off." Kate huffed. "Some guys never get the hint that a woman doesn't want to jump their bones."

"**Did he have money?**" Tessa asked.

Lainey turned to Tessa. "How would she know, and why would you ask a stupid question like that?"

Because, little sis, most rich guys think the almighty dollar will get them laid no matter how ugly they are. It's been my experience that a man is like a bank account. Without a lot of money, they don't generate much interest. She smirked. **Admit it. A guy who flashes around a wad of cash garners immediate**

attention, even if it's obvious he'd need a bag over his head for any kind of sexual contact.

Despite herself, Maddy laughed. "Why am I not surprised that this is your idea of expert advice?" She turned back to Kate. "Does this Roger guy have a last name?"

"If Deena mentioned it, I've forgotten it. She did say he drove an expensive car. Made it a point to let her know that."

Maybe our naive sister is smarter than we think about men and their money.

"Having an expensive car doesn't make him rich," Lainey said. "Maybe he was leasing it. Besides, Kate said Deena got away from him as soon as she suspected that he was married."

"Deena also said that after the bouncer gave him a come-to-Jesus lecture, he backed off a little, but still stared at her and made her uncomfortable," Kate added.

"I'll make a run out to the Stallion and get a look at the credit card receipts to see if one with a Roger something or other pops up on any of them. Maybe someone there remembers the guy." She gave a thumbs up to Kate. "Good recall, Sis."

"And if the man's married, maybe there's a wife hanging around who wasn't real happy with her husband courting a possible mistress," Kate said.

You may have hit on something there, Katie, Tessa said before grinning. **You know what they always say about extra-marital affairs.**

Maddy shook her head. "I don't suppose we can stop you from telling us."

Not a chance. One girl's piece of crap husband is another trashy homewrecker's prince charming.

They all laughed before getting serious again.

"What do you want us to do, Maddy?" Lainey asked.

"We found her phone on the side of the road, so there's no use calling her. We just have to wait until she decides to contact one of us. In the meantime, we're checking out her credit cards, bank accounts, airlines, places she frequents. And speaking of places she liked to haunt on weekends, let me check out the Stallion and the guy's wife. I also want to talk to the head honcho at Warner Chemicals to see if he can shed some light on all this." She refilled her glass. "We might as well finish up the sangria. It'd be a shame to let it go to waste."

"Okay, then I have to run. I gotta prepare for my gig on Saturday. I'm interviewing a woman who claims she can talk to birds." Lainey sighed. "Being the weekend anchor on the morning show is chock full of excitement," she said sarcastically before adding, "I'll text you all after I talk to Mom."

Thirty minutes later, Maddy was in her car heading home. Tessa had disappeared by then, allowing Maddy time to recap her conversation with her sisters. She was glad she'd involved them. When they put their heads together, they were a force to be reckoned with.

She couldn't help thinking about Kate's story about the horny cowboy. If, in fact, there was a jealous wife, it was a possibility that she was involved somehow. What if she'd followed Deena to Foster's house that night and killed both him and Linden? Or worse, what if Deena had wrestled the gun from her, and it went off and killed them? Maybe she had taken Deena prisoner and was torturing her right now—or worse.

Stop! She couldn't let her mind go there. First thing in the morning, she'd try to find out who this Roger guy and his wife were and pay them a little visit. In the meantime, she'd hold off on telling Mitch or Ryan about it just yet. It might turn out to be nothing.

But then again, it might not.

7

M addy woke up the next day with a pounding headache. Red wine usually did that to her—something about the sulfate in it. Climbing out of bed, she headed to the kitchen and brewed a cup of strong coffee before popping two Excedrin Migraine tablets. Every time she suffered through one of these, she swore it would be margaritas only the next time she decided to drink.

Then she smiled. Who was she kidding? Her mom's sangria was too good to resist even though only two glasses usually brought on morning–after consequences.

At the thought of her mom, she wondered how her conversation with Lainey had gone the night before. Lainey's text had been vague and only said that their mom was okay. She'd give her sister a shout later to see if she needed to call her mother herself to reassure her, despite the fact that there was still nothing positive to report about Deena. The only thing that kept her from totally losing it was that there was no Jane Doe in the morgue.

After the coffee, the pills, and lying back down for a half hour nap began to work their magic on her headache, she called the police station to let them know that she wouldn't be coming in until late that morning so she could follow up on a new lead. She was glad that Mitch hadn't answered the phone as he would have pried the details from her about this new lead and insisted on going with her. She wanted to check things out on her own before she brought it to the team.

Plus, he had a way of bullying people for information. If there was one thing that she'd learned from her mother, it was that you catch more flies with honey than with vinegar. Truth be told, she wasn't averse to batting her eyelashes if the situation called for it. It had gotten her a lot of useful info over the years.

After standing under the shower head for nearly fifteen minutes with the hot water massaging her scalp, she felt almost human again. Another cup of coffee would put the headache to bed completely.

Finally, around 9:30, she walked out to the garage, slid into her car, and was on her way to the Wild Stallion Saloon to see if she could find out any information that might help Deena's case. She prayed that someone there would remember a good-looking guy named Roger who drove a high-dollar car.

The Stallion, as it was known to the locals, was across town on the border of Vineyard and Cordova. Traffic was light at this time of day, and she made it to the parking lot a little after ten. On her way to the front door, she turned back to see if Tessa was with her. She wasn't, not that she would have been any help since she'd never been to this bar. It had opened after her sister died.

She knocked on the front door and waited.

After a minute or two, a man that had to be at least six-five opened the door. "We're not open for business. Come back after seven tonight," the giant said as he started to pull the door shut.

Maddy put out her hand to stop it from closing. "Are you Josh?" she asked, thinking that a big guy like this had to be the bouncer. When he narrowed his eyes and frowned, even she was intimidated—and she had a gun.

"And who would you be?" the big man asked, unashamedly letting his eyes wander up and down her body.

She had to count to ten to keep from pointing to her face and saying, "Hello. I'm up here."

Instead, she pulled out her badge. "I'm Detective Madelyn Castillo of the Vineyard Police Department. I'd like to ask you a few questions."

"About what?" He moved closer to the door to further block her entrance.

"About a missing woman. You helped her out of a bad situation not too long ago."

Josh squinted in thought. "I get paid to help a lot of people out of bad situations, so you're going to have to be more specific than that. Otherwise, I got work to do behind the bar."

Maddy debated whether to remind him that they could have this conversation down at the station if he preferred, then remembered her mother's advice about honey and vinegar. She'd play nice a little bit longer.

"The woman was being harassed by an aggressive man a couple of weeks ago and asked you to get him off her case," Maddy explained, before adding, "I think his name was Roger, and it's possible that he drove a luxury SUV."

His eyes lit up with recognition. "You talking about Deena Rodriguez? She's missing?"

Finally, a little cooperation. "I am, and yes, she is missing. Deena is my sister. Any information you can give me would be helpful."

He opened the door wider and motioned for her to come in. "Damn! Come on in. Want something to drink?"

She shook her head, remembering her migraine from earlier. She was still a little nauseated and even a Coke sounded awful. "I'm interested in this Roger guy. Any chance you might know his last name?"

"I think I know who you're talking about, but right off the top of my head, I can't come up with a last name. If it's the guy that I'm thinking about, he's a heavy drinker. Usually does tequila shooters and always runs up a big bar tab. Let me go back to my boss's office and fill him in. I'm sure he'll give you permission to go through the credit card receipts to see if something pops up."

Again, Maddy held her tongue. She didn't want to resort to reminding him to tell his boss that she was in the middle of an investigation and there was no chance in hell that she would walk out of this bar without getting a look at those receipts. If necessary, she could have a warrant in her hand in less than an hour. She might even be tempted to mention that *said* warrant might also include a visit from the fire marshal and quite possibly, the state liquor commissioner.

She waited for him to return, prepared to do what she had to if they weren't willing to cooperate.

Fortunately, Josh returned from the back with a large box and a smile on his face. "Carl is more than happy to do anything to help Deena. We all love her here." He pointed to a large, framed picture of the Budweiser Clydesdale horses behind the bar. "Sam's from St. Louis and has been wanting one of those for a long time but could never score one. Somehow, Deena managed to not only get this one, but she had it signed by the head of the Anheuser-Bush Corporation himself." He pulled out a barstool and motioned for Maddy to sit down, then placed the box in front of her. "Here are the receipts for the past two weeks. If this Roger guy ran a tab, then you should find one with his name because I distinctly remember that he was here two weeks ago. Not sure if he's been here since."

Maddy felt her hopes rise at perhaps, the first real lead. "And my sister was here as well, right?"

Josh nodded. "Yeah, but the guy stayed away from her and was focusing on some other woman, a blonde from Cordova who sometimes frequents the Stallion."

"So, Deena didn't make any contact with him at all?"

Josh shook his head and stood up to leave before turning back to Maddy. "Wait a minute. Now that you mention it, I did notice that he was standing next to Deena at the bar towards the end of the night. I was about to go over there and chase him away from her when another woman walked over and squeezed in between the two of them."

"Was it the blonde that he'd been hanging around with earlier that evening?"

Josh shook his head. "No. I remember thinking that this woman didn't look like one of his usual female playthings."

"How so?"

"For one thing, he usually goes for leggy, well-built girls. This one was short, a little stocky, and wearing clothes that made her look like a librarian. Usually, he likes his women in skimpy, tight clothes." He paused. "Or in Deena's case, really attractive ones."

"What happened then? Did the short lady leave or did she confront him?"

"Oh, she confronted him, all right. I was about to go over there and tell them to take it down a notch when they both turned and walked back to the tables. I don't know what happened after that."

"So, the other woman was definitely angry?"

Josh inhaled sharply and blew the breath out in a loud gust. "More like ready to kill the guy. I remember thinking that he was in for a beatdown of some kind from her. I almost felt sorry for the dude."

"And you don't know who the other woman was?"

He shook his head. "Actually, I don't ever recall seeing her here before. Like I said, she was clearly not like all the other women he usually picked up." He plopped down on the stool beside her and pointed at the box of receipts. "I've got about an hour before I have to get things ready for tonight. I can help you go through these if you want." He smiled before adding, "Deena is one of my favorite people, so anything I can do to help her, I will."

"Thank you. I can use the help. All I know is that I'm looking for a guy named Roger who drives a luxury car."

He reached for the gloves that she handed him. "Just a precaution in case we can lift any prints from the receipts," she explained before donning her own gloves.

Silently, they rummaged through the boxful of receipts together.

About forty-five minutes later, Josh yelped and waved a receipt in the air. "Mr. Roger Kennedy."

"Terrific," Maddy said as she pulled an evidence bag from her pocket and reached for the receipt in Josh's hand. With her gloved hand, she shoved it in and sealed the bag. "We'll get this back to you as soon as we can." Then she finished with the last of the receipts just in case there were two Rogers who paid their bar bill with a credit card in the past two weeks.

"No hurry. His account has already been charged. We hang on to the receipts for a few weeks to make sure there's not a problem with a credit card company." He stared at her for a few minutes. "You know, you look a lot like our Deena."

Maddy smiled. "I've been told that." She thanked him again and walked out the door.

Heading to her car, her heart was racing. Who was the lady who'd been unhappy to find this Roger dude flirting with her sister? What was her connection?

Could it have been Mrs. Kennedy?

And if it was Roger's wife, was she mad enough to do something crazy?

Maddy reached for the name that Josh had scribbled on a sticky note and called the station to get Flanagan or Landers to look him up without mentioning why she was interested in the guy. It didn't take long for Danny to get back to her. Fortunately, there was only one Roger Kennedy listed in the immediate area, and he lived about fifteen miles away from the Stallion. She checked her watch. If she hurried, she could pay the man a visit on the slight chance that he might be at home and get back to the office before lunch. Then if she got lucky and garnered any info that might help her sister's case, she'd share it with both Mitch and Ryan.

She punched in the address and headed that way. Fifteen minutes later, she pulled up at the curb in front of a two-story brick house that, other than needing some work on the lawn and the flower beds, seemed to be well-maintained. She couldn't help thinking how ironic it was that her sister could have given the front yard a fabulous makeover—if only Roger Kennedy hadn't been married.

She walked up to the door and rang the bell. When there was no response, she rang again. After a few minutes, she was about to leave when she thought she heard a soft knock. Followed by a muffled whine that sounded an awful lot like the word "help."

Definitely probable cause.

Pulling out her cell phone, she called for back-up, knowing there would be hell to pay for not waiting for reinforcements. She retrieved her weapon from the shoulder holster and tried the door. Covering her other hand with her shirt, she broke the side window and reached in to unlock the door.

"Vineyard Police," she yelled. "Show yourself."

When there was no response, she moved slowly down the

hall, making sure there was no one with a gun waiting for her in the living room or the kitchen. Hearing the barely audible voice once again, this time calling for help from the second floor, she made her way up the steps cautiously.

Again, she heard the faint voice say, "Help."

After clearing the first two bedrooms and not finding the source of the voice, she was at least feeling confident there was no one was lurking there. Then she opened the door to what was obviously the master bedroom. At first glance, nothing looked out of order.

Where the hell had that voice come from?

The bed was unmade, the comforter was on the floor, which didn't seem strange to her since her own bed at home was never made. A while back, she'd read that making your bed every morning was the biggest waste of time ever. That made it okay in her mind.

She scanned the room and saw a large desk which took up most of the corner and was cluttered with a slew of papers.

As she walked slowly toward the bed, she spotted a foot off to one side. Hurrying across the room, she found a woman lying in a pool of blood, her fist clenched and still trying to knock on the wooden floor, and a bleeding gash over her swollen right eye. But most alarming was the massive chest wound that was covered in more blood.

A bloodied butcher knife lay on the floor beside her.

Quickly, Maddy slipped on gloves and bent down to check the woman's pulse. Weak and thready but still palpable. She was about to check out the wound to see if she could stop the massive flow of blood still pouring onto the floor when the woman opened her eyes and whispered, "Don't leave me."

With one hand applying pressure on the chest wound, Maddy pulled out her phone with the other and dialed 911. "This is Detective Madelyn Castillo of the Vineyard Police

Department. I need an ambulance at 3124 Locust Street. I have a woman with an apparent knife wound to the chest in need of immediate transport. Hurry." Before she hung up, she heard sirens in the distance and figured it was probably the police back-up she'd requested. No ambulance could have gotten there so quickly, although she wished they had. From the look of the woman's ashen color and her extreme loss of blood, it was obvious that every second counted.

Putting pressure now with both hands on the woman's bloody chest, she glanced down. "I'll stay with you. I promise."

A few minutes later, she heard Mitch's booming voice screaming her name.

"Upstairs," she hollered back. She glanced down once again at the wounded woman who had now slipped into unconsciousness. "Mitch, find out where the hell the ambulance is."

"They're about a minute away," he responded. "Are you okay?"

"I'm okay. I checked the house before I came upstairs and didn't find anyone. Ask Landers to do a thorough check of the closets and any place that someone could be hiding. Also, call the crime scene guys and get them over here as fast as possible. The sooner we can get this house secured as a crime scene, the more evidence we can preserve."

She checked the woman's pulse again, and this time there was nothing. She was about to start CPR when the EMTs burst into the room and took over. Within minutes, they had an IV in her arm and dripping wide open to deliver the possible life-saving saline. One of them inserted an endotracheal tube and attached it to an Ambu bag to breathe for her. The other started chest compressions then looked up at her and shook his head. Within minutes, they had the wounded woman on the gurney, loaded into the ambulance and on their way to the hospital. But it didn't take a brain surgeon to know that more than likely, the woman would be DOA. You can't lose that much blood and survive.

A call a few minutes later confirmed her suspicions. The woman died in the ambulance about a mile from the hospital, and they were unable to revive her.

She had no idea if this was Mrs. Kennedy or one of Roger's girlfriends, but she was leaning toward the former, given Josh's description of the woman who had confronted him in the bar on Saturday.

"Who is this woman, Maddy? And why are you even here in the first place?" Mitch asked after they were alone in the room waiting on the CSI guys.

A tear slid down Maddy's cheek, and she brushed it away, guilt rearing its ugly head. If she'd just arrived a few minutes earlier, they might have been able to save this poor woman. It would be hard to forget the terrifying look on her face when she'd begged her to stay with her.

"Last night Kate told me that Deena was being harassed by a good-looking guy at the Stallion. All she remembered Deena saying was that his name was Roger and that he drove an expensive car. Evidently, at first, Deena had welcomed the attention until she'd discovered that he was married. Josh—that's the bouncer—remembered that a few weeks ago, the guy apparently saw Deena sitting by herself at the bar and snaked his way through the crowd to stand beside her, no doubt to try to convince her that he really wasn't married. Josh said that a woman he'd never seen in there before marched up to the bar and squeezed in between him and my sister. The woman began arguing with the guy so loudly that Josh was on his way over to intervene when the two of them left the bar area."

Mitch rubbed his forehead. "And how in the hell did you come to the conclusion that this was a house you needed to visit? By your own admission, you didn't even know the guy's last name."

Maddy blew out a slow breath, knowing she was in for a scolding. "Josh remembered that the guy always rang up a big bar tab, so he and I went through all the credit card receipts for the past two weeks."

"Obviously, you found this dude and came to his house? Is that how it went down?" Mitch shook his head. "Do you have any idea how dangerous that was? I'm your partner, Maddy. Why didn't you call me so that I could meet you here?"

"I know. I should have, but when Josh found a receipt signed by a Roger Kennedy, he was pretty sure that it was our guy. Said the man I was looking for always did tequila shooters with a beer chaser, and the bill had five or six of them on it. Since it was only a fifteen-minute drive from the bar, I was just gonna stop by before I headed back to the station. I wanted to see their faces when I questioned them. You, yourself have preached to me on multiple occasions to count how important that first contact is before someone has time to think up an alibi."

"I did tell you that, but never in my wildest dreams did I think you would go and do something as stupid as interviewing a possible murder suspect by yourself. Good Lord, Maddy, you could have been killed, and no one even knew where you were." He swallowed hard. "You and I will have another discussion about this later, but for now, I repeat my question. Who is the victim? Is she the wife and was she the one who confronted him at the bar?"

"I don't know. I've never seen either of them, but this is their address, so I have to believe that she is the wife. Whether or not she was the one who argued with him at the bar is unknown." Maddy walked over to the dresser, where there was a picture of a man and woman standing in front of the Marriott Hotel in Maui. She studied it before showing it to Mitch. *Roger and Nancy*

2015 was imprinted on the bottom. Although it was obvious that the victim was Mrs. Kennedy, until DNA confirmed it, it would have to remain only an assumption. Still staring at the picture, something caught her eye. If this was Roger Kennedy in the picture with the victim, he was definitely tall and ruggedly handsome, but something about his eyes grabbed her attention.

She turned and scrambled down the stairs and out to the garage, expecting to find a black luxury SUV. But there was only a Ford sedan.

Mitch caught up to her, panting from trying to keep up with her. "What are you thinking, Maddy?"

She sighed. "Something about his eyes makes me think I may have seen him before. I thought maybe he was the guy I saw outside her apartment."

"I'll put out an alert to be on the lookout for any high-dollar cars within our jurisdiction. Not too many Vineyard citizens can afford something like that. In the meantime, I'll call Ryan and have him do a deep dive on our Mr. Kennedy. We need to know where he worked so that we can pick him up for questioning."

"He definitely is a person of interest," she said, rushing back to the bedroom with Mitch right behind her. Careful not to step in the blood and contaminate the evidence, she quickly removed the bloodied gloves and put on a fresh pair before moving slowly over to the desk in the corner. After searching through a pile of scattered papers, she gasped. "Oh my God!"

Mitch was beside her in a matter of seconds. "What?"

She handed him a receipt from a rental car company. "Roger was driving a Cadillac Escalade. My gut tells me that I was right. He could be the guy I saw two times at Deena's apartment in that black luxury SUV."

Mitch grabbed the rental car receipt out of her hands and punched in the number on the receipt. After speaking with the clerk, he turned to Maddy. "They said he rented the Caddy last week. Said his car was in the shop waiting on a part."

"How did you get him to give you that information without a warrant?"

"I have my ways." He smiled before explaining. "I said I was calling about the Caddy and wanted to know when it had to be returned. The guy took the bait and said I could keep it until the part came in for my car."

"You are aware that a good defense lawyer will have a field day with that, ill-begotten fruit and all."

"That's not gonna happen. I never really said I was Kennedy. The clerk just assumed I was." Mitch began dialing another number on his phone. "I'll put out a three state APB for the car. In the meantime, if he is the killer, he probably knows that you've been snooping around. You're moving in with Sara and me until we get to the bottom of this. And when Jessie comes home from band camp, she is, too."

"That's not necessary, Mitch. I'm a big girl with a gun. Don't forget that. I can take care of myself."

"Oh, I won't forget that. But you're still moving in with me. Go home and pack a bag and then meet me at the station where we can fill Colt in on the details of today's events. I can already predict his reaction. I want to be sure to be there so he doesn't kill you."

She opened her mouth to protest before he put up his hand to stop her from speaking.

"And just so you know, if Colt doesn't kill you, I'll personally put a bullet in your kneecap if you ever pull a stunt like this again."

8

The minute Maddy walked into the police station, she knew that something was up. She'd had Mitch drop her off at her house so that she could get out of the bloody clothes. She glanced toward Danny Landers, who immediately looked away. She got the same reaction from Sean Flanagan.

Oh boy, those two never missed an opportunity to razz her about being the boss's favorite when she came in late, but this time they wouldn't even make eye contact with her.

Mitch got up from his desk and walked over to her as she was about to sit down at her own desk. Fortunately, she'd convinced him—at least for now—that she'd be fine at her own house. She hoped he wasn't going to try to change her mind.

"Don't get comfortable. Colt wants you in his office right now."

She stared at her partner. "Is this about me going on my own and finding the body at Kennedy's house?"

He shrugged. "Not sure, but Landers said his face was beet red, and it looked like he was about to blow a gasket."

"What else could it be?"

Mitch raised his eyebrows. "Oh, I don't know. Maybe he heard about the secret meeting with your sisters last night."

Maddy opened her mouth to deny it, then thought twice about it. "And how would he know about that?"

"Your mother wasn't convinced that Lainey was telling her everything when she talked to her last night. She tried to call you a couple of times today to get more information, but it went to voice mail both times, so she called me about it. When I told her that I didn't know anything, she did the only thing she could think of—she called her son-in-law." He narrowed his eyes. "And why wasn't I invited to the sister meeting? Everyone knows that I'm like your sister with balls."

At another time Maddy would have laughed at that, but right now she was more concerned about her mother. She grabbed her phone and pulled up the recent call list. Sure enough, there were two calls from her mom that must've happened when she was smack dab in the middle of trying to save a woman's life.

She frowned. "Colt couldn't have figured out that my sisters and I were having a secret meeting about this investigation just from what my mom said. Lainey was only going to tell her that Deena was missing but that we weren't worried about it. That we figured she partied with her girlfriends and just lost track of time."

"Yeah, well, that ship has sailed. Your mom is too smart to buy that lie. She told him that wherever Deena was, her sisters were on top of it. Said that when her daughters put their heads together with a plan to find their sister, nothing would stop them. Still, she wanted to hear it from the horse's mouth about Deena because she said that her own flesh and blood treated her like she was some kind of breakable Kewpie doll who would fall apart if she knew the truth."

"Oh God. Colt couldn't have been too happy hearing that, given the many times he's warned us to back off one of his investigations, but at least he doesn't know that I went to a possible killer's house by myself today."

Mitch shrugged. "For God sakes, Maddy, Colt's the police chief. Of course, he knows that. The minute you called for backup, the entire room was abuzz with speculation."

Maddy blew out a frustrated breath. "Great! I'm not sure that being part of his family will be enough to save my butt this time." Her eyes pleaded with Mitch. "You're my partner. Please tell me that you're gonna walk through his door with me. I could really use your support."

Mitch shook his head. "Wish I could, but he specifically said he only wanted to talk to you privately."

"That sounds ominous." She shoved her purse into the bottom drawer of her desk. "It's time to face the music. If I get fired you need to know that I loved being your partner, Mitch."

He laughed. "Get fired? That ain't gonna happen. You're too good of a cop for him to can you over one screw-up. My guess is you'll get a slap on the hand or possibly a written reprimand in your file, but let you go? Never."

"Hope you're right." She inhaled sharply and headed toward Colt's office. As she passed Angie Winter's desk, the dispatcher looked up at her, and Maddy would have sworn that the woman's face was covered with sympathy.

Crap! It was worse than she thought if even Angie, who was as hard-nosed as they came, was feeling sorry for her. She opened the door and slowly walked over to her boss's desk. "Colt? You wanted to see me?"

The chief had his back to her, and when he turned around, he had two cups in his hand.

Handing her one, he said, "Black with a Sweet'N Low, just

the way you like it." He motioned for her to sit in the chair facing his desk.

For a second, she allowed herself to breathe a little easier. If he was giving her coffee, maybe it meant that he wasn't as angry as she had imagined. The minute he narrowed his eyes and glared at her, that little bubble of hope burst like a water pipe in a Texas ice storm. She braced herself for what she knew was coming.

He took a sip of his hot coffee before addressing her. "Have I not asked you on multiple occasions to let the police do their job without you and your sisters going all Sherlock Holmes on me?"

"I am the police, Colt," she fired back. When she saw his face harden, she lowered her eyes, afraid to meet his hard gaze straight on. Finally, she looked up. "But this time is different. This time—"

He slammed his hand on the desk, spilling a little of his coffee on the papers strewn across it. "Damn!" He grabbed a tissue and dabbed at the spilled coffee before turning his stone face back to her. "Different? Why? Because it's your sister that you think is in danger? Hell, I'm worried about her, too." When she nodded, he continued. "That's exactly why this investigation needs to be played out strictly by the book. It can't be a family thing." He paused. "I won't let you involve my wife and your sister, Kate, in an investigation where there might be a killer out there who's not real happy with the prospect of you being on his or her trail."

"I would never put my sisters in harm's way. I was only—"

For a second time he slammed his hand on the desk, this time a little easier so as not to spill his coffee again. "You already have, Maddy. And any idea that you and your siblings have about concocting a plan to help has got to be put to bed right here and now. Do you understand me?"

She nodded, hoping that would be the end of this conversation. "I do, but this time is diff—"

"And what makes it so different?" His voice jumped to the next octave. "Because you and your sisters think you are better qualified than a trained police force to find a missing person who may very well be a witness to a double homicide? That—"

"Tessa's back," she interrupted, her voice barely a whisper. "That's what's different."

She watched his expression change from anger to confusion. He lowered his voice. "Why would Tessa show up if she thinks Deena is in danger? Doesn't she usually make her grand entrance only to the one who might be in trouble?"

"Usually, but here's the thing. This time all of us can see and hear her. That's never happened before. That's how we know that Deena might really be in danger."

Colt stood up, walked around his desk, and sat on the edge before addressing her, his voice barely a whisper. "Does your *dead* sister have any information that we don't have?"

"Unfortunately, no, but give me a little credit, Colt. We know it's got to be serious if all of us can communicate with her." Her voice cracked as she continued, "This is our sister we're talking about. You can't expect us to sit on our hands and wait around doing nothing."

"Fair enough, but again I have to make sure that you understand how important it is for your sisters to leave the police work to the actual police. Not only are you endangering them but think about the legal ramifications when we do find the killer. A good lawyer will have a field day with the fact that a doctor who delivers babies, a TV anchorwoman, and a ghost that nobody sees but the sisters, have been snooping around without just cause or following rules of evidence. He'll throw the case out faster than the district attorney can open his mouth to argue with him."

Resigned, she nodded. "I get it. I'll talk with the sister squad. But you must know how close we are. I have to keep them and my mother updated."

"I'm okay with that, and now that we have that settled, let's move on to the next issue." He walked back around his desk and sat down. After taking another big gulp of his coffee, he said, "Even a rookie cop knows not to pursue a possible killer by herself."

She opened her mouth to give her side of the story before he put his hand up to stop her from speaking.

"Don't bother explaining. Mitch did that for you. Despite his trying to make it seem less dangerous, you and I both know it could have gone south in a New York minute."

"I know. It wasn't my best decision, but Colt, we're talking about Deena here, not just some random missing woman. She's been my best friend since we were toddlers. When I found out there was a guy who'd been hitting on her at the Stallion and discovered that he lived only minutes away from the bar, I just made a decision. I'll admit now, it was a bad one, but it seemed logical at the time. You can't blame me for doing everything I can to find her."

"No, I can't, but you're a better cop than that, Maddy. We pride ourselves on being a team and always having each other's back. You have to know that the entire Vineyard police force would have come running if you had only said the word *before* you charged into that house by yourself. I don't even want to imagine what could have happened if you had come face to face with a crazy killer with a gun and you with no backup." He blew out a slow breath. "I had every intention of suspending you to allow you some time to think this through, but I'm not going to do that. However, I do need your promise that what happened this morning will never happen again—and I mean never. I love you too much to allow you to put yourself in that kind of danger again if I can help it."

"I know you're right. It's not just me that I have to think about. There's Jess. That's probably the biggest reason to heed your words."

For the first time since she'd walked into his office, he smiled. "So, we're good?"

She smiled back. "Yes. And thanks for not suspending me. I'll do better, I promise."

"That's good enough for me." He stood up. "Now get out of here and go do your job."

"Yes, sir." She stood up, gave him a quick salute, then walked out of his office.

This time everyone was smiling at her. Landers even gave her a high five as she passed him. It was obvious they had expected her to come out of Colt's office and clean out her desk.

She winked at Mitch, who looked like he was about to burst into tears at any moment. "Thanks for sticking up for me."

"That's what partners are for." He grabbed her in a bear hug. "The reason life works so well is that everyone in your tribe isn't nuts on the same day. Today just happened to be a good day for me. But hear me when I say that if you ever do anything like that again, I swear I'll kill you myself."

"I would expect nothing less." She plopped down at her desk and glanced over at Nick Ryan, waiting for him to lecture her or, at the very least, to nail her with a disapproving glare.

Instead, he smiled. "Glad to see you just got your butt handed to you and nothing worse. But for the record, though, I agree with your partner that what you did was stupid and risky."

"I know. Consider me fully chastised." She exhaled slowly and closed her eyes for a second. When she opened them, Tessa was sitting on the edge of her desk.

Of all my sisters, you were always Colt's favorite. Tessa grinned. **Of course, after Lainey started sleeping with him, that all changed. You were relegated to number two.** She leaned closer. **Now, the important question is, are you really gonna shut down the Garcia girls' investigation, or was I sent back here for nothing?**

Maddy smiled and shook her head. She'd only promised to talk with her sisters and hadn't actually said they'd back off. She had only agreed to be more careful. When she was sure no one was watching her, she gave her dead sister a thumbs up. After all, they were the Garcia sisters, she was the police, and one of their own was in danger.

"What's with that grin all over your face? Didn't your boss just rip you a new one a few minutes ago?" Nick asked.

Tessa pointed to the NCIS cop. **Go ahead. Tell him about me. I'm sure he'll think you're smokin' something.** She laughed. **Sometimes, I think about how weird this all is and even I'm freaked out.**

Maddy jerked around to see Ryan staring intensely at her. The last thing she needed was for him to suspect that she was talking to herself—let alone a ghost. "Thought of something funny that Colt said while he slapped my hand. Couldn't laugh in there, but I can't stop thinking about it now."

"Care to share? I could use a good laugh."

"What was said behind Colt's closed door should stay private. You'll have to get your jollies somewhere else." She shot him an end-of-conversation look and grabbed a folder from her desk, flipped it open, and pretended to read it.

"I have something that will make you smile," he said, shrugging. "But maybe it should also remain private."

"What?"

"You first."

She took a deep breath, hoping she would sound convincing. "He asked me what he had to do to keep me and my sisters from interfering in this investigation." She smirked. "Like he really had to ask. He's the chief, for heaven's sake."

"Your sisters? How many do you have?"

"There were five of us, but the middle one, Tessa, was murdered several years ago. So, it's just me, Colt's wife Lainey, my sister Kate, and of course, Deena."

"And are you and your siblings planning on interfering?"

"Of course not." It was hard lying to him when he was staring at her with those mesmerizing blue-gray eyes. Besides, there was a difference between interfering and investigating. "Now what's your secret?"

He picked up a notepad from his desk. "Just got off the phone with the financial manager at Warner Chemicals. Got him to tell me that Foster hadn't requested a loan on his 401K recently like he did a few months ago."

"And why would that make me happy?"

He grinned. "So where was he gonna get the money to pay off the gambling debt? Remember that he told the head honcho at the sports joint that he would have the money by that weekend. Maybe he really was planning on blackmailing Pamela Linden? Or maybe he was planning to ask your sister for the cash? Either way, it gives us another angle as to why he and Linden were killed."

"You're forgetting about the fact that both Foster and Linden were restrained."

"I'm not, which has me thinking that we need to look into the loan shark guys a little deeper. The crime scene techs went over Linden's house with a fine-tooth comb and found nothing, other than the fact that someone did a number on the inside and both her laptop and phone are missing, which we already knew. And they weren't able to find any shell casings or fingerprints from the Ring camera that was used for target practice outside her front door."

"What's your gut telling you?" she asked.

"That this is sounding more and more like a professional hit as opposed to a jealous rampage."

She nodded. "I agree. Did the crime scene guys find anything of interest when they searched the Kennedy house?"

"I haven't heard." He picked up his phone. "Let me give them a call and light a fire under their rear ends."

She watched silently as he spoke to the forensics department. When he hung up, he shrugged. "Nothing that gives us a clue about who murdered her, but they're pretty sure the victim was Nancy Kennedy, the wife of Deena's stalker. They're not ready to make that public until the results of the DNA come back, though. And get this. They found photos of Roger Kennedy and your sister dancing at the bar. They say that the photos appear to be professional, which makes me think that Nancy Kennedy may have hired a private investigator to spy on her husband." He paused. "Hold on. They just sent them."

"She knew about my sister?"

"Looks like it. We'll go through her bank records and find out who was getting money from her, and then we can talk to the PI to verify just how long Mrs. Kennedy suspected her husband of cheating on her."

"So, she could very well have had a reason for wanting to see my sister out of the picture."

He glanced down at his phone. "Now, this is really gonna make you smile." He shoved the phone over to her. "I saved the best part for last."

On every one of the pictures, Deena was either slow dancing with Roger Kennedy or at the bar sharing what looked like some kind of flirtatious banter, given the way the man touched her sister playfully and the way her sister smiled up at him.

She looked over at Ryan, who was now grinning like a Cheshire cat.

"This could definitely be our motive," he said.

She looked back down at the pictures. Deena's face had been obliterated with a black magic marker on every one of them.

"I'd say it's a pretty damn good one."

Tessa walked behind Maddy and glanced at the photos over her shoulders. **This doesn't look good. Jealous women have been known to go bat-shit crazy,** she said before she disappeared.

9

Maddy frowned when she turned around and realized that her sister was no longer there.

Oh, great! Way to drop that little jealous woman tidbit on me and then disappear.

Tessa was right, though. A jealous woman could be unpredictable and, as her dead sister had so eloquently put it—bat-shit crazy.

There were so many questions that couldn't be answered right now. If only Deena would call, these things would all be cleared up in no time. For instance, did Nancy Kennedy follow Deena to Foster's house that night? Or maybe *she* had actually followed her husband there. If Maddy allowed herself to entertain that idea, then it wasn't that much of a stretch to imagine that Nancy, already suspicious about Roger Kennedy cheating on her, may have waited and watched for the perfect moment to confront both of them.

It had already been established that the gun was registered to Carl Linden, who said that he gave it to his wife when she left him. Could Mrs. Kennedy have wrestled this away from the

Naval officer and accidentally killed her before turning the gun on Foster? Or was Mr. Kennedy the culprit?

Where is he, anyway?

So many theories, none of which could be proven at this point. All of them brought even more questions. Like where was Deena if it had gone down like that? As much as Maddy hated to let her mind go there, she knew the person that Nancy Kennedy wanted out of the picture the most was probably her sister.

Could the jealous woman have killed the other two and taken Deena somewhere? But why? If her sister was the one Nancy was after, why not kill her with the other two?

A disturbing thought ran through Maddy's mind. Maybe that was the point. If it could be proven that Deena had been there at the time of the murders and had suddenly disappeared, it stood to reason that the police would assume Deena was the killer. At the very least, she would be a person of interest—which she already was.

Maddy shook her head, trying to clear her thoughts. Nothing made sense since it was obvious from the DNA on the condom at Foster's house that Deena had slept with him at some point. Had she run by his place for a quickie before heading to Warner Chemicals? Was it possible that the condom had been in the trash for several days, and that maybe Deena wasn't even there that morning? Hadn't spent the night? But her lipstick on the wine glass suggested otherwise. The perfectly made bed didn't offer any help with that, either, because if Deena had spent the night, she would have made the bed before doing anything else. That's just the way she was.

A part of her prayed that her sister had indeed been spared for whatever reason, but another part knew that if that was how it went down, her sister was still in a lot of danger—if she was even alive.

Maddy shuddered. Just thinking about it was too much to

handle right now. But a nagging thought brought her back to her sister's cell phone. Why had they found it demolished along the side of the road going out of town? Right now, the forensic techs were trying to lift any info off Deena's extremely damaged device, but it didn't look promising.

Where the hell are you, Deena?

However, there was still the reality that both Linden and Foster had been restrained. That blew the whole theory about Nancy Kennedy wrestling the gun away from the helicopter pilot and led Maddy back again to the possibility of a professional hitman.

And if Nancy Kennedy wanted Deena dead, who brutally murdered her?

She sat down at her desk and rubbed her forehead, hoping the answers to all her questions would magically pop into her brain. But none did. It was so confusing. Just as she was about to open up the file and reread everything they had so far about the investigation, her phone rang, nearly causing her to jump out of her skin.

Caller ID showed that it was Warner Chemicals. She wondered why they would be calling her. Had her sister shown up as if nothing had happened?

Oh, God, she prayed that was true.

She grabbed the phone. "Detective Castillo."

"Detective Castillo, this is Martin Warner of Warner Chemicals. We spoke the other day about your sister missing an important meeting. I was just checking to see if you'd heard from her. We're all so worried since it's not like her to just up and disappear."

"Who said she disappeared?"

A short silence ended when he cleared his throat. "I guess I just assumed that she had since I never heard from her—or you for that matter. Your sister still has unfinished business here, and I would have thought she would have at least called to let us know if she was sick or if, for some reason, she had to take some time off and delay the renovations."

"To answer your question, I haven't heard from her." Maddy blew out a breath and closed her eyes. "Deena is nothing if not conscientious about her work, which is why I expect to hear from her soon with a logical reason why she hasn't called me."

"I'm sorry to hear that. If there's anything we can do to help, let us know. If your sister's in trouble, we all want to help."

"I don't suppose she left her computer over there, did she?" Maddy knew that was a long shot but couldn't stop herself from asking.

"Wish she had. Then I could have used it to give her presentation myself the other day. It wouldn't have been as good as Deena's would have been, but my execs are dying to see what kind of awesome decorating she has in mind for their offices."

"The computer's missing as well as—" Maddy stopped talking before she blurted out that they'd found her sister's phone smashed to smithereens outside Vineyard city limits. That kind of information was best kept under wraps at this early stage. "Hold on a minute," she said as Danny Landers slid a stack of reports across her desk. Glancing down, she realized that the top one was the official results from the crime scene technician who had processed the Kennedy house. Along with them were the photos of her sister they'd found on the woman's desk. Staring up at her was a woman with her face blacked out, but despite that, Maddy immediately knew it was Deena. The only other interesting thing was the analysis of the fingerprints found on the butcher knife used on Nancy Kennedy.

Deena's prints aren't there, thank God.

The only other prints on the knife beside Nancy Kennedy's were that of an unidentified female and an unidentified male. She would get the evidence guys to take a razor or a toothbrush from Kennedy's bathroom to the lab for DNA and fingerprints. But that wouldn't prove that Roger Kennedy was the killer. There were so many reasons why his prints might be on the knife, most of them not related to homicide.

So, how did that other female's prints get on the murder weapon? Could it be as innocent as being the prints of a friend who had come over for dinner and helped Nancy chop the salad or cut the meat? Could this unidentified woman possibly be the blonde that the bouncer at the Stallion had seen hanging all over Roger that fateful night? Another possibility was that someone killed Nancy Kennedy for another reason that didn't involve Deena. Maybe dirtbag Roger had several women on a string.

Whatever it was, it was apparent that they needed to do a deep dive into Nancy Kennedy's life, along with her husband's. Another trip to the Stallion was also warranted to see if the bouncer remembered said blonde's name or maybe even seeing Roger making nice with more than one female.

Suddenly, Maddy remembered that she still had Martin Warner on the phone. An idea popped into her head before she spoke. Deena had been working for Warner Chemicals for a few months. Maybe she had confided in someone, or maybe one of her conversations with someone had been overheard. It was worth a try. They were running out of leads, and she was fighting to ward off desperation.

"Mr. Warner, are you still there?"

"I am, but I'll need to end this conversation soon. I have an important meeting in fifteen minutes."

"No problem. I was just wondering if I could swing by there and talk to some of your employees?"

"Why would that help? I'm sure nobody has any more information than I do. Your sister was very professional when she was here. I never saw her talking to anyone but the people she needed to discuss renovations with." He paused. "And of course, David Foster, God rest his soul."

"Sometimes the least little thing that might seem inconsequential might prove to be helpful."

After a long pause, the CEO said, "I still don't think it will help because your sister was so private, but you're more than welcome to give it a shot. When would you like to come by?"

"What about tomorrow morning? We can be there around ten."

"We?"

"My partner and me."

"Again, I believe you will be wasting your time, but like I said, you're welcome to try. I'm looking forward to meeting you in person."

Before Maddy could respond Warner hung up, and she was left wondering if he was right about them wasting their time.

But time was definitely something they were running out of, and she would be remiss if she didn't check out every possible angle. If, in fact, Deena was still alive—and for her own sanity, Maddy had to believe that she was—they had to work fast.

"Sorry, Colt," she mumbled to herself. The sisters couldn't just sit by with Deena missing and possibly in trouble. They'd just have to find a way to stay under his radar.

After hanging up, she took another look at the pictures that Ryan had forwarded to her phone. Although Deena's face had been X-ed out with a marker, she could still see her eyes, which were looking up at Kennedy and apparently laughing at something he'd said. The picture must have been taken before her sister found out that the man was married. Ever since Deena's own cheating, humorless ex had been killed several years before, her sister had vowed to only look twice at men who made her smile and treated her like a friend and ally. From the pictures, it looked like the guy made her laugh.

Unfortunately, he had also committed a major, mortal sin in her sister's eyes.

Roger Kennedy was a cheater.

"Are you getting any clues looking at those pictures I sent to you?"

She looked up to see Ryan staring intently at her, and she shook her head.

"I couldn't help overhearing your conversation about your sister. Care to share that with me?"

Every instinct in her body told her to lie about it, but a twinge of guilt made her kick that thought to the curb. After all, she and Mitch had promised not to withhold information from the NCIS cop, especially since he was now a big part of the investigation. Truth be told, he was kinda growing on her in a quirky sort of way and always shared his information about the double homicide victims with them.

"That was the CEO of Warner Chemicals where my sister was contracted to do a major makeover." She stopped when her voice cracked. After a few seconds, she continued, "They haven't seen or heard from her, either."

His eyes grew serious. "That doesn't mean your sister..." He paused, then moved on, apparently not wanting to finish his thought. "Don't overthink this, Castillo, is all I'm trying to say."

"I know, but sometimes I can't help it." She sighed. "Anyway, I'm going to go over there tomorrow morning to talk with some of the employees. Maybe one of them had a conversation with Deena and can remember something that seemed off."

"You're not going alone, are you?" He didn't wait for her answer. "I was planning to swing by the Sporting Place tomorrow morning before I head this way, but I can do that on the drive home tonight and go with you tomorrow as backup."

She shook her head. "You go talk to the betting place people tomorrow. If we're leaning toward Foster getting a beatdown-gone-too-far from one of the loan shark enforcers, they just might slip up and say something we can use. Besides, Mitch would pitch another hissy fit if I didn't take him with me after warning me that he would kill me himself if I ever went solo again." She smiled. "Thanks, anyway. Here's hoping that we both find out something that might help us find my sister."

Ryan nodded. "Oh, on another note, I asked Flanagan and Landers to pick up Carl Linden and bring him here for more questions. Want to do the interview with me?" When she looked confused that he would ask her to join him, he added, "I distinctly recall that you were able to open Linden up about his alibi back at his house. Apparently, you got under his skin."

She tried not to smile. "I've been told that's one of my many annoying talents."

Before he could respond, his attention was diverted to the door when the two young officers walked in with Carl Linden in tow. "Come on. Hopefully, that annoying talent will prove useful today."

He got up and walked to the interrogation room with the two cops and the suspect. Maddy was right behind him, wondering if Mitch would consider her a traitor for doing this without him.

She looked around the station. *Where was Mitch anyway?*

Ryan must have read her mind. "Your partner left a little early today. Something about his wife and rabbit food."

Maddy laughed. "It's a long story. Don't ask."

When she and Ryan were seated across from Linden, she asked if he wanted a drink.

"I'd give my left nut for a double whiskey right now, but from the scowl on your face, I know that ain't happening anytime soon," he responded. "What's this about anyway?"

Ryan shoved the picture of Roger Kennedy across the table. "You recognize this man?"

Linden shook his head. "Never seen him before in my life. Who is he?"

"Just someone we need to speak with about your wife's murder," Maddy responded.

Linden's eyes teared up at the mention of his wife and murder in the same sentence. "He killed her?"

"We don't know. Right now, he's just a person of interest, like you are."

"Me? I would never kill my wife. I loved her. Hell, I was doing everything in my power to get her to come back to me."

"It must have pissed you off that she rejected you—that she couldn't stand the sight of you," Maddy fired back. "That she was partying every weekend without you and even got a judge to say that you couldn't get within a hundred yards of her."

Linden slammed his hand hard on the desk. "Damn right it did, but like I said, I loved her. She was the only thing I ever *did* love. I would never kill her."

"Yeah, yeah. So why don't we believe you?" Before he could respond, Maddy answered her own question "Oh, I don't know. Maybe it's because ballistics prove that it was your gun that killed her and the man she was with."

"Add in the fact that your whereabouts on the night of the murder can't be verified, and to anyone with even a smidgeon of common sense, it seems reasonable to surmise that you're a lot more than just a person of interest," Ryan blurted.

Linden shot out of his chair and raised his fists at them. Both Maddy and Ryan jumped up. Maddy reached for her gun, ready to use it if necessary, before the man glared at her with a look so evil, she shivered.

Realizing he was outnumbered, Linden sat back down. "Look here, lady. I told you that I parked outside her house the night before. Nothing else. And I was more than a hundred yards away, so don't try to pin this on me."

"And you didn't see her at all the next morning?" Maddy stared him down.

"Hell no. Are you deaf? How many times do I have to tell you that?"

Just then Flanagan knocked on the door and stuck his head in. "Maddy, I have to talk to you right now."

She looked at Ryan and shrugged, then got up and walked out of the room. After the door closed behind her, she faced the younger cop. "What's so damn important that you interrupted an interview, Sean? You know how vital it is to keep a suspect talking. We had him ready to kill us, and we both know that's when a suspect says something he later regrets."

"I know, Maddy, but this is really big." He showed her his phone. "If you remember, Foster's neighbor from across the street was out of town when we tried to talk to him the morning of the murder. He—"

"Please tell me that he saw something before he left," Maddy interrupted.

Sean shook his head. "He was already on a plane to Atlanta for a business meeting."

"So, we still have nothing?"

Flanagan's lips curled in a half smile. "I didn't say we had nothing, Maddy. The man was out of town, but his Ring camera wasn't." He pointed back down at his phone. "Look closely."

There was a picture of a car parked in front of Foster's house timestamped at 8:45 a.m. on the day of the murder.

"Pamela Linden's Lexus," Flanagan said.

"That's fifteen minutes before her scheduled meeting with Foster, according to her own notes. But what does it prove? We know she was there. I'm hoping that you've got something better than this for me."

He used his fingers to enlarge the picture on his phone.to

show the rear end of a pickup parked farther down the road. "See that truck?"

"Yeah, so what?" she said. "Now if you had an image of the killer walking down the street towards Foster's house, that would imp—"

He held up his hand to cut her off. "Look again. This time check out the license plate." He wiggled his eyebrows up and down, Groucho-Marx style. "And who do you think this truck is registered to?"

She couldn't help herself and laughed. He could be such a drama queen sometimes, and she was anxious to get back into the interrogation room. "Roger Kennedy?"

"Nope. The Silverado is registered to the guy waiting for you in the interrogation room right now. None other than Mr. Carl Linden."

Maddy grabbed the phone from his hand and enlarged the photo even bigger. Although only a little of the front of the truck was visible, something was very clear to her as she stared down at the vehicle. "There's no one in the truck."

"Jackpot! Just where in the hell was Linden?" Sean asked, grinning now like he'd just shot a three-pointer to win the state basketball championship.

10

———

"You did good, Sean." Maddy blew him a kiss before opening the door and walking back into the interrogation room.

Ryan looked up, his eyes questioning. She had to bite her lower lip to keep from smiling because of what she'd just learned. Instead, she sat down next to him. After taking a deep breath, she focused on Carl Linden "Can you tell me once again where you were the night before your wife was murdered?"

He closed his eyes and took a deep breath himself. "Look, Officer, I don't know how many times I have to tell you before you believe me." He stopped and made eye contact with her, probably hoping that would end the interrogation. From the way his hands were shaking, it was obvious he was seriously in need of a stiff drink or two.

Like that was ever gonna happen.

"Why don't you tell me one more time?"

He took a drink from the bottle of water that Danny Landers had placed in front of him before responding. "I drove by her house and sat out front for a few minutes. I swear I was always a hundred yards away."

"Go on," Ryan prompted when Linden stopped talking.

"That's it. After about ten minutes I got bored and went home. I've already told you I woke up the next morning with a killer migraine. After that I took some medicine and fell asleep. I only woke up when you pounded on my door. End of story."

"Are you sure about that? Think long and hard before you answer, Linden." She leaned closer and in almost a whisper, added, "And keep in mind that more than likely I already know the answers to my questions before I ask them."

He stared at her for a few minutes before he replied. "You can try and intimidate me as much as you want, but my story will stay the same. Seems to me that you're barking up the wrong tree and wasting precious time on me when you should be out there looking for whoever killed my Pammie."

Maddy turned to Ryan with mischief in her eyes. "Do you see his nose growing right in front of us?"

He looked confused for a second before going along with her. "I believe I do."

Maddy turned back to Linden. "Out of the goodness of my heart, I'm going to give you one last chance to tell the truth."

"Dammit, woman. How many times do I have to explain it before you believe me?"

Maddy pulled up the picture that Sean had sent to her phone and showed it to Ryan before pushing it across the table toward Linden.

After glancing down, he shrugged. "So what? We all know that my wife was there that morning. That's her Lexus."

Maddy stood and walked around the table by him, then leaned in and enlarged the photo with her fingers. "And whose Silverado is that?"

The man's face lost all color, and he shook his head. "Okay, you got me. I lied about the migraine. Big deal."

"Oh, it's a big deal, all right," Ryan said, glancing up at

Maddy when he finally realized where she'd been going with all the questions. "Why don't you stop lying and tell us what you were doing in front of David Foster's house fifteen minutes before the homicides most likely occurred?"

Linden took another drink of water before looking away. Finally, he turned back. "It's not what you think. I already told you that I parked up the street from her house the night before, hoping she'd come out and I could talk to her. I had a lot to drink that night and must have fallen asleep. When I woke up the next morning, I started to leave when I saw her garage door open, so I decided to follow her." His eyes pleaded with them to believe him.

"You never got out of the vehicle?" Maddy was ready to play her trump card if he lied.

"No. I swear."

She used her fingers to enlarge the picture even more. "I must be blind or something. Sure looks like the truck is empty."

This time his face flamed, and he tried to stand. Landers was at his side immediately and pushed him back into his chair.

He grinned. "Nature called. I got out to take a leak."

Maddy shook her head. "Do you have any idea what is involved in a murder investigation? We check every angle, every camera available to us. Fortunately, nowadays, almost everyone has a Ring camera on their front porch." She leaned over and fast-forwarded to ten minutes after ten when he was seen walking back to his truck and driving away.

"Let's see. That's twenty-five minutes total that you were out of your car. Even old guys with prostate problems don't take that much time to pee."

"Okay. Okay. I'll tell you the truth now."

"Do you honestly think we're gonna believe you after all the lies we've caught you telling?" Maddy asked.

Linden narrowed his eyes and zeroed in on Ryan as if he'd

had enough of her questions. "I needed to know what she was doing in that house."

"Funny. I distinctly remember that your wife divorced you," Ryan said. "And that's exactly why she took out a restraining order against you. You were stalking her."

"What happened after you got out of the car?" Maddy asked before Linden could react.

"All I did was walk around to the back of the house and look in the window."

"And?"

"And I saw Pammie and an older guy sitting on the couch."

"Cut the bullshit and tell us what happened after that. Did you see her in Foster's arms, and in your rage, break into the house and kill them both?"

He looked surprised that she would even consider that. "I loved her. I only watched her for a few minutes before I went back to my car. I swear I never went into the house. I had a little scotch left in a bottle in my car. I was anxious to get back to it and drown my sorrows."

"Was there anyone else there with your wife and the older guy?"

Maddy held her breath waiting for his answer, hoping that if he said no, it might mean that her sister wasn't even there when the murders occurred.

"Not that I could see. I waited for a few minutes, then left. The next day you guys showed up at my doorstep and told me that my wife had been murdered." He swiped at a tear that had escaped down his cheek.

"Unfortunately, by your own admission, there were only two people in that house, and they were alive and well when you looked into that window. We've looked at videos all the way up to 10:30 that morning when the housekeeper arrived and found the bodies, and no one else entered or left the house. That makes you the only one who could have killed them."

Maddy glanced toward Ryan and nodded.

He nodded back before motioning to Landers who'd been standing behind Linden ever since he'd gotten angry and tried to jump out of his chair. "Read him his rights and book him on capital murder charges," he instructed.

Landers cuffed him as he recited the Miranda rights, then led him out of the interrogation room.

Once they were alone, Ryan turned to Maddy. "What are you thinking?"

She shrugged. "Not a hundred percent sure he's our guy, but he's all we have right now." Then she grinned. "And I'm beginning to think that my sister wasn't even there when this all went down."

"So, where is she?"

"That, my friend, is the 64,000-dollar question."

HE CLOSED his eyes as he sat in the car down the road from his house. The cops and the crime scene techs had left over an hour ago, but he couldn't bring himself to go in there even though he wanted to grab a few things he'd need on the run. There was the danger of them realizing they'd missed something and reappearing, only to catch him red-handed in the house.

He'd gone there earlier, determined not to take no for an answer. This time he intended to force her into divorcing him, one way or another. When he'd confronted her, he'd been furious to discover that the bitch had hired a private detective to follow him around. Even had pictures of him and Deena dancing. When she admitted that she had been monitoring his barhopping for over two months, he'd punched her in the face and then rushed from the house in a fit of anger. Right then, he couldn't stand the sight of her.

The liquor store was his first stop after that, and he'd downed nearly half a bottle of whiskey before returning to force her into giving him a divorce. He'd asked many times, but she'd always said they could work things out. He had fallen out of love with her several years before and discovered how much fun he could have as a single guy. The sex wasn't always the best, but it beat the hell out of Rosy Palm and her five sisters. Some women were so desperate that it hadn't taken much effort to get them into bed. Of course, afterwards, he would dump them like a bag of rotten potatoes. Why would he want to be tied down with just one woman when the world, especially the bars, was like a smorgasbord of needy women just waiting for a good-looking man like him to pay them a little attention?

That had been his MO until about six weeks ago when Deena Rodriguez walked in and smiled at him. He knew then that no matter what it took, somehow, he had to convince his wife to let him out of the loveless marriage. He didn't care what he had to give up. He was done. It had been a long time since he and Nancy had been intimate—a long time since they had even been civil to each other. He focused on how he would convince Deena to see him as the man who would worship her. He'd known that she was special that night he'd first laid eyes on her. After much flirting and bantering with her, she'd finally agreed to dance with him.

When he closed his eyes, he could still feel her body next to his as they slow danced. She definitely wouldn't have been a one-night stand. Even now, he could imagine what life with her would have been like. She was everything he ever wanted in a woman—smart and funny, not to mention gorgeous.

But things hadn't worked out the way he'd planned. When she'd noticed the tan line on his ring finger, everything changed. She'd called him a lying cheater and never looked his way again.

He couldn't give up on her, though, convinced that once she really got to know him and understand his situation with his wife, she would come around. He'd been stalking her for over a month now. That's how he'd discovered that she was seeing another man. He followed her when a man picked her up outside the bar and then sat in his car, hoping for a chance to talk to her. He left the next morning when he saw another woman drive up and walk to the door.

When he heard about the double homicide at the guy's house, he hoped and prayed that it wasn't his Deena who was the victim. He was more than a little elated to find out the dead woman was the other woman he'd seen enter the house.

But if it wasn't Deena, where was she? He tried finding her with no luck—sat for hours in the parking lot of her apartment building, hoping to get a glimpse of her, hoping to convince her to give him a second chance.

That thought was still in his mind as he stood over Nancy, who had looked so pitiful begging for him to help her, and he'd almost done exactly that. But that thought had lasted about half a second before he remembered how she was ruining his life.

So, he'd looked her right in the eyes, bent down, and pulled the knife out in a single jerk, knowing he was signing her death certificate as blood spurted from the now gaping wound. He realized his prints would be all over the knife, but it would be hard to prove when he had handled the knife. After all, he had lived in that house for over ten years.

Ten miserable years.

He'd slipped out of the house, feeling more hopeful than he had in a while. Maybe now that Nancy was dead, he could convince Deena to give him a second chance. He would no longer be a cheater in her eyes, and his wife's death might even warrant a little sympathy from her since he was now a widower.

He had to try. He had to have her, no matter what he had to do to accomplish that.

11

———

"How was your trip to tofu land yesterday?" Maddy asked, trying unsuccessfully not to smile as she watched his reaction to the question.

Mitch pointed his finger at her. "I see what you're doing here, partner. You know damn well how that little excursion went. You're just trying to rile me up." He sighed. "My God! The woman made me eat a fake burger. I still have that nasty taste in my mouth." He paused to take a drink of his coffee and swish the liquid around in his mouth before swallowing. "Promise me you'll take me to a real burger joint for lunch today." He pulled a paper sack out of his desk drawer, raised it up for all to see, then tossed it into the trashcan. "Nobody should have to eat this crap."

"You know I can't do that. Taking you to eat behind Sara's back would be like I was betraying her." Maddy knew that eventually he would break her down, and there would be a loaded hamburger and lots of fries on their lunch menu, but she couldn't help herself. He looked so adorable when he begged, and she had never been able to say no to anything he asked of her. She loved the guy like the older brother she never had.

"Come on, Maddy. It could be our little secret. Sara would never know."

"She'll know if you end up in the Emergency Room again with a burger attack like the last time. It should—"

"That was a burrito," he interrupted. "I probably went a little crazy with the hot sauce."

"Whatever! I have a rule. I don't go to burger joints with just anybody. I'm watching my weight too, you know. When I do go, I usually ask for something in return."

Mitch grinned, probably knowing he had her, just like always. "And what would a sex- starved nymph like you want? Because I can get one of these young bucks here to service you." He made a sweeping motion around the room with his arm.

Maddy slapped his arm. "Why is it that a man's mind always assumes everything is about sex?"

"Oh, I don't know. Maybe it's because that's about ninety percent of what we think about all day."

"And the other ten percent?"

"Wondering how to get it." He laughed. "Here's a fun fact. Sex burns off as many calories in thirty minutes as running eight miles in the same time frame." He winked. "Got you there, princess."

Number one. No man has ever lasted thirty minutes on the sex clock. And number two, no man has ever run thirty miles in eight minutes, Tessa said, suddenly appearing and sitting on the end of Maddy's desk. **"Tell Mister Chubbs here that when it comes to his wife and her health journey for him, he needs to chin up—or in his case, chins up."**

Maddy walked over to stand beside her dead sister before addressing her partner. "Name one person that you know who can run eight miles in thirty minutes, or for that matter, have sex for that long?" she quoted Tessa. She held her hand up in the air and pretended to touch Tessa's hand.

Mitch squinted, then recovered. "For a minute there, I thought you had high-fived the air." He blew out a breath. "Okay then. You got me there, but Maddy, please, I can't go home to carrot soup or some other crappy thing that Sara is going to force me to eat. She still believes that this awful food will magically transform me into Brad Pitt."

Tessa laughed. **No chance of that, big guy.** She turned back to her sister. **And I kinda like him a bit chubby because I still have a million fat jokes left in me. Besides, look at him all hopeful over there. You know what they say about not taking life too seriously. No matter how healthy you are, nobody ever makes it out alive. I predict there's gonna be a lot of health nuts feeling pretty stupid when they wake up in the hospital dying of nothing one day,** she quipped, before shrugging. **Do the humane thing, Maddy, and put him out of his misery. Let him have his carbs.**"

Maddy sat down at her desk and faced her partner. "Okay. I give up. If you want to go behind your wife's back and sneak food, who am I to stop you? But, if you're asking for my opinion, you need to have a serious conversation with Sara about all this. Maybe there's a compromise you can come up with."

You know what they say about opinions, Maddy. They're like buttholes. Everyone has one and most of them stink. Tessa wiggled her eyebrows. **Yes?**

Maddy ignored her and stared at her partner, waiting for his response.

"Can I assume that this means what I think it means?" Mitch asked.

Maddy nodded. "If you promise to have a serious talk with your wife so that I don't always feel like a traitor."

Mitch jumped up from behind his desk. "Done. Now, let's talk about that new Five Guys hamburger joint in the mall. I heard they have awesome burgers and fries to match, not to mention all the free peanuts you can eat while you wait. I may even get two of everything." He licked his lips. "Wonder if they have dessert?"

"No way," Maddy said. "One burger, one order of fries, and that's it, but only if you go with me to Warner Chemicals afterwards."

"Why are you going to Warner Chemicals? Did I miss something that came up about our investigation?"

She shook her head. "Not really. I spoke to Martin Warner yesterday and asked if we could come over and talk to some of his employees to see if any of them overheard anything that could be a clue to where Deena might be."

"Does this Warner guy think it might be helpful?"

Again, Maddy shook her head. "Just the opposite. He said that Deena was the quiet type and hadn't really made friends with many people there. Apparently, she did her job and stuck to herself."

"That sounds like Deena. She was always the responsible sister and probably thought making friends with those people might somehow jeopardize her job." He shook his head. "Except for David Foster, that is."

"I can't wait to hear that story," Maddy said.

"If we don't find anything, we can at least cross that off our list of people to talk to. And we might even get lucky and find someone who remembers something that might prove helpful to us." He grinned. "And hey, I'm getting a burger and fries out of this little fishing expedition. That's the best part."

"So, you're good with going with me?" When he nodded, she continued. "I arranged to meet Warner at 1:30 today."

Mitch glanced down at his watch. "It's already eleven. We need to hustle to get to Five Guys beforehand." He grabbed the keys to the squad car and threw them at her. "You drive."

Maddy caught them midair and headed for the door before

turning back to him. "And if you're a good boy, I might even turn on the sirens to beat the lunch crowd."

"Oooh! I got chills just thinking about it. You really know how to turn a guy on, partner."

"One of these days, I'm gonna turn you in for on-the-job sexual harassment."

"Ha! Look at me. No one would believe you." He nudged her forward. "Let's go. I'm hungry enough to eat the whole cow."

AFTER PIGGING out at Five Guys, Maddy and Mitch headed north to the Texas/Oklahoma border. Warner Chemicals was located just on the Oklahoma side in a small town called Rosemont, a forty-five-minute drive from Vineyard. They were stopped at the gate by a guard who most definitely was concealing a weapon under his jacket. The man checked their badges, glanced down at his clipboard, and then opened the gate to allow them to proceed.

"Mr. Warner's office is in the building on your left. Third floor."

After thanking him, Maddy drove down a long driveway, spying two buildings in the distance. Both sides of the road were lined with colorful flowers, which was a nice addition to the otherwise nondescript concrete driveway. She wondered if this had been Deena's idea.

"Over there." Mitch pointed to the three-story building down the road from what was probably the factory and covered the remainder of the block. "Whoa! I had no idea this place was so big. Deena must have been excited when she was offered the job sprucing it up."

"She was," Maddy said. "She said that working on this place

was a big deal, and if she did a nice job, it might jumpstart her designing career."

They got out of the car, headed for the door of the smaller structure and walked in. In the middle of the room there was a fountain with a beautiful sculpture in the center, the silver lights reflecting off it like dancing stars.

"Deena," they both said in unison as they stared at the sculpture.

"She told me once that they had her on a budget, but that she was able to find sales at Market Hall in downtown Dallas."

"May I help you?" the attractive redhead sitting behind the front desk asked as they approached.

Maddy flashed her badge. "Detective Madelyn Castillo and Lieutenant Gary Mitchell from the Vineyard Police Department here to see Mr. Warner."

After checking the computer in front of her, Courtney, according to her name badge, pointed to the elevator to the left of where they stood. "Mr. Warner is expecting you. His office is on the third floor."

As they waited for the elevator door to open, Mitch eyed her and grinned. "We're about to meet Darth Vader's long-lost sister."

Maddy looked at him, confused before he responded just as the door opened.

"Meet Ella—you know Ella Vader."

She couldn't help herself and laughed out loud. "If you have any plans of ever working the comic club circuit, I advise you not to give up your day job."

"You're not allowed to make fun of me. I heard you laugh," he said as they entered the elevator and the door closed behind them.

They ascended for a few moments in silence, and when the elevator stopped, they stepped out onto the third floor.

"Hey, nobody said Warner's office was the *entire* third floor," Mitch said, scanning the large area.

"They must make a lot more money than I thought," Maddy responded as she checked out the decor. The walls were painted a pale shade of yellow with beautiful images of waterfalls and awesome scenery pictures.

"Five bucks says this is Deena's handiwork," Mitch said, following her eyes to the walls.

"Of course it is. Her own apartment is painted with this same subtle color of yellow." Maddy sighed. "The girl does have talent."

After checking in with yet another attractive redhead at the desk in the middle of the room, they were led to a back office where they got their initial look at Martin Warner.

The CEO was not what Maddy had expected. She'd assumed that a company this huge would have an older person in charge. Martin Warner looked to be in his late thirties, tall, well-built, and wearing a suit that for sure had not come off the racks at Suits Warehouse.

Warner came around the desk and shook Mitch's hand first, and then hers, holding it a bit longer than normal.

"You look just like Deena. Is there any news about her?" the head honcho asked.

Maddy shook her head. "I was hoping that we could get a clue or two from some of the people she worked with here."

"Like I told you on the phone yesterday, your sister was somewhat of a loner. You are welcome to talk to the people in this building about her, but don't bother going to the warehouse. She only worked in this building."

"Thank you," Maddy said. "Is there anyone in particular who might have known her better than some of the others?"

"Other than Foster, I really can't say. But that isn't much help to you." Warner walked around and sat back down at his desk.

"Then, if it's okay with you, we'll just check around and see what we can find out. We promise not to stay too long," Mitch said.

"That will be fine. I hope you do find something useful. We'll help in any way we can. Your sister is a special lady with enormous talent."

As they headed for the door, Warner called out to them. "Wait a minute. You might want to talk to Jeff Donovan. If I recall, I sometimes saw them eating lunch together in the cafeteria."

"Jeff Donovan?"

"He's the company lawyer, and his office is downstairs on the second floor." He pushed a button on his phone. When the receptionist answered, he asked her to give Donovan a call to let the lawyer know that he was sending two Vineyard police officers to his office.

"Thanks. You've been very cooperative, and we appreciate that. I'm sure Deena thinks a lot of you."

He smiled. "Like I said, the feeling is mutual. Good luck."

Heading down to the second floor, Mitch turned to Maddy. "How did a guy so young become top dog of this monstrous company?"

Maddy shrugged. "It's a family business. My guess is that he was next in line."

"You're probably right." He gave her a mischievous grin. "Good looks, all that power and money—you might want to take a shot at that. He had a sweet smile for you."

She playfully slapped his arm. "You don't even know if he's married."

"I kinda do," Mitch responded. "All the pictures in his office were of him and two kids. No wife. No ring."

"You need to worry about not having a heart attack with all

the junk food you eat and leave my social life to me," she fired back.

"What social life?" he asked, before backing away from her before she could slap his arm again.

When they reached the second floor, they were greeted by another attractive receptionist, but this one had what Maddy would call chestnut hair—brown with just a touch of red.

"Mr. Donovan is waiting for you. It's the last office at the end of the hall."

As soon as the door opened, they walked in and flashed their badges at Jeffrey Donovan, who was sitting at his desk.

He looked up and smiled. "Martin said you looked just like your sister, but the resemblance is really uncanny." He motioned for them to sit in the two chairs opposite his desk. "So, what can I do for Vineyard's finest?"

Maddy leaned forward. "We're looking for anything that might help us find Deena. Mr. Warner mentioned that sometimes you had lunch with her downstairs."

He nodded. "Your sister and I hit it off the minute she started working here—even went out a few times before we both agreed that we were better friends than anything else."

"Did she ever mention David Foster?" Mitch asked.

Donovan scowled. "David Foster was a lowlife. Why Martin ever hired him as the director of sales is beyond me."

"So, you and Foster weren't friends?"

"Hell, no. I despised him, and I'm pretty sure he felt the same way about me. I can't tell you how many times I tried to talk Deena out of dating him, but she didn't listen. Against my better judgment, I even told her that he'd had multiple complaints about harassing some of the young girls who work here. Several sexual harassment lawsuits ended up costing the company a lot of money. It was weird, though. He had some kind of strange hold over her. She never saw the bad in him. Said she knew that they had no future together but that he was fun and made her laugh."

"Sounds like my sister." Maddy paused before speaking again. "Mr. Donovan, is there anything you can tell us about her from the day she disappeared?"

Donovan shook his head. "Sorry, I was in D.C. at the time testifying before Congress. I flew out Thursday night." He smiled at her. "And call me Jeff. I—"

"About what?" Mitch interrupted. When Donovan finally took his eyes off Maddy and shifted them in Mitch's direction, he added, "Why did you testify in Washington?"

"Not sure why that might be important." He paused as if deciding whether to answer or not. "Here at Warner Chemicals, we make the fluoropolymers used to coat water towers and airplanes, among other things. The senators were looking for ways to make the metal on military planes less likely to crack under pressure. I was there with three other companies testifying."

"Did you win?" Maddy asked.

He smiled at her, and for a minute, she felt a tingle up her spine.

"Still waiting to find out, but I did my best." He walked around to her and flashed another of his smiles her way. "Tell you what. I'll take some time tonight to try to remember if there's anything that might help you. Leave me your number, and I'll call so we can meet up."

Mitch stepped in front of her and shoved his own card into Donovan's outstretched hand. "Call the station if you have any new information." He gave Maddy a nudge toward the door.

In the elevator he turned to her. "Now that was a player."

"Wow! What happened to the guy who was ready to have one of the young studs back at the station service me? Or the guy who encouraged me to hit on Martin Warner?"

"Something about Donovan didn't sit well with me."

"What?"

"He smiled at you like he was undressing you."

"Get outta here. He did no such thing."

"I can't put my finger on it, but there's no way I'm letting him have your phone number. He can deal with me from here on out." He shrugged. "Girl, you've been out of the game too long if you don't even recognize when someone is flirting with you."

"What if I liked him flirting with me?"

"Now, you're messing with me. I know you can spot a womanizer as easily as I can."

They got off the elevator with him mumbling. "And what's with all the redheads?"

12

When Maddy and Mitch walked back into the station two hours later, Nick Ryan looked up from his desk and greeted them with a wave.

He spoke to her, totally ignoring Mitch, who was now glaring at him. "Hopefully, you found something that might be useful to our investigation or to finding your sister."

"Nothing that we didn't already know. Deena didn't socialize much on the job," Maddy responded.

"Bummer. We could use a break in the case." Ryan shook his head. "I'm beginning to think we need to expand our investigation."

"What do you mean, Ryan?" Mitch asked, plopping down into his desk chair and continuing to glare at the NCIS cop. "Are you implying that Maddy and I are slacking off on the job?"

"A little sensitive, are we?" Ryan quipped and then turned to concentrate on Maddy. "But no, that's not what I'm saying. I'm thinking we need to lean a little harder on Carl Linden. I think there's a lot he's not telling us."

"Possibly. We can get him back into the interrogation room

later today," Maddy said. "In the meantime, have there been any hits on the BOLO out on Roger Kennedy?"

"No, but Landers told me they'd discovered that he owns his own Orthodontic clinic on the other side of town. He and Flanagan went there and were told that Kennedy took a few days off for personal reasons." Ryan shook his head. "How does a dentist disappear off the face of the earth after allegedly killing his wife? Every cop in the surrounding areas and even out of state are looking for him."

Maddy laughed. "Obviously, you don't have kids. An orthodontist is a braces guy. It cost me a small fortune when my daughter had to have them." She sat down at her desk and faced him. "Kennedy will eventually show up. But, back to our day at Warner Chemicals. Although we didn't get any real clues about my sister, we were able to talk to several women who hated Foster enough to want to do him harm."

Ryan's eyebrows hitched. "Well, that's something. What did the guy do to piss off so many of the fairer sex?"

"Apparently, he couldn't keep it in his pants," Mitch deadpanned. "Rejecting a woman after that is more than enough to bring out her claws." He smirked. "But then again, you probably know all about that, right, Ryan?"

The Navy cop threw back his head and laughed out loud. "I'll admit that I've probably pissed off a few women in my day, but never badly enough to need a bodyguard. Can you say the same?"

"If you two boys are done exchanging insults, we need to review what we know about this investigation, or do we need to bring out the ruler and see who has the biggest one?" When neither of them answered, she continued, "Lose the testosterone, both of you, and let's move on." She turned her attention back to Ryan. "Was there any excitement here while we were gone?"

"A little. I had a lot of time to think about Pamela Linden and decided to review all the notes we had on her. Figured there was probably a lot we didn't know—like why she had a scheduled meeting with David Foster the morning they were both murdered."

"Unfortunately, neither of them can tell us," Mitch said. "So, what else did that pea brain of yours come up with?"

Ryan ignored the jab. "Is it possible that we're taking the easy road by pinning the murders on her drunken, angry ex? I wondered if that might be the case, so I began digging into her personal life. Carl Linden did say that she was a frequent flyer on the weekends at the local honky-tonk. Thought maybe there could be a jealous boyfriend in the picture."

"Good point. We should take another run at the bar. I wanted to talk to them anyway to see if there might have been any other jealous women hanging around Roger Kennedy. Josh, the bouncer there, mentioned a blonde. My guess is there were more since he was another one of those guys who obviously couldn't keep it in his pants."

"Let's plan on that trip to the bar sometime tomorrow." Ryan faced Mitch this time. "On another note, I drove over to the Cordova Helicopter Services and had an interesting chat with Ernie Sheridan, the owner of the company and Lieutenant Linden's boss."

"Was he able to shed any light on the case?" Mitch asked.

Ryan shook his head. "Not really, but I did find out why she was able to afford that huge ranch. Before I went to the helicopter place, I checked public records and discovered that Linden inherited the ranch when both her parents perished in that big airline crash several years ago at DFW Airport. Apparently, she was part of a multi-million-dollar settlement with the airlines. She moved in after she and Carl split up and was granted an agricultural property tax exemption because she leases out 300 acres of the land farthest from her house to neighboring ranchers who house their livestock there. That saved a helluva lot of money on property taxes, which I understand were nearly forty grand, despite her exemptions."

"Holy cow!" Mitch exclaimed. "Even with her inheritance and the settlement, she'd still need money to run the place. How does a helicopter pilot who flies city tours get that kind of money?"

"That's just it. According to Sheridan, Linden made north of 150K."

Maddy whistled. "For sure, I'm in the wrong business. That's airline pilot money."

Ryan grinned. "It's amazing what you can find out on Google if you look in the right places. When I questioned Sheridan about how a tour helicopter pilot could make a salary like that, he took me to school. Said that the notion that his company only flew tourists around was a misconception in today's day and age. According to him, the only time they do flying tours is over the Labor Day weekend when Vineyard puts on a three-day celebration. Apparently, the entire town turns out to party, as well as a crowd of people from neighboring cities."

"Don't tell me they make their money taking people on those copter excursions where the wannabe cowboys shoot feral hogs from the air for sport?" Maddy made a face. "That's disgusting."

"Not exactly." Ryan stood and walked over to stand beside Maddy's desk. "With ranches growing larger and operations becoming more challenging, there's an increased need for advanced technology to run them efficiently. Most of the big ranches are using helicopters nowadays to meet that challenge."

"Cordova is home to some of the biggest ranches in Texas," Mitch said, getting up and walking over to stand beside Ryan, obviously more interested now. "I can see where that might be lucrative."

"You would be correct," Ryan said. "According to Sheridan, they have contracts with most of those ranches. Linden got the big bucks because she was good at what she did and kept the ranch owners happy."

"What exactly do those helicopters do?" Maddy asked.

"A variety of tasks, such as herding cattle and tracking the livestock. They also check fences and irrigation systems to make sure the cows don't get out, and that they have enough edible grass and water, especially in high-heat seasons and periods of drought, like right now." He paused. "According to Sheridan, they're affectionately called Aerial Cowboys and are an absolute necessity for ranchers. They no longer use real cowboys on horses, trucks, or ATVs in today's changing times."

"So, our dead woman was not hurting for money. From all indications, David Foster was a sleaze and probably knew that. With all his gambling debts coming due, he may have viewed her as a cash cow, pardon the pun," Mitch surmised.

Maddy jumped up from her chair. "That's it! Remember the head honcho at the sporting place in Fort Worth told you that on the weekend of the murder, Foster mentioned that he would be coming into some money?"

Ryan nodded. "I've been thinking about that, too. The CEO said that Foster let it slip that he would be able to pay off the entire 100K debt after the weekend."

"Sounds like it could be a motive for Linden's death if she refused to give him the money, but there's still a little problem with that theory. Foster was tied up and killed as well," Mitch offered.

"I thought that, too, and came to the same conclusion. Knowing how rich our lady pilot was, I dug deeper into her financials."

"Go on," Maddy urged.

"You'll never believe what I found."

"What?" Maddy said. "You're killing me, Ryan."

"Anything this good is always worth the wait." When Maddy cupped her hand and pointed it up to keep him talking, he added, "Apparently, Pamela Linden never got around to changing her will. Guess who gets that two-million-dollar ranch and a 401K worth almost that much?" He raised his eyebrows. "And that's not even including her 200K life insurance policy."

"Carl Linden," Both Maddy and Mitch said in unison.

"Bingo!"

"How DID you get away from the house without alerting Colt?" Maddy asked as she joined her two sisters at the bar around the corner from the hospital.

Both Kate and Lainey turned to greet her before Lainey responded. "I told him I was meeting my agent. Said Sam was in Dallas to interview a potential new client and needed to talk to me about my contract with WFFA, which I told him was about to expire this year."

"What's going on with your contract, Sis? Are you finally going to quit so you can run the vineyard full time?" Kate asked.

"Nothing's going on. I lied about the contract. I've got another two years. And no, I love my job too much to give up the weekend anchor slot. Besides, I have extremely capable people who can run the vineyard and the wineshop for those two days every week."

Maddy looked surprised. "And your chief of police hubby bought that story?"

"It's partially true. Sam *is* interviewing a new client, but he doesn't need to meet with me. You all remember me talking about Jason, my co-host? Well, he's having problems with his own agent and wanted me to set him up with a face-to-face with mine."

"Still, you and I both know that your husband, my boss, is already suspicious, thanks to Mom calling him. I wouldn't be surprised if he checked out your story."

"Already got that covered," Lainey said. "Sam's booked at the Conquistador Hotel next to the airport. If Colt does check registrations, I think that will satisfy him." She paused, then grinned. "And I gave Sam the lowdown. He's prepared to lie if Colt does call. He'll say that I just left, and if that happens, he'll call to warn me."

"I should have known that you had it all figured out," Kate said before turning to Maddy. "So, what's going on with your investigation and finding Deena? I'm worried sick about her."

"We all are. Unfortunately, nothing useful to report. I'm going to file an official missing person report tomorrow." Maddy sighed. "And then—"

"Before you start talking, Maddy, let's get another round of margaritas." Lainey held up her empty glass and licked the salt off the rim. "God, I need to get out more."

You'd better slow down, girlfriend. We wouldn't want you to get picked up for a DUI and then have to have your already-suspicious husband bail you out of the pokey.

They all stared as Tessa slid into the booth next to Maddy.

Hello, bitches. You really didn't think you could have a clandestine meeting without me now, did you?

"Wouldn't think about it." Maddy held her drink in the air. "Too bad you can't have one of these. They were always your favorite."

Tell me about it. Being dead sucks. She turned toward Maddy. **Find out anything at Warner Chemicals today?**

"You went to Warner Chemicals?" Kate asked. "Why?"

"I thought I might find someone who may have befriended

Deena. Somone who might remember something that she may have said or done before she disappeared."

"And did you?" Lainey asked.

Maddy shook her head. "We wasted a couple of hours talking to everyone in the building who may have had any contact with Deena. There were a few people who remembered seeing her around, but no one had any idea where she might be right now. We all know how private she is. Obviously, she followed the golden rule about keeping her private life separate from her business one."

"Apparently not with David Foster," Lainey said, sarcastically.

"That one's a mystery to me, too. The CEO there never even mentioned Foster except in passing. He sent us to Jeff."

"Jeff?" Kate squinted. "Who's Jeff?"

"Jeffrey Donovan, Warner Chemicals' chief lawyer. Although he really didn't have much to add to our investigation, he did let it slip that he despised David Foster. That he'd warned Deena about him many times. Said there was a folder full of sexual harassment claims from a lot of the young women there that had cost the company a bunch of money. He commented that he never could figure out why Martin Warner hadn't fired the guy."

"What could our sweet Deena have possibly seen in a guy like Foster?" Lainey asked.

"I don't know. That also remains a mystery. Donovan thought he might have some kind of weird hold on her or something."

Tell them about the murdered woman, Tessa prompted.

That got their attention, and both sisters leaned forward to hear better.

Maddy pointed to Kate. "Thanks to you for remembering about the married man who was trying to get cozy with Deena at the Stallion." When Kate looked confused, she added, "You know, the dude with the expensive car."

"Oh, yeah. He killed someone?"

"Not sure. But after you told me about him, I went to the Stallion and found out that his name is Roger Kennedy. Since his address was close to the bar, I decided to pay him a little visit."

"Was Mitch with you?"

Maddy shook her head. "And before you even start on me about why that was such a bad idea, forget it. Colt has already raked me over the coals about it, and Mitch threatened to kill me himself if I ever did anything like that again."

"I should hope so, Maddy. The dude could have killed you, and—"

Tessa raised her hand. **Let her finish the story, Lainey. It's a good one.**

Maddy nodded to her dead sister. "Like I said, I went to his house and found a woman on the floor of her bedroom dying from a gaping chest wound and a bloodied butcher knife beside her."

"Oh, my God! What did you do?"

"I dialed 911 and then called for backup. I tried to save her, but she had already lost too much blood. She died in the ambulance on the way to the hospital."

"Was it Kennedy's wife?" Kate asked, leaning so far over the table now that Maddy could almost touch her. "Did he kill her?"

Maddy shrugged. "It was Nancy Kennedy, but we don't know if her husband was the one who killed her. There were three sets of fingerprints on the knife. Hers, one set from an unidentified male, and the other from an unidentified female. The lab is still processing them, but so far, no hits."

"Holy crap! You're the cop, Maddy. What do you think?" Lainey asked.

"The prints could be from Kennedy since he's never been in trouble with the law and has no fingerprints on file. The lab took two toothbrushes from the bathroom and is checking out the DNA now. The female prints could be from the actual killer or just a woman friend who helped the dead woman chop up the meat or a salad for dinner."

"You're not thinking that the guy could have hurt Deena, are you?" Kate asked, unable to hide the worry in her voice.

"Don't even go there. We have to keep believing that Deena is hiding out somewhere and can't communicate with us for whatever reason."

It's that 'whatever reason' that has me worried, Tessa mumbled.

Maddy blew out a slow breath. "I know. But to answer your question, Kate. We have no idea if Kennedy killed his wife, but I doubt that he had anything to do with Deena's disappearance."

"Why would you say that?" Lainey asked.

"For starters, we're not even sure that he *was* the one who killed his wife. Even if we find his fingerprints on the butcher knife, that's not a smoking gun. Any good lawyer would shoot that down in a nano second since it was his house, and he might have used it while he was cooking. Second, right after I found out that Deena hadn't shown up at work, I went to her apartment, twice to be exact. The first time, I saw a man who was lingering outside her door, and the other time I saw what I think was the same man sitting in his car outside her apartment. Although I never got a good look at the man's face, there's a good chance it was Kennedy. We found a receipt for a rental the day of the murder, a black Cadillac SUV like the one I'd seen at her apartment. That makes me think he was there hoping to talk to her or something."

"What did this Kennedy guy say about his wife's murder?"

Maddy shrugged. "Unfortunately, nothing. He's in the wind. There's a BOLO out on him as we speak."

"So, what you're saying is that we really don't have much to go on to help us find our sister, right?" Kate blew out a frustrated breath.

"True. The unknown is a killer, pardon my use of that word." Maddy glanced first at Lainey, then Kate before speaking again. "But there is one other bit of hopeful information I can share with you guys." She took the last sip of her margarita and then set the glass down. "We interviewed Carl Linden, the husband of the woman who was found dead next to David Foster."

"And?"

"We booked him for the double homicide."

"And how would that be good news for Deena?" Kate asked.

"A Ring camera across the street caught Linden's car in front of Foster's house right at the estimated time of the murder. We were able to see that Linden had gotten out of the car, and although he lied at first, he finally fessed up that he'd gone around to the back of the house and peeked into the window."

You could have heard a pin drop as the sisters waited for Maddy to speak again.

"He said that Foster and his ex were the only ones in the living room."

"Does that mean that Deena wasn't even there?" Kate asked, letting the hope come through in her voice.

"Possibly, although she could have been in the bedroom. Remember, evidence proves that she'd been at the house at some point and that she'd had recent sex with him." Maddy glanced down at her watch. "Gotta run. Mom's coming into town tomorrow, and I've got to clean up before she gets here. You know how she is about clutter. That's where Deena gets her neatnik thing."

"Oh Lord, don't let her come near my apartment." Kate giggled. "Bet she wishes we were all like Deena."

"I'm sure she does," Maddy said, getting up. "So, until I have more news, let's just play it cool. I'll call another meet-up when I have something more to tell you."

"What about Mom?" Kate asked.

"We definitely don't want to let her know any of this," Lainey said. "She'll run straight to Colt with it. I swear, she likes him more than me." She tsked. "Let her think she's helping us a little and then get her mind busy with something else—like working toward world peace."

Seriously, Lainey, world peace? Hell, Coke and Pepsi can't even be on the same menu at restaurants, and you think there can be world peace? Tessa wisecracked.

"Do you have a better idea?" Kate asked.

Tessa shook her head. **For now, don't tell her any of the stuff you've learned, Maddy. Definitely not the stuff about the Cadillac guy. She'll want to go over there and interrogate him herself.**

They all agreed. As soon as Maddy was by herself on the way home, she thought back on the conversation with her sisters. Something kept nagging at her about the investigation. She had to be missing something.

But what?

She was deep into thought when her phone rang, nearly causing her to wreck. She looked at Caller ID before answering. "Mitch, why are you calling me so late? Are you OK?"

13

"When you didn't answer my calls, I drove by your house. Where are you?" Mitch paused. "It's not those damn burritos that will be the death of me, Maddy. It's you."

Maddy glanced at the clock on the car dashboard—eleven-fifteen—before responding. "I had drinks with my sisters."

"It wasn't one of those secret meetings that I wasn't invited to *once again*, was it? 'Cause if it was, I'm—"

"Relax. Our mom is coming into town tomorrow, and we were trying to figure out what to do with her."

"Make sure that Sara and I get an invite when she makes her fabulous enchiladas," he said. "Sara tried to make them, using your mom's recipe, but they weren't even close."

Maddy breathed a sigh of relief that he wasn't going to pressure her about the sit-down with her sisters. Normally, her partner could read her like a book, but obviously, the thought of her mother's Mexican food was enough to grab his undivided attention and make him forget everything else. Well, that and the appeal of eating something other than the diet food his wife served him.

"Why the urgency to talk to me at this hour, Mitch? Aren't

you usually in bed by now, all cuddled up with your sound machine blaring?"

"For your information I was in bed, and I can't help it that Sara snores louder than I do. We both need the volume up on the machine. Anyway, I got a call from Flanagan. He said the cops in Jackson Heights picked up Roger Kennedy in a bar across the county line."

Maddy pulled into her driveway, then put the car in reverse to back out. "I'll meet you at the station in about ten minutes. Don't you dare interview him until I get there."

"Don't bother. Flanagan said the Jackson Heights cops are transporting him to our station as we speak, but there's a little problem. He's so drunk he can barely walk. He'll be sleeping it off for the next several hours. I just wanted to let you know so that you can plan to come in a little earlier tomorrow. We'll tag-team him with questions like we always do and maybe catch him in a lie or two."

She switched back to drive and pulled forward. "What about Ryan? Does he know?"

"He has nothing to do with this case, Maddy. Neither Kennedy nor his wife were ever in the military."

"I know, but I think we should include him. He did share all that info about Pamela Linden's financials earlier today." Maddy turned off the engine and walked into the house, thinking how empty it felt with Jessie still at band camp until the Friday before Labor Day.

"You're probably right, but as far as I'm concerned, we already have Linden's killer behind bars. Ryan's part in that investigation should be over. Maybe now, he'll go back to Fort Worth and do his thing there. I can't say I'll shed a tear over that."

"Come on, Mitch, he's not that bad. I'm kinda getting used to him."

"You seem to have a thing lately for good-looking men. Sounds to me like you need to get laid. But, hey, if he can put a smile on your face and make you forget how worried you are about Deena for even five minutes, more power to him."

"What?" She laughed. "You assume that I need a man to fulfill me. Well, listen up, buddy, I'm here to tell you that I don't, so quit trying to pimp me out."

He snickered. "If you say so, Maddy. Gotta run. With a little luck, I can still get a few more hours of beauty sleep before I meet you at the station. See you bright and early tomorrow."

After disconnecting, Maddy couldn't help herself and grinned. Her partner might not be as far from the truth as she'd tried to make him believe. She had been tense lately, and in the course of only a few days, she'd met three attractive men who just might have the goods to make her smile again.

Nick Ryan threw his suitcase into the trunk, then slid into the driver's seat and headed toward Vineyard, still thinking about the call he'd gotten late last night from his sister. Julie was on her way to Leroy from El Paso because their mother had fallen and broken her hip. Stephanie Ryan was scheduled for surgery that afternoon.

He reasoned that more than likely, Carl Linden was responsible for Pamela Linden's death, and he was already locked up in the Vineyard jail. Until the trial or more evidence surfaced proving Linden's guilt or innocence, there really was no reason why he couldn't take a few days off and go back home to help his sister. He'd hit the road as soon as he got things wrapped up at the station and be there before his mom got out of surgery.

But he couldn't stop the nagging voice in his head that

wondered if "more than likely" was enough to positively pin Pamela Linden's murder on her ex.

Yeah, they had the murder weapon with Carl's fingerprints on it, but he'd insisted that he'd bought the gun for his wife. Said she told him she didn't need it. But when he'd looked for it that first day they'd met him at his house, he'd been surprised to find it missing. As suspicious as that sounded, knowing the guy regularly consumed more than his share of alcoholic beverages might be enough to convince a judge that Carl could have been in a blackout and didn't remember his wife taking the .22 that was found at the scene.

But if that were true, why had Pamela Linden carried the gun with her when she went to see David Foster? Was she afraid of him for some reason? And if so, why didn't she call the police?

The only other bit of evidence they had on Linden was that, by his own admission, he'd followed his wife to Foster's house and watched her sitting on the couch with the guy. Of course, that could be easily argued away by a good defense lawyer, especially since Carl's fingerprints weren't found anywhere in Foster's home.

Nick decided he'd take one last look at Linden when he got to the station, then head west to Leroy. The case could wait three or four more days until he could be sure his mom was out of surgery and back in her room. He'd be able to help his sister with their mother's immediate post-op care and planning for her long-term recovery.

When she'd called, Julie had repeated the doctor's recommendation that, because of the severity of the break, their mother stay in a rehab facility for two weeks post-op to learn how to walk again and to master the basic skills of taking care of herself after the hip had healed. But Nick knew his mother. Knew that she would fight them tooth and nail if she had to go anywhere other than her own home after the operation. He'd heard her say many times that after seeing several of her friends get "kidnapped" and shoved into a nursing home, she would never let that happen to her. Convincing her that rehab was not a nursing home would take a great deal of persuasion and more than likely, require both of her kids doing the persuading.

Especially if the doctor kept referring to the place as skilled nursing. The words sounded way too much like nursing home rather than the rehab facility it was.

But if he were being honest with himself, he knew there was a good possibility that at the very least, his mom would end up in an assisted living facility even after the rehab stay. He'd researched hip fractures after his sister had called, and according to most of the articles he'd read, some degree of help was usually necessary with the daily activities of living long after the hip was repaired. There was no way his mother could live by herself, at least not for a while. He didn't even want to think about how difficult convincing her would be if that happened. But he couldn't waste time thinking about that. They'd cross that bridge when they came to it. For now, just getting her through the surgery was priority number one.

Julie was a nurse with three kids and worked full-time in the ER at Mercy Hospital in El Paso. Her job was not only stressful but sometimes required her to do double shifts or stay later than normal. Bobby, her husband, was the regional sales rep for a large corporation and traveled three or four days a week. He'd taken personal days to keep the kids while his wife went to Leroy, but this was the busiest time of the year for him, and he couldn't take much time off right now.

No, his mom would not like it if she had to move to another place, but if she wasn't able to take care of herself, there might be no other options. And although it would be the first time he would step foot in Leroy General since his wife, Sharon, had died, he hoped he'd be able to get through that without breaking down.

He pulled into the parking lot at the police station, noticing a lot of cars were already there. He figured something must be up and hoped it wouldn't delay his trip to Leroy.

"What's going on?" he asked as soon as he walked in and sauntered over to his desk.

Castillo looked up. "They found Roger Kennedy. Mitch and I are getting ready to interrogate him. Want to sit in?"

He shook his head before sitting down and breathing a sigh of relief that the commotion was not about Carl Linden. On the surface, Roger Kennedy had nothing to do with his homicide investigation into Lieutenant Linden's murder. With a little luck, he could still wrap things up and head out the door right after lunch.

MADDY WALKED into the interrogation room with Mitch right behind her and got her first look at Roger Kennedy. Although she wasn't 100% sure he was the man she'd caught a glimpse of at Deena's apartment that week, a few good questions might trick him into admitting that it had indeed been him.

Danny Landers entered the room and set a bottle of water in front of Kennedy. Then he took his position behind the suspect in case the man decided to get rowdy. Maddy stared at Kennedy, thinking that he didn't look like a killer, sitting there in handcuffs, looking like he could really use a couple of Excedrin for a hangover headache.

Dressed in a T-shirt and wrinkled jeans with splotches of dirt all over them, Kennedy could have been any other ordinary guy. Except for the fact that his eyes were still bloodshot from all the liquor he'd consumed the night before, and he was being interrogated for the murder of his wife. Maddy held his gaze even though it unnerved her the way he kept staring at her.

She looked away for a second to regain her composure before facing him again. "Good morning, Mr. Kennedy. I hope you had a restful sleep. The question on my mind is why you were hiding out in Jackson Heights."

His eyes narrowed in defiance. "Who said I was hiding out? My wife and I had a little argument, and she kicked me out. She knows I have needs and usually turned a blind eye. For some reason, this time it was different. I was waiting till she cooled down and called to beg me to come back home, like she always does after one of our tussles."

"So, you and your wife had fought before? Did it usually end up with you in a motel?"

"Sometimes, but like I already told you, we always work it out."

"Oh, you're gonna play that game, are you?" Mitch leaned forward, scrunching his nose when the combined odor of BO and alcohol hit him in the face. "Explain why we have your fingerprints on the weapon you used to kill your wife."

Kennedy tried to stand before Landers roughly pushed him back down. "I didn't kill Nancy." He sniffed back a crocodile tear. "I didn't even know she was dead until the cops told me last night."

"Is that so? We know you were stalking Deena Rodriguez. Explain that."

"Who?"

"Cut the crap, Kennedy. Do we look like rookie cops to you? I've seen you at my sister's apartment twice. That counts as stalking to me, right Mitch?"

Mitch nodded as Kennedy continued to stare at Maddy.

"Deena was your sister? I should have known when I first saw you that day."

Maddy grinned as Mitch slapped her leg under the table, their version of a secret high five. "So, you admit to being at her apartment?"

"Where were you Friday morning when she disappeared?"

"Not proud of this, but I'd passed out in some rinky-dink hotel with some woman I'd picked up at the bar. Woke up the next morning with the worst headache I've ever had. Went straight home and crashed."

"And what time was that?"

"I don't know. It was a little after noon because the asshole clerk tried to charge me for an extra day."

"Can you prove that?"

"It was the Vineyard Landing. I paid with a credit card, You can easily check that out." Kennedy lowered his head.

Maddy made eye contact with Mitch. According to the coroner, Foster and Linden were found by the housekeeper at 10:30 that morning. If his alibi checked out, there was no way he could have been at the scene.

"Why were you at Deena's apartment, then?"

"She wasn't answering my calls, and I was worried about her. That's all."

"Really! I have it on good authority that she'd quit taking your calls long before you showed up at her apartment."

A flash of panic spread across his face. "I didn't say that I never called her before that. I liked your sister and wanted to make sure she was all right. I worried about her." He shrugged. "Ask her yourself. She'll tell you that I called almost daily."

"Did she answer?" Maddy asked, unwilling to let him know that not only was Deena missing, but also, that her cell phone had been destroyed.

Kennedy shook his head. "I should have just let it go. She made it perfectly clear that she wanted nothing to do with me after she realized that I was still married. I was about to give up on her when I discovered that my wife had pictures of her and me dancing as well as a few of me making out with another woman in the corner of the bar."

That got Maddy's attention, and she glanced toward Mitch. When they'd found Nancy Kennedy dying in her house, the only pictures they'd found were of Deena and Roger Kennedy.

"What other woman?"

"Just someone I partied with sometimes. I had no feelings for her like I had for Deena."

"Does this other woman have a name?"

"Christine something or other. Like I said, with her it was just sex."

Maddy shook her head in disgust, thinking this guy was a real sleaze. "And you don't even know her last name?"

A slight smile creased his eyes. "Do you know the last name of everyone you have sex with?"

"Of course, she does. Most people do," Mitch said, barely able to hide his grin and slapping Maddy's knee under the table once again. "But we're not talking about most people, Kennedy. We're talking about you and the pictures you found at your house. Sounds like that pissed you off. Is that why you killed your wife?"

"Hell, man, I told you I didn't kill my wife. Nancy was the daughter of one of the biggest real estate moguls in Texas. Her dad made me sign a prenup that said if we divorced or if she died before me, I got nothing. He even went as far as having his high-dollar lawyer draw up a will for Nancy that cut me out completely. Knowing all that, how stupid would I have to be to kill her?"

"Pretty stupid, but you don't strike me as a brainiac, Kennedy," Mitch said. "Is that why you were stalking Deena—to tell her that you were free now to pursue her?"

Kennedy lowered his eyes, then lifted them up to meet

Maddy's. "I honestly cared a lot about your sister. I only wanted to warn her that my wife had hired a private investigator and had those pictures. Nancy was a jealous woman and could get really ugly at times. With her daddy's money, she could have hurt Deena's career."

"That still doesn't explain why your prints were on the murder weapon," Maddy interjected.

"There's a lot of reasons why my fingerprints would be on a butcher knife from my own kitchen," he said. "Any good cop would know that."

A smile curled Mitch's lip. "Like I said before, you're not a brainiac." He high-fived Maddy above the desk this time before turning back to Kennedy. "Nobody said that your wife was killed with a butcher knife. We haven't even released that information to the press."

Kennedy blew out a breath before speaking. "Okay, you got me. When I walked into the house that day, I found Nancy on the bedroom floor. I couldn't stand looking at the knife in her chest, so I pulled it out." He paused, obviously pleased with himself for that explanation.

"So, why did you run?"

"Wouldn't you have run? I was scared. Knew no one would believe me that she was already dead when I found her and that I would be your number one suspect. I was still hung over from the night before and needed some time to think it through."

Maddy leaned in, nailing him with narrowed eyes. "So, your wife was dead when you found her? That's when you pulled the knife from her chest?"

"Yes, do you believe me now?" He looked hopeful but soon changed his expression when Maddy shook her head.

"Obviously, you don't know that I was the one who found your wife that day."

"So?"

"So, I personally know that although she was critically wounded, she was still breathing and able to talk to me."

When he realized that he'd just been caught in a lie, his expression changed from pleased with himself to sheer panic.

Maddy went in for the kill. "And just so you know, Mr. Kennedy, the butcher knife was on the floor beside her, which tells me that if what you say is true about pulling out the knife from her chest, your wife was still alive when you ran out and left her to die."

She nodded to Landers. "Read him his rights and then book him."

14

Nick Ryan looked up when Maddy and Mitch walked out of the interrogation room. "You're both smiling. Does that mean that you got Kennedy to confess?"

Maddy shrugged. "Not a confession, per se, but the next best thing. He knew his wife was killed with a butcher knife even though that little tidbit has not yet been released to the press."

"Did he say why he killed her?"

Mitch shook his head. "Said he didn't do it. Said he found her dead with the knife in her chest, and he pulled it out. He also said he had lost a boatload of money because of her death."

When Ryan looked confused, Maddy chimed in. "Apparently, his father-in-law is extremely wealthy, and he made Kennedy sign a prenup that cut him completely out of his daughter's will if she died before Kennedy did. Guess Nancy's father knew what kind of man she was about to marry and wanted to protect her."

"Man, that's cold," Ryan said. "Are you thinking that maybe Kennedy came home drunk one night and decided the money wasn't worth it after all?"

"Could be. But from something Kennedy said in the interview room, his wife knew about his indiscretions and was apparently okay with it until recently. Said they'd usually argue about it, she'd kick him out for a day or two and then beg him to return home. He thought she must have realized that his feelings for Deena were different from the other women he'd bedded because she hired a private detective to keep tabs on him. He saw the PI photos of him and my sister—which we already knew about—along with pictures of him with another woman."

"I wasn't aware there were pictures of the guy with anyone but your sister."

"It was the first we'd heard about this other woman, too. Our next step is to locate her to see if she can shed some light on all this."

"We're cops. That shouldn't be too hard with today's technology."

"That would be true if we had the other woman's last name. The scumbag only knew her by her first name." Mitch grinned. "When Maddy confronted him about that, he asked her if she knew the last name of every man she'd ever slept with."

Ryan bit his lower lip to hide his smile and turned to Maddy with a pseudo-serious look. "And do you?"

Maddy glared at Mitch and then Ryan. "First of all, it's none of your business, and secondly, of course I do. And because I have more manners in my pinkie than the two of you combined, I won't ask either of you the same question."

Mitch winked at Ryan. "Now, you went and got her all riled up. She's gonna be hard to live with for the rest of the day."

"You started it." Ryan made eye contact with Maddy. "As much as I'd like to stay and hear about your social life, I need to finish up a few things here and then drive to Leroy this afternoon."

Mitch grinned. "So, this is goodbye?"

"Don't look so happy, Mitchell. I still have a lot of work to do on Pamela Linden's homicide." He lowered his eyes and took a deep breath. "I got a call from my sister before I left the apartment. My mother fell this morning and broke her hip. She's having surgery at noon."

"I'm so sorry, Nick," Maddy said softly. "Let us know if you need us to do anything with Carl Linden while you're gone."

"That's the first time you've called me by my first name." He smiled at her. "But no, I think things can wait for two or three days while I take care of my mother. I should be back before Labor Day weekend."

"Spend as much time as you need with her," Maddy said. "We're good here."

"I appreciate that. Like I said, if all goes well, I'll be back by Thursday or Friday."

"Just in time to see how Vineyard celebrates Labor Day." Maddy looked down at her watch. "It's almost noon. Why don't you pack up and head out right now? Mitch and I will hold down the fort until you get back."

"That's probably not a bad idea. I'm useless here, anyway. I can't stop thinking about her and what will happen after the surgery." He stood up. "I'll talk to Chief Winslow and then head out."

"You go on. You've got a two-hour drive to Leroy, and I'm sure your sister could use the support while she waits for your mom to get out of surgery," Maddy said. "I'll let Colt know your plans."

He nodded his appreciation, picked up a file from his desk, and headed toward the door.

When he was gone, Maddy turned to Mitch. "I pray that his mom comes through the surgery okay. I can't even imagine what a basket case I'd be if it were my mother going under the knife."

Mitch sat down at his desk. "Speaking of your mother, isn't she supposed to be coming into town today?"

"Her plane gets into DFW at 6:10 tonight. My sisters and I are going to meet her and then take her out to dinner."

"So, what's our next move, partner?"

A slight smile curled Maddy's lower lip "I'll make you a deal, Mitch. If you go with me to the Wild Stallion Saloon, I'll buy you lunch afterwards."

"You're on!" His eyes lit up and then narrowed. "And just why are we going to the

Wild Stallion?"

"To see if we can find out the last name of that mysterious other woman that Kennedy was fooling around with. She might be able to give us something we can use on Kennedy."

"You go tell Colt about Ryan's mother, and I'll go put the lunch that Sara packed for me where it belongs—in the garbage." He stood up and grabbed her in a bear hug. "I think I love you, kiddo."

"Be sure and remember that the next time Sara has to haul your chunky ass to the ER."

ON THE FIFTEEN-MINUTE drive to the Stallion, Mitch was like a two-year old on his way to an amusement park. You'd have thought that Maddy had promised him season tickets to the Cowboys games instead of just a cheeseburger with onion rings.

She hoped that she wouldn't be the reason something happened to Mitch because she enabled him to sneak behind his wife's back and eat unhealthily. She also hoped that Sara wouldn't kill her if she found out.

"I think I may get two cheeseburgers and keep one in the fridge at the station for when Sara packs more tofu in my lunch," he said, preening like he was so proud of himself for thinking of that.

"Oh no, you don't. I feel bad enough, already."

"Come on, Maddy, you've seen what she's making me eat. Even you wouldn't eat that crap."

"I know. I just feel like I'm lying to Sara every time I indulge you."

"Better that you feel like that way once in a while than me living the rest of my life like this."

She snuck a peek at him and for the first time, she felt empathy for her partner. Nobody—at least not anybody she knew—would like to eat kale and tofu every day. She decided she'd invite Sara to lunch soon, confess to her about the cheeseburgers, and then try to talk her into implementing a diet that wasn't so hard on Mitch. Maybe even suggest that she and Mitch see a nutritionist and work out a more realistic diet that he could follow.

And possibly an exercise routine, although Tessa had once reminded her that a whale swims all day, eats fish, and is still fat. She had also quipped that when people go to a gym, the first thing they tell them is to wear loose-fitting clothes. Tessa had continued with that thought by saying that if these people had loose-fitting clothes, they wouldn't need a freakin' gym in the first place. Maddy chuckled. Her dead sister came up with the darndest things sometimes, but if she were being truthful, she'd have to admit that a lot of them made sense.

"Park in front," he said when they pulled up to the bar. "I don't think I can walk all the way from the back since I don't have any carbs in me," he said with a serious face.

"Get outta here. Of course you can." Against her better judgment, she pulled up to the front and stopped to let him out. "I'll park the car while you get Josh to let us in."

"Josh?"

"The bouncer. Tell him you're with me."

When she walked in several minutes later, Josh and Mitch

were sitting at a table laughing about something. She smiled. Her partner could be very cordial when he wanted to be—which wasn't very often.

She walked over to them as Josh stood up to pull the chair out for her.

"Chivalry is not dead, I see," she said. "Thanks."

"So, Mitch here tells me that you're looking for a woman who may have spent time here," he said when she was seated.

"We are. I'm sure you heard about Nancy Kennedy's murder."

"Mitch said you were the one who found her, right?" Josh asked.

"I did. And this morning we booked Roger Kennedy for her murder, thanks to your help in finding him." Maddy paused. "But that's not why we're here now. The last time you and I talked, you shared the video footage of the night my sister went missing. At that time, you told me about another woman who you thought might have gotten friendly with Kennedy after Deena rejected him. Do you remember?"

"Yes. She was a blonde who comes in the bar every now and then, but I don't know her name. Funny, she only started coming here in the last month or two. I don't recall seeing her before that or even lately."

"Kennedy mentioned that he was having a fling with a woman named Christine. Could that have been her?"

Josh frowned and stroked the back of his neck. "I know I probably heard her name once or twice, but for the life of me, I can't remember it. All I know is that she had long blonde hair and a great figure. I feel sure that her name wasn't Christine, though. I would have remembered that since my sister's name is also Christy."

Maddy pulled out her phone and brought up the video

footage she'd copied the last time she was there. "Take a look at this and see if anything jogs your memory."

She and Mitch sat silently and watched as the bouncer concentrated on the video. He paused it on a picture of Deena standing at the bar talking to a blonde.

"That's the woman I've seen Kennedy with around here, but I still can't help you with her name. Sorry."

Maddy took the phone from him. "No worries. This may not be anything, but I'm sure we'll find her." She stood up. "Thanks again for taking the time for us, Josh."

"Anytime." He grinned. "And I don't notice a ring on your finger. Maybe one Saturday night you'll come here and dance with me."

Maddy laughed out loud. "Why do all you men think I need a social life?"

"Because you do," Mitch said before he stood up. "Let's get out of here so you can make good on your end of our bargain."

On the way to the restaurant, Maddy asked, "I wonder what my sister and the blonde were discussing."

Mitch shrugged. "Could be as innocent as what drink they preferred or perhaps something more relevant to our case. But unless we either find Deena or this mysterious woman, we may never know."

"Don't you mean *until* we find Deena?" Maddy reminded him.

"Sorry. I know we'll find your sister very soon."

"From your lips to God's ears," Maddy whispered, saying a silent prayer that "very soon" would be the outcome.

After pigging out on good burgers and excellent onion rings, the two of them headed back to the police station when Maddy's phone rang. She looked down at the caller ID before she answered. "Mom? Are you at the airport?"

"I've got some bad news, honey. On the way to Orlando International, some idiot ran a red light and T-boned us."

"Oh my God! Are you guys okay?"

"I'm just banged up and bruised. Hit my head on the dashboard pretty hard. The doc says I probably have a mild concussion and told me to take Tylenol for the headaches. Chuck, on the other hand, took the brunt of it since the car plowed into his side. I'm at the hospital now waiting for him to return from getting a chest MRI."

"But he is okay, right?"

"As far as we know, honey, but they think he's got a couple of broken ribs, and he's having difficulty breathing. The MRI will show if one of those ribs punctured a lung, and if that's the case, they'll admit him and put in a chest tube."

"I'm so sorry, Mom. You're sure you're okay?"

"Yes, honey, I'm a tough old broad, as you know. Needless to say, though, I'm not going to be able to come to Vineyard anytime soon. Please let the girls know how much I was looking forward to seeing all of you."

"Don't worry about that, Mom. In a few months it will be Thanksgiving, and hopefully Chuck will have recovered enough so that the two of you can come to celebrate with us."

"That sounds wonderful." She paused. "And you still haven't found where Deena ran off to? I'm trying hard not to panic. It's so not like Deena to disappear without telling someone."

"I know, Mom, but Tessa..." Maddy stopped talking, hoping that her mother hadn't picked up on that slip of the tongue. They hadn't told her about her middle daughter appearing to them for fear that it would only upset her.

But Carolyn Garcia had always been as sharp as a tack when it came to sniffing out one of her daughters trying to get away with a lie. The times that Maddy and her sisters had been able to squeak by with telling one were few and far between.

"Tessa?"

"I meant Lainey, Mom. I just got off the phone with her, and she mentioned how much she missed Tessa."

"Well, all right then, I've got to go. I need to be in the room when they bring Chuck back. I love you. Tell all your sisters that I love them, and that I'll be waiting to hear that you all have located Deena."

"We love you back, Mom. And don't worry. I'll let you know when there's news about Deena. I'm sure she'll show up any day now."

After she hung up, she told Mitch about her mom and step-dad. She was surprised when he didn't question her about lying to her mother. He knew she hadn't just talked to Lainey, but for some reason, he let that slide. She also knew that Mitch was almost as good as her mother at spotting a lie. Sooner or later, they'd have to tell him about Tessa's ghost, but now was not the time.

Now, they had to find Deena.

15

———————

When they arrived back at the station, the first thing Maddy noticed was that, except for Angie Winters, the dispatcher, the room was empty.

"Where is everyone?" Maddy asked her.

Angie pointed to the conference room. "They're waiting for you to update them on your investigations."

"Thanks." Maddy turned toward the conference room with Mitch right behind her.

As soon as they walked in, Colt motioned for them to sit. "I thought with so much going on right now, we needed to bring everyone up to speed on both investigations."

"With Carl Linden behind bars for the double homicide of Foster and his ex-wife, we're concentrating on Roger Kennedy," Mitch said as he took the seat next to Sean Flanagan. "Right now, we're holding Kennedy for his wife's murder, but we're still looking for stronger evidence to convict him."

Danny Landers cleared his throat. "Don't shoot the messenger, Mitch, but Linden was released about an hour ago."

Mitch scowled. "What?"

"All the evidence we had on him was circumstantial, and the

prosecutor wasn't willing to move forward with formal charges. Linden's public defender wasted no time pointing out to us that the forty-eight-hour hold on his client was up." Colt leaned back in his chair. "We either had to charge him with the murder of his wife or let him go."

"Ryan is not going to be happy about that," Maddy said. "Have you told him, Colt?"

The chief nodded. "I called right before you and Mitch returned from lunch. He'd just arrived at the hospital. As unhappy as he was about Linden's release, his concern for his mother was greater. He said he'd see us all in a few days and start from scratch with the investigation."

"So, we really don't have much to go on since Linden and Kennedy were our only leads," Maddy said.

"And we're sure that Kennedy wasn't involved in the Foster house murders?" Colt asked.

Mitch nodded. "He had a solid alibi for that night, plus there's no reason to believe that he knew either of the victims."

"But we do have him for the murder of his wife, boss," Landers interjected.

Maddy agreed. "He looks really good for that one. Right now, we're trying to locate a woman he was supposedly having an affair with. He said his wife had pictures of him with her as well as with my sister. She may have some information we can use."

"Good. Get on that right away. I've got the mayor on my tail about these investigations, so the sooner we solve at least one of them, the sooner he'll get off my back." Colt stood up. "On another note, how are the baseball practices coming, Mitch? Please tell me that we're gonna kick some major Cordova butt this weekend. I can barely stomach hearing Chief Rivera bragging about how they beat up on us last year. If they win again this year, he'll be insufferable."

"I would hardly call winning by a walk-off run as beating up on us, but to answer your question, practices are going really well, Colt," Mitch said. "We lost our catcher when Parker moved to Oklahoma last month to be closer to his grandkids. But lucky for us, Joey Henderson, a new young firefighter from Firehouse II, is as good as—and maybe even a little better—than Parker. We're hoping he'll be the difference for us on Sunday. Nothing I'd like better than to shove a baseball down Larry Sullivan's throat."

"Ah, Mitch?" Flanagan lowered his eyes. "There's something I need to tell you."

Mitch turned to him "Spit it out, kid."

"Right before I came in here, I got a call from one of my buddies over at the firehouse. He said they'd just returned from a five-alarm fire over on Grand Avenue."

"So?"

Flanagan looked first at Colt and then back at Mitch. "Apparently, Joey Henderson fell through the ceiling and was badly injured. He's at the hospital now with internal injuries, and they're getting ready to take him to surgery to insert pins into his lower leg."

"Damn it!" Mitch shouted before he lowered his voice. "Sorry. You all know how much I liked Joey. Instead of crying about the ballgame on Sunday, I should be thinking about what I can do to help an injured fellow first responder."

"Maybe we should call it off this year. Make up some excuse for why we can't do it. It's only a game," Maddy said.

"It's only a game if you're losing, Maddy. We'd never live that down." Landers turned to Mitch. "I played catcher in Little League a long time ago. I'll fill in for our team."

Mitch gave that some thought. "Thanks for stepping up to the plate, pun intended. Not many people would volunteer for that job, Danny, especially when lard-asses like Sullivan will look for ways to take you out."

Maddy couldn't help herself and quipped, "Isn't that a little like the pot calling the kettle black, Mitch? If I remember correctly, you took out poor one-hundred-and-sixty-pound Martinez at the plate last year."

That got a big laugh until Mitch narrowed his eyes at her. "If I were you, I'd be careful, Maddy. I'm sure you wouldn't want me to tell any of your secrets."

"Okay, *mea culpa.*" She winked at him. "Later, I'll need you to tell me what secrets you think you have on me."

He was silent for a few seconds before giving her a shit-eatin' grin. "Then, they really wouldn't be secrets, now, would they?"

"Enough. Personally, I don't want to hear about Maddy's secrets. All I care about right now is getting Mayor Cusack off my back." With that, Colt got up and headed for the door. "I'm counting on you all to find me some killers."

When they were back at their desks, Mitch shut down his computer and announced, "I'm gonna run over to the hospital and check on Henderson. Then I'm heading home from there. Tomorrow, we'll go through all our notes again, and hopefully, we'll catch a break and find a clue or two."

"Sounds good," Landers said. "Mind if I go with you? I shared a beer or two with Joey, and we hit it off."

"I'm sure Joey would appreciate that." Mitch bent down and opened the top drawer of his desk, grabbed the keys to his car, and then walked out the door with Landers right behind him.

After Flanagan left, Maddy and Angie were the only ones left behind, except for Colt who was wrapping up things in his office with the evening shift who had just arrived. She decided to use the quiet time to go back over her notes to see if she'd missed something. Jessie was coming home from band camp the Friday before Labor Day, and she might not get the chance to stay late again. She smiled, thinking that the last time she spoke to her daughter on the phone, Jessie had been so excited about all that she'd learned. She still hadn't told her daughter about her Aunt Deena being missing, but that could wait until Jess was home. Why ruin her adventure at camp when there was nothing she could do about it, anyhow?

Her thoughts were interrupted when Angie yelled from across the room.

"Maddy, there's a gentleman on the phone who says he has information about your sister, and he'll only talk to you."

"Transfer it," Maddy said, unable to stop herself from hoping this might be the break they needed. She picked up the receiver. "Hello."

"Detective Castillo, this is Jeff Donovan at Warner Chemicals. We met the other day when you and your partner were here asking about your sister."

"I remember," Maddy said. "You have new information about Deena?"

"I'm not sure how much it will help, but I do remember something that your sister told me the day before she disappeared."

Maddy caught her breath. *Let this be what we need,* she prayed to herself. "What did she tell you?"

He was silent for a moment before speaking, "It would be better if we met face to face."

"And why is that, Mr. Donovan?"

"Please call me Jeff. Because when I tell you, you may be able to add something that will help me remember if there was anything else that might be significant, something that didn't seem important at the time."

Maddy didn't believe his ridiculous explanation for one second and wondered if this man thought she was as naïve as other women he might have tried that line of BS on. She'd known from the moment that she and Mitch had walked into his office that Jeff Donovan was a player.

But still... She looked around, thankful that Mitch wasn't there listening to the conversation. She decided to humor Donovan in case he really did know something important.

"When did you want to meet?"

"How about tonight over dinner?"

If she had any doubts about his intentions before, she was positive now. Still, he said he'd had lunch with Deena the day before she disappeared. She may have mentioned something to him. And if there was even the slightest possibility that whatever it was might help, what would it hurt to indulge him?

Since she no longer had to pick up her mother at the airport, she'd cancel dinner plans with her sisters. On the off chance that Deena may have told Donovan something, it was too important to pass up. Besides, she knew how to handle guys who hit on her. "How about if we meet at La Cantina in Denton at eight? That's about halfway for both of us."

"Perfect."

She hung up, a little excited not only about possibly finding new information to help locate Deena, but also about the prospect of having a nice dinner with a man who seemed pleasant and was definitely easy on the eyes.

Maybe Mitch was right. Maybe her social life did need a reboot.

She packed up her things, her mouth watering with thoughts of margarita swirls and loaded nachos.

MADDY TRIED on at least five outfits before she settled on a simple flowered blouse and black Chico pants, going for a look that could only be interpreted as business casual. Her sisters were more excited than she was when she called to explain why she had to cancel dinner. Kate even suggested that a hot date with the good-looking lawyer might bring more rewards than just getting information about Deena. It gave them something to think about besides worrying about their missing sister.

Maddy had quickly shot that idea down, reminding them that this was strictly police business. But was it? Since Jake had moved to California a year ago, she hadn't even thought about making herself available again. If that happened, no one would be happier than Mitch, and it just might get him off her case about her social life—or lack thereof.

She laughed, remembering Mitch's reaction when he thought that Donovan was flirting with her that day at Warner Chemicals. He was going to freak out when he found out that she'd gone to dinner with him.

She gave her hair a final flip and turned from the mirror.

Well, look at you, getting all dolled up for a date, I hope, Tessa said, sitting on the edge of Maddy's bed. **Wear high heels. It'll make it easier to look down on him.**

"Tessa where have you been? The last time you showed up was at Kate's house a week ago."

Like I told you, I go where they send me.

"So, why are you here now? I'm only having dinner with a man who might have information about Deena."

Is he good looking?

Maddy grinned. "And then some. But he's also not the kind of guy you want to bring home to your mother."

Tessa laughed out loud. **Our mother could spot a rotten egg from a mile away.**

"He's not really a rotten egg, but I also wouldn't call him a golden one, either. Maybe somewhere in between."

Tessa gave her an imaginary shove towards the door. **Let's go. This is going to be good.**

"What? You're coming?"

Wouldn't miss it for the world. Since Mom isn't here, I

have to watch out for you. Tessa paused. **By the way, where is Mom? Thought she was coming to town to help with finding Deena.**

"She was, but she and Chuck were involved in an accident. Come on. I'll tell you all about it in the car."

On the way to the restaurant, Maddy relayed the story to Tessa, then admitted that she'd slipped and blurted out her dead sister's name.

Oh my! Did you fess up that I'm still hanging around?

"God, no. But the more I think about it, the more I think she needs to know. Maybe we'll break it to her at Thanksgiving."

Probably a good idea, Tessa said, as Maddy pulled into a parking spot at La Cantina. Walking into the restaurant, Maddy stole a glance behind her to see if her sister was still there.

She was.

An attractive, college-aged hostess came up to her, but before she even had a chance to speak, Jeffrey Donovan appeared and touched her elbow.

"I've got a table for us in the back. It's quiet there." He led her through the restaurant, pulled out the chair for her, and then smiled. "You look gorgeous, by the way."

"Thanks," Maddy said when she was seated across from him. "So, what did my sister tell you?"

"Let's order a drink first," he said just as the waiter walked over. "What's your fancy?"

Maddy looked up at the server. "I'll have a margarita swirl— light on the tequila—and a glass of ice water, please."

Donovan ordered a vodka martini, then squinted at her. "Light on the tequila?"

"I get headaches from too much liquor. I'm sure it's a message from above to keep me from drinking too much and making a fool of myself."

Wouldn't hurt you to make a fool of yourself with this guy.

And remember that despite the ads that say kisses come after a gift from the jewelers, hot sex comes after a lot of alcohol. I, for one, never went to bed with an ugly person after imbibing too much, but I sure as hell woke up with a few. Tessa said, plopping down in the chair next to her. **You never mentioned that this guy was eye candy. Now, if only he's a good egg.**

Maddy ignored her and turned her attention to Donovan. "Can you tell me what you remembered?"

"I'm afraid it might not be as helpful as you'd like it to be."

"Let me be the judge of that," she said when their drinks arrived.

He took a long sip of his before setting it down. "If the food's even half as good as this martini, I'd say we're in for a treat."

"It is. Now, back to my sister, please."

"Oh, yes. I had lunch with her on Thursday. She was really excited about showing Martin the PowerPoint presentation she'd made with her ideas for decorating the rest of our offices." He stopped to take another drink, and Maddy had to bite her tongue to keep from screaming at him to get to the point.

"Anyway, she was also excited about going to the Wild Stallion that night, not only to celebrate, but also because she was going to speak to a woman who'd called her and wanted to meet up with her. Deena said it sounded important. She—"

"Did she say the woman's name?" Maddy interrupted.

Donovan shook his head. "Just that she was really curious about why this woman wanted to talk to her."

On a whim, Maddy lifted up her phone and scrolled to the video footage from the bar. When she came to Deena talking to the blonde, she showed it to Donovan. "Do you recognize the woman with my sister?"

He started at the image, then shook his head. "Sorry. I've never seen her before. Do you think she might be the one Deena was meeting?"

"It's possible. It looks like they're deep into a conversation about something. We're working on locating her, but so far, no luck."

"Did they find out who killed Foster and that other woman?" he asked, changing the subject.

"We have a suspect in custody, but nothing's firm."

"Well, kudos to whoever took Foster out. That man was a nasty piece of work."

"You hated him so much that you're glad someone took him out?"

"Me and a whole lot of other people. Like I said, he was not a good human being." Donovan picked up his drink and drained it. "Do you want another margarita?"

"I'm good." Maddy took a second to watch him as he ordered another one for himself.

Wonder if he hated Foster enough to do the deed himself? Tessa asked, almost as if she'd read Maddy's mind.

"You mentioned that you were in Washington for a congressional hearing on Friday. Can I ask what time you returned home?"

Donovan tilted his head and stared at her before speaking, "Am I a suspect?"

Maddy laughed. "Everyone is at this point."

"To answer your question, the hearing lasted until after six, and I missed my earlier flight. I spent the night at the Radisson and flew out at 11 AM on Saturday." He picked up his drink as soon as the waiter set it down. "Here's to getting some great Mexican food into our stomachs and to finding out where the night takes us after that."

Tessa stood up and walked around behind Donovan's chair and sniffed his hair. **I don't know, Sis, I'm starting to smell a rotten egg.**

16

———

Nick Ryan and his sister sat quietly in the visitor's lounge at Leroy General Hospital waiting to speak to their mother's surgeon. Except for a nurse telling them two hours ago that surgery was going as well as could be expected, they knew nothing.

"Want another cup of coffee?" Julie asked her brother.

"No, thanks. I've had about as much caffeine as my body can handle. He glanced up at the big clock on the wall. "What's taking them so long?"

"The doctor warned us that it would be a complicated surgery," Julie responded.

"I know, but it's been..." Nick stopped talking when the doctor came through the double doors and headed their way.

Still dressed in full operating room garb, his expression confirmed their worst fears—that the news was not going to be good.

"Your mom had a serious injury called a comminuted fracture of her femur. What that means is that the thigh bone was broken in two places and required metal rods and plates to repair it. Although she came through the surgery like a trooper, she has a long road ahead of her if she is ever going to walk again."

"How long are we talking, Doc?" Nick asked.

"Her recovery will start with a two-week stint in rehab. Then she's looking at potentially a year or more of intense physical therapy to help her regain strength and mobility. In other words, the goal is to teach her how to walk again, although I must warn you that she may never be able to bear weight on that leg." He paused to let that sink in. "Unfortunately, recovery comes with a lot of pain and swelling, which we'll control with meds."

"When can we see her?" Julie asked.

"She'll be in the recovery room for an hour or so to allow her to wake up. Four hours under anesthesia is a long time for anyone, but especially for a sixty-three-year-old woman. Then she'll be transferred to surgical ICU where she'll spend a few days to make sure there are no early complications. You can see her there."

"Are you expecting complications?" Julie asked, swiping at the tears trickling down her cheeks.

"There's no reason to think she won't do well in the hospital. Your mother is a strong, otherwise healthy woman. These first few weeks will be hard on her, sometimes even unbearable, but like I said, we'll make sure that she stays comfortable. Now, if you have no other questions, they're waiting on me in the operating room." With that, he turned and walked back through the double doors.

For a few minutes, neither Nick nor Julie spoke, both still stunned by what the doctor had just told them. There was a possibility that their mother might never walk again.

Finally, Julie turned to her brother, still dabbing at the tears in her eyes. "I don't know how we're going to do this. I can't just up and leave my job and ask Bobby to take care of the kids. He can't do it, Nick." Julie lost it, and this time she sobbed.

Nick moved closer to her on the couch and wrapped his arms around her. "Don't worry about that now, Jules. You took care of Mom most of her life. It's my turn to step up. If I have to, I'll move back to Leroy or take her to Fort Worth with me. Whatever it takes."

"No, Nick, I know how hard it was for you to walk into this hospital again because of what you went through with Sharon. That's the reason you moved away from here in the first place. I—"

He placed his finger on her lips. "Shh! Let's just concentrate on getting Mom through the rest of her hospital stay and cross that recovery bridge when we come to it. I promise we'll find a way." As soon as those words left his mouth, he made the decision to do whatever he had to. If that meant changing his life as he knew it, so be it.

On the drive home from the restaurant, Maddy thought about what Jeff Donovan had told her. Her sister was meeting someone at the Wild Stallion Saloon the night before she disappeared. Could that have anything to do with the murders at Foster's house the next morning? And if so, how?

She pulled into the garage and got out of the car, still thinking about Deena. Once inside, she made a cup of coffee, sat down on the couch with it, and pulled up the video from the bar again, hoping against hope that something would jump out at her. Nothing did at first, then she focused again on the picture of the blonde talking with Deena. When she zoomed in, she realized she'd missed something all the other times she'd reviewed the tape.

Deena had that expression on her face that she always got when she was talking about something unpleasant. Only those who knew her would pick up on that signature Deena look, and Maddy wondered how she and her siblings could have missed it. It was obvious that her sister did not like whatever the blonde was saying to her. Was it possible that the mystery woman was telling her to back off Roger Kennedy? Maddy shook her head. Probably not, since Deena had already broken away from the guy a few weeks before.

So, what could have upset her?

Maddy thought about showing the picture to a lip reader but realized that the blonde was doing all the talking, and her back was to the camera.

She picked up her empty coffee cup and placed it in the kitchen sink, then headed to bed. Tomorrow was another day. Maybe with the alcohol out of her system—even though she'd only had one margarita—she'd figure it out.

The next morning, Maddy called Mitch and arranged for him to pick her up. He arrived thirty minutes later.

As soon as she slid into the passenger seat, he joked, "Hope you got a couple of apple fritters on your mind."

"Really, Mitch. Is food all you think about?" She didn't wait for his response. "I've been doing a lot of thinking about that blonde in the video with Deena. I know that my sister was excited about meeting a woman at the Stallion that night. She—"

"And how do you know that? Are you psychic?"

Maddy blew out a breath and prepared herself for a beat-down. "I had dinner last night with Jeffrey Donovan, the lawyer at—"

"I know who he is," Mitch interrupted, "And just what in the hell were you doing with that jerk?"

"He called me at the station and said he remembered something that Deena had mentioned to him at lunch the day before the murders."

"And obviously, he also remembered how he'd like to do the horizontal boogie with you." Mitch groaned. "You know as well as I do that Donovan is not your kind of guy, Maddy."

"Believe it or not, Mitch, I'm a big girl, and I can take care of myself. This isn't my first rodeo with guys who want to jump my bones, you know. But I had to find out if he knew something that might help me find my sister."

"I get that, Maddy, but couldn't he have told you in his office? Or better yet, over the phone?"

"I'm not the naive young thing that you see me as. I knew exactly what his ulterior motive was." She stopped before she blurted out that she also knew that Tessa had her back.

Mitch took a deep breath. "Tell me you didn't."

"Of course, I didn't but meeting him was something I had to do." She paused. "Anyway, I'd like to run by Roger Kennedy's orthodontic clinic right now and talk to his staff. Maybe one of them either knows a woman named Christine or possibly can recognize the blonde in the video."

Mitch picked up his phone. When Danny Landers answered, he asked, "Can you let Colt know that Maddy and I are going to interview a couple of people about Kennedy?" He paused before adding, "And Danny, I need you to comb through the financials of both Nancy and Roger Kennedy again. I'm specifically interested in money paid to a private detective. If you find that information, take Flanagan and go have a little chat with whoever it is."

"Will do," Landers said.

Mitch grabbed Maddy's arm and led her to the door. "Maybe we can stop at that restaurant again afterwards. I had dreams about those mouthwatering onion rings last night."

"I'm done going behind Sara's back. Whether you like it or not, I plan on having a sit- down with you and her to plead your case." When she saw disappointment cover his face, she held up a bag and added, "I brought leftover taco salad for lunch today. It's not enough to do much harm, but it's the best I can do, and it's yours if you want it."

"You're the bomb, Maddy," Mitch said as they drove across town to Vineyard Orthodontic Clinic.

He pulled into the strip mall where the office was located and parked the car in a handicapped spot.

"Mitch!"

"This is official police business, Maddy. Limp if it makes you feel better." He gave her a look that dared her to argue about it.

She resisted the temptation. As incorrigible as he was, it was hard to argue with him when he made that face like a kid who'd just been told that he couldn't have ice cream. She got out and headed for the door.

"I called ahead to make sure the office was open today. I spoke to a woman named Monica Townsend, who said that she'd be the only one there and that we were welcome to stop by."

They walked into the small room with several photos of smiling children on the wall. At the empty desk, Maddy called out, "Hello? Monica?"

"I'm in the back. Be up front in a minute," a female voice shouted from somewhere down the hall.

"I'll start the conversation. You follow my lead," Maddy whispered to Mitch as they waited.

"Yes ma'am. Ordinarily I wouldn't let you boss me around, but that taco salad gives you a little leverage."

A young lady emerged from the back hallway and smiled. "Sorry. I must have eaten something that didn't agree with me at dinner last night." She sat down at the desk, wiping her mouth with paper towel. "What can I do for you, officers?"

Maddy took a second to look her over. The twenty-something woman wasn't what she would call beautiful, but she had a great smile and, even in the baggy scrubs, a nice figure. Her short, strawberry-blonde hair was styled in a flattering way that brought out her blue eyes.

"I'm Detective Castillo, and this is my partner, Lieutenant Mitchell. We'd like to ask you a few questions about your employer, Doctor Kennedy."

"Of course. Everyone here is saddened by what happened to his wife, so we'll do anything we can to help."

"Where is Dr. Kennedy?" Maddy asked, fishing to see how much this woman knew about the case.

"He called in a few days ago to say that he was taking a couple of days off. Something about his grandmother."

Yeah, right, Maddy thought as she stole a quick look toward Mitch. His reaction was the same as hers. "Can you tell me how many people work in this office?"

The woman smiled, displaying a perfect set of white teeth. Maddy wondered if everyone who worked here had been treated by the missing orthodontist. Maybe she should look into getting her teeth whitened when these investigations were over.

"There's an orthodontic assistant, two technicians, an administrative assistant, a treatment and financial advisor, and of course, Doctor Kennedy."

"And which one are you?"

"I'm the administrative assistant. I do all the billing and scheduling." Monica looked down at her watch. "How much longer do you think you'll need to talk to me? I only came in today because I have a stack of bills to send out, and I have another appointment this afternoon."

"I promise we won't take up too much more of your time, Monica. We only have a few questions," Mitch said. "You're familiar with all Dr. Kennedy's patients?" After she nodded, he continued, "We wondered if there was anyone associated with him named Christine?"

"Christine?" Monica shook her head.

Maddy pulled up the video and showed it to her. "Do you recognize the blonde woman talking to the brunette at the bar?"

She could have sworn that Monica caught her breath, but if she had, she quickly recovered.

"I'm sorry. I don't. What's this all about?"

"The brunette is my sister, and she's missing. We're just following up on a few leads," Maddy said.

Mitch handed her his business card. "We'd appreciate it if you'd give us a call if you think of anything that might prove helpful. Also, if you'd ask your fellow coworkers if anyone knows a woman named Christine, we'd appreciate that, as well."

"Of course. Sorry, I wasn't much help. Dr. Kennedy should be back in the office in a few days, and you can check with him about the woman you're looking for."

Back in the car, Mitch turned to Maddy. "My gut tells me, she knows more than she's willing to tell us."

"I've known you long enough to trust your gut," Maddy responded. "We'll give Monica a few days to mull it over, and if we still haven't found this Christine woman, we'll pay her a return visit and introduce her to our old good-cop, bad-cop routine."

"Okay, but I get to be the good cop this time," Mitch said with a grin.

Maddy smirked. "Seriously? Do I look like a bad cop to you?"

17

———————

When they returned to the station, Danny Landers was waiting by Mitch's desk. "We found weekly payments made out to a Joshua Gelding. He's a PI with an office in the Charleston Bank building downtown. We went there to chat with him."

"And?"

"Be patient, Mitch. I'm getting to that. Gelding seemed genuinely saddened about Nancy Kennedy's death and didn't want to talk to us about it until we convinced him that it would take less than an hour to get a warrant with cops tearing up his office. Nancy must have been serious about keeping tabs on her husband because she paid this guy a thousand bucks a week." He whistled. "We're all in the wrong business."

"Tell me something I don't already know," Mitch said. "So, what'd you find out?"

"He said he'd followed Roger Kennedy around for several weeks. Said the guy left his practice around six every day during the week, then went straight home afterwards. Only partied hard on weekends."

"Did he know the blonde in the pictures that Roger's wife had?"

"No, but since he only had a few photos of her with Roger, he assumed that she was just another one of his one-nighters. According to Gelding, the man had a lot of those. He also told us that a month ago, Nancy instructed him to concentrate more on Deena."

"But we still don't know who the blonde is. Did this Gelding guy recognize the name Christine?"

This time Flanagan responded, "No, but he showed us a lot of pictures of Kennedy with Maddy's sister, even ones with only Deena in them."

"Sounds like, along with her husband, Nancy Kennedy was obsessed with my sister," Maddy observed. "Sean, were you able to run those pictures of the blonde through facial recognition?"

"We tried, but Gelding never really got a good frontal shot of her."

"Well, crap! I was hopeful there for a minute," Mitch said as he sat down at his desk. "But, hey, nice work, you two, even though it looks like another dead end."

"Yeah, sorry." Danny turned to Mitch. "On another note, I'm curious what you think about my work at the plate?"

Mitch made eye contact with Maddy before answering. "You're no Joey Henderson, but you hold your own. We really need you in centerfield, though."

"I'm getting better at every practice, Mitch. I should be solid by Sunday," Danny said, grabbing Flanagan and heading for the door. "We'll be back after lunch."

"Where are you going? Maybe you can pick up something for me?" Mitch said, his voice hopeful.

Maddy glared first at Landers then at Flanagan. "If you do, I'll have to kill both of you. Now get out of here before he tricks you into telling him where you're going."

"Spoilsport," Mitch said when they were the only two people in the room. He glanced toward the chief's office. "Looks like our NCIS cowboy is back. I knew his departure was too good to be true."

"What's with your obvious dislike of the guy, Mitch? Even you have to admit that he's proven himself to be a pretty good cop, and he always cooperates with us on the joint investigation."

"Something about him bugs the hell out of me," he said, just as Ryan came out of Colt's office and walked over to his desk.

"Happy to see me?" Ryan asked.

Mitch grunted. "I've got to talk to Colt for a minute. Try not to screw anything up out here, will you, Ryan?"

"I'll do my best." When he was sure that Mitch was behind closed doors, Ryan turned to Maddy. "I hate that we had to let Linden go. I was pretty confident that he was our man."

"So was I," Maddy responded. "We've got a few more days before Labor Day weekend. Let's just take a deep breath, relax, and enjoy the festivities. Thursday, we'll all get together and powwow over our notes again."

"Sounds like a plan." He sat down at his desk. "So, how's your investigation into the Kennedy murder coming? Did you find anything to positively nail the guy for his wife's murder?"

Maddy shook her head. "Mitch will hate me for this, but we could use a third pair of eyes on that case."

"Anything I can do to help, although I'm not sure how much longer I'll be here in Vineyard."

Maddy looked surprised. "We just talked about starting fresh on our double homicides. Is it your mother, Nick?"

He smiled at her use of his first name again and proceeded to tell her about his mother.

"I'm so sorry she's going through all that, but whatever you have to do for your mom, I know you will. I wish there was something we could do to help you."

"Solving Pamela's murder would go a long way to making me feel less guilty about leaving the investigation to another NCIS officer."

"Family is always the most important thing," Maddy said as Mitch came out of the office and sauntered over to his desk.

"What about family?" he asked.

Maddy glanced toward Nick. If he wanted Mitch to know about his mother, he would have to be the one to tell him.

"The doctor told my sister and me that my mother is going to have a long, painful recovery, and even with the best physical therapy, she may never walk again."

Mitch opened his mouth to say something then closed it and shook his head. "I know we've had our differences, Ryan, but if there's anything we can do—"

"I appreciate that. You and the rest of the team may have to continue with my replacement to get justice for both victims if my family needs me."

Mitch turned to Maddy. "Speaking of family, I just spoke to your brother-in-law about how Danny isn't working out as our catcher and how Kenny Phillips can't throw the ball far enough to reach second base from the outfield. Colt agrees that we need Danny back out in centerfield."

"He's not gonna like that. He thinks he might be the next Johnny Bench," Maddy said. "Who will replace him at the plate?"

"Glad you asked. With all the injuries, we barely have enough bodies to field a team." Mitch paused and held her eyes. "So, I need you to play catcher for us."

"Me? No way. I'm your biggest cheerleader in the stands."

"We have no one else. We're desperate, Maddy."

"What about one of the firemen? Surely, you can get one of those big, strong dudes to play for you?"

Mitch shrugged. "Believe me, I've tried. Both of the guys who played with us last year have problems. One guy had his knee scoped last week. There's no way he can squat behind home plate and catch even if he wanted to, and another one's wife had a baby and is having problems. They transferred her to Parkland, and he's taken a leave of absence."

"What about all the others? I know there are more than two guys at the firehouse."

"They all have excuses. As much as I hate to do this to you, you're all we've got."

"Be reasonable, Mitch. I weigh 120 pounds. Those big firefighters and policeman from Cordova will knock me into yesterday. You wanna be the one to explain to my family how you're the reason I'm in a coffin at the funeral home?"

"Maybe you didn't hear me when I said we were desperate. If things don't work out, I'll move you to left field, but it will be hard to take an experienced player out of a position he's good at and throw him behind the plate." He hugged her and then walked to the breakroom to pour himself another cup of coffee as he hollered over his shoulder, "Don't get all whiney on me. Hopefully, with my pitching skills, they won't even get a hit. I'm just asking you to think about it for the team."

"So, you weigh 120 pounds?" Ryan asked when Mitch was out of hearing range. "I would've guessed you weighed a little more."

"Shut up! Maybe I fudged five or ten pounds." She giggled. "Okay, maybe fifteen, but I had to make a point. There's no way I can be a catcher playing against a team full of big guys."

"It baffles me why they would even ask you," Nick said. "You look nothing like an athlete."

"You heard Mitch. They're desperate. And bite me for that smartass, athlete remark. For your information I played volleyball all four years in high school. I was even voted all district my senior year."

"That was meant as a compliment. You're rough around the edges, but underneath, anyone can see the feminine side of you."

"I suppose that was meant to be a compliment as well?"

"Take it any way you want to, but now I have something over you. If you cross me, I'll tell Mitchell that you're lying about your weight."

"You wouldn't dare. If you do that, I'll suggest that he put you behind the plate and let those big guys roll all over you."

"They wouldn't roll all over me."

"A little cocky, are we?"

"Would it surprise you to know that I went to the Naval Academy on a baseball scholarship?"

"You did not."

He nodded. "You're looking at the guy who helped Navy win the NCAA Division I championship his senior year."

"Were you drafted?"

"I might have been, but I chose to fulfill my commitment as a midshipman. It turned out to be a good deal for me because they sent me to the police academy and then trained me as an investigator."

Maddy narrowed her eyes. "Does Mitch know about this?"

"Why would he? He barely speaks to me."

Maddy sat down at her desk, her mind racing like a hamster on a wheel, but she tried to remain calm until Mitch came back and sat down at his desk. Turning to him, she said, "Hey, Mitch, did you know that Ryan here plays a little baseball now and then?"

"Now, why would you think I'd be interested in that?" he grumbled.

"Oh, I don't know. Maybe because you need an extra player on your team for Sunday's game."

"You think I'd ask this scrawny guy to play baseball with us? He probably doesn't even know how to hold a bat."

"How much do you wanna bet on that?" She waited for his response. When there was none, she blurted. "For your information, Mister Smart Guy, he went to the Naval Academy on a baseball scholarship and helped his team win the championship his senior year." Maddy almost lost it when Mitch's jaw nearly dropped to the floor.

He whirled around to face Ryan. "No shit! You really played baseball for Navy?"

Ryan nodded. "I really did."

Mitched moved closer to him. "And would you be willing to play baseball with us on Sunday?"

"Thought you hated my guts." From the smile that inched across Ryan's face, it was obvious he knew he had Mitch by the cajónes.

Mitch shook his head. "I don't hate you, man. I just had to act like I was in charge."

Maddy knew how hard it was for her partner to admit that. He had to be beyond desperate.

"I'll think about it, but if I get a call that my mom isn't doing well, I'm out of here."

"That's good enough for me," Mitch said, slapping him on the shoulder, as if they'd been buddies for years. "Hang on while I call that jerk-off Sullivan. He's head of the rules committee, and I'll have to get his approval for you to play since you're not a regular Vineyard first responder."

Mitch dialed the Cordova police department, and when

Sullivan picked up, he put him on speaker. "This is Mitchell. We've got a little problem over here concerning Sunday's game."

"I'd say you've got a lot of problems over there."

Mitch ignored the sarcasm and explained all the injuries to his players. "I'm not even sure we can field a team, and we may have to postpone the game."

"No way," Sullivan yelled. "Either you play or you forfeit the game, although given my preference, I'd like you to play. It will give us a chance to kick your ass again."

"Like I said, if we can't find nine healthy players, we won't have a choice." Mitch held the phone away from his mouth and grinned like a Cheshire cat before saying. "There might be a way, though, if you agree."

"If you're thinking that we're going to lend you one of our players, think again, fat boy. No Cordova cop would be caught dead in a Vineyard uniform."

Mitch narrowed his eyes at the fat boy slam, but to his credit, kept his voice calm. "Nothing like that. Do you remember the NCIS officer from the double homicide a few weeks ago?"

"What about him?"

"He's been working with us on that case because the dead woman was retired Navy. Matter of fact, Colt gave him a desk at our station, and we've been collaborating on the murders."

"So?"

"So, he's kind of a Vineyard cop right now, and if you're okay with it, he could be our ninth player."

"We are talking about the skinny guy from Fort Worth, right?" Sullivan asked.

"Yes. As much as I'd like to put him on the field where he won't hurt us too badly, right now it looks like our major vacancy is at the catcher position since Joey Henderson is in the hospital."

"Yeah, I heard about that. Hope he's okay." There was a pause before Sullivan continued, "Catcher, you say?"

Mitch held the phone out and covered his mouth so Sullivan wouldn't hear him chuckle.

"Yes. So, as the head of the rules committee, can I assume you're good with that?"

Sullivan laughed out loud. "Hell, yeah. Bring it on."

"One last thing. Could you put that in writing and fax it over just to keep it on the up and up?"

"On it now. You should get it in the next ten minutes. See you on Sunday, chump." Again, Sullivan laughed. "I can't believe you're putting that skinny guy behind the plate. Hope he doesn't end up in the hospital like Henderson."

Mitch hung up and shook hands with Ryan. "Welcome to the team. I take back every bad thing I ever said about you."

"Apology accepted. When's the next practice?"

"Tonight. We meet at the high school field from six till eight. Sometimes, we even go until nine." Mitch paused. "Please tell me you can catch."

"If you liked me a little before, you'll really love me now." Ryan grinned. "I was an All-NCAA catcher."

Mitch slammed his hand on the desk. "I think I'm gonna kiss you."

Ryan held up his hand. "Please don't. I can only handle so much of you being nice to me."

CARL LINDEN COULDN'T EVEN MAKE it home without a drink and stopped at the local liquor store for a fifth of scotch. Sitting in his car, he opened the bottle and took several long swigs before he felt his nerves calming down and his shakes lessening. When he finally felt like he could drive home, he turned on the ignition and headed in that direction.

After pulling into the garage, he climbed out of the car and went into the house. Normally, Luke would greet him as if he'd just returned from a year-long vacation, even if he'd only run to the 7-Eleven for a six pack. But when he entered the kitchen, there was no dog to greet him. It was just an empty house, and for the first time since he'd lived there, he noticed a foul odor. He decided that he might have to splurge and get his carpet cleaned and sanitized, but right now, he didn't have the funds for that. Truth was, he really didn't even have a pot to piss in, and his rent was coming up. His landlord had already given him a warning last month when he was only a day late with the check.

He went outside and walked over to his neighbor's house to retrieve his dog. Luke was so excited to see him, he nearly knocked him over, covering his face with wet, sloppy kisses.

At least someone loves me, Carl thought.

Back home, he had several more drinks before falling asleep on the couch. He was awakened a few hours later by a loud knock on the door. He stood up and made his way there, nearly stumbling twice.

When he opened the door, he came face to face with a stranger dressed in fancy clothes. "Whatever you're selling, I don't want none," he grumbled.

"Mr. Linden, I'm from Cross Timbers Insurance Company. Several years ago, your ex-wife took out a $200,000 life insurance policy and named you as her beneficiary. I'm here to talk about the specifics with you."

Carl grinned. Pamela must have loved him, at least a little, if she had left him all that money. The hell with cleaning his carpet, he was going to get all new stuff. Maybe even a new house in a better neighborhood. His life was going to change in a big way.

He was about to become a rich man.

"Give me a minute to put old Luke here in the back room." When he returned, he grinned from ear to ear. "You've just made my shitty day a whole lot better."

He opened the door as wide as it would go and motioned for the stranger to enter.

"Come on in."

18

Maddy got through the rest of the week with little progress made on either of the investigations. She'd gone to the last two baseball practices just to see how Nick Ryan was working out. Apparently, his skills behind the plate had made him very popular and even had Mitch singing his praises.

On Wednesday, Maddy had dinner with Sara and Mitch at Lombardi's, a popular Italian restaurant across town. She'd thought about inviting Colt and Lainey but decided it might make it too uncomfortable for Mitch who might feel like they were ganging up on him. Before dinner, she'd spoken to her brother-in-law to get his thoughts on whether she was doing the right thing with Mitch or not. Colt agreed that it was a good idea to intervene—that Mitch was too good of a cop to lose over bad eating habits. Everyone at the station knew that Mitch was cheating on the unrealistic diet that Sara forced on him, and they also knew that the guy hadn't even lost one pound—everyone, that is, except Sara.

Maddy hadn't looked forward to confronting her friend about seeking professional help for her husband, but to her surprise, Sara was almost relieved and jumped at the suggestion. She had called Maddy on Thursday to thank her and to let her know that she had called a highly recommended nutritionist in Dallas. Although, the first appointment was not for six weeks, she had gotten a call back that there was a cancelation. They were heading to Dallas on Friday for the consultation and to look into alternatives to the tofu diet that he was on.

Both Vineyard and Cordova were anticipating the big Labor Day celebration to be held in downtown Vineyard. Main Street was closed with the festivities beginning on Friday afternoon and ending with the baseball game between the rivals on Sunday. All proceeds from the game were going to the battered women's shelter, a charity that received a limited amount of federal funding and counted on local donations to survive.

Only a skeleton crew manned the police station on Friday with both Danny Landers and Sean Flanagan taking the day off, although they were instructed to keep their phones nearby and charged.

Maddy used the quiet time to catch up on paperwork for the investigation into the murder of Nancy Kennedy. They still hadn't identified the woman in the video with Deena, but she and Mitch planned to make a return trip to talk to Monica, the administrative assistant at Roger Kennedy's orthodontics office, to see if Mitch's hunch was right—that Monica did know more than she was telling them.

Maddy jumped when her cell phone rang, and she reached into her purse to retrieve it. Caller ID indicated Pearlie Williams at the other end. Pearlie was an older woman who had lived next door to Maddy and her family in Grand Fork when their father had been reassigned to the Naval Air Station in Fort Worth early in his military career. Maddy remembered her as a sweet lady who used to dote on the Garcia sisters because she and her husband had no children of their own.

"Hello, Mrs. Williams. This is quite a surprise," Maddy said when she answered. "Is everything okay?"

The woman laughed. "Of course, dear. I'm trying to get in touch with your mother, but I don't have her number now that she's moved to Florida."

"Mom went all techy on us and doesn't have a landline anymore. I can text you her cell phone number."

"Terrific. I need to talk to her about something, and it's rather urgent."

"Unfortunately, my mother and Chuck, her new husband, were in an automobile accident this week. Both are banged up but healing nicely. Is this urgent matter anything that I can help you with?"

"Oh, dear. I'm glad they're doing well." There was a pause before the woman continued, "It's just that I'm getting married on Monday, and Bill and I are leaving for Colorado right after the ceremony."

"Congratulations," Maddy said, wondering why this woman needed her mother and what was so urgent about a wedding? As far as she knew, other than a yearly Christmas card, her mother hadn't stayed in touch with Pearlie Williams.

"Yes, after Walter died four years ago, I thought I would never find love again, but the Almighty had plans of His own. No one fought harder than I did not to fall for my electrician, but here I am getting ready to say I do and run off to Colorado to be closer to his kids."

"That's pretty awesome," Maddy said. "But why do you need my mother?"

"Well, dear, your mother always loved my hutch that has been in the family for years. Bill and I are going to live in one of those tiny houses, and I have no room for it. I can't bear the thought of just anyone having it, and knowing how much she loved it, I want her to have it."

"I'm sure she'll be excited. Can you rent a storage unit for it? Then when my mother comes to Vineyard on Thanksgiving, we can pick it up. I'll pay for it, of course."

"I haven't the time for all that. Like I said, Bill and I are getting married on Monday." She paused. "Do you think you could make a trip down here and pick it up before Monday?"

"I'm sorry. I can't. This weekend is really going to be busy for me, but if you agree, I will try to make arrangements for somebody to come and move it into a storage facility. There are always firefighters and cops looking to earn extra money on the side."

"That won't work, dear, since Bill and I will be gone until late Sunday night. Would it be possible for you to drive down here and pick it up on Monday morning? Maybe you could even stay for the ceremony."

"I wish I could, but—"

"Please, dear. It would mean so much to me and be such a wonderful surprise for your mother. Plus, I'd love to see you."

Maddy thought about it. With a limited crew at the station, there really wasn't anything to keep her from going. Grand Fork was a little over an hour's drive from Vineyard, and all the Labor Day festivities would be over by Sunday night. "How big is the hutch?"

"Not too big. It comes apart in two sections, so I'm pretty sure it would fit into the back of an SUV."

Maddy wanted to say no, but this woman had been so good to the Garcia girls when they were growing up, and the hutch would really be a nice surprise for their mother. "What time are you getting married?"

"We've planned it for two in the afternoon, but a friend is officiating, so if we have to change the time, it's doable." She stopped and sniffed. "Please, dear, I really want your mother to have the hutch, and our flight for Colorado leaves at six that night."

Maddy tried to think of more excuses about why she couldn't do it, but nothing came to mind. What would it hurt to take that relatively short drive to Grand Fork to see an old friend who had been so sweet to all of them growing up? She could use the momentary distraction from worrying about her sister. The nostalgia of the small town located west of Fort Worth might just do that for her. "Okay. I'll be there around 10:00-ish."

"That would be terrific. Maybe I'll even take you down to The Square and buy you a homemade ice cream cone like I used to when you were younger."

Maddy laughed. "I've never forgotten how good that banana ice cream was. I'll definitely see you on Monday."

JESSIE GOT HOME from band camp on Friday evening, and she and Maddy met her sisters and their families on Saturday afternoon at the festival. Jessie was really upset when she told her about Deena being missing, but she'd assured her that they'd find her aunt soon. She seemed to accept that, bubbling with excitement about being back in Vineyard. She talked her mother into going on all the rides until Maddy thought she would throw up.

Sara and Mitch were there, acting like newlyweds instead of an old married couple. Apparently, Sara had broken down and cried. Seeing his wife cry was Mitch's kryptonite, and he would have promised her anything. Fortunately, the nutritionist they'd seen on Friday had worked out a low-carb diet where Mitch could still enjoy hamburgers and hot dogs occasionally—without the buns, of course. He'd agreed to give it a try, and if it didn't work out, they would revisit the nutritionist and see about Plan B, C, or even D if necessary. Maddy smiled and gave him kudos when he bought a corn dog and pulled off all the cornbread before eating it.

By the time they got home Saturday night, both she and Jess were ready to collapse into bed. After a quick shower, that's exactly what she did, sleeping like a baby until 9:00 AM on Sunday morning. Feeling refreshed and excited, she looked forward to losing her voice at the game cheering on her team just like she had the previous year, even though it had taken almost a week before she could speak normally again.

Jess was spending the rest of the weekend at her friend Carla's house to recap all the awesome events they'd shared at band camp. Carla had a pool in the backyard, which only added to Jess's excitement.

After dropping off her daughter at her friend's house, Maddy arrived at the ballpark. Most of the team was already there, dressed in the traditional green and white uniforms that represented Vineyard and its official city flag.

She walked over to the Vineyard dugout and hugged Mitch. "You know I'll still love you even if we get slaughtered. I want you to know that I am eternally grateful that I don't have to buy a coffin. I just hope that Ryan doesn't need one. I will be my same old, loudmouthed cheerleader that you know and love in the dugout keeping the morale up." She let go of him and addressed the entire team. "Give it your best shot. No matter what the outcome is, we've got pizza and enough cold beer to start our own brewery after the game. So, go get 'em."

She smiled at Ryan, who looked adorable in his uniform. He'd returned from Leroy with good news about his mother, who apparently was adjusting well and getting ready to transfer to the rehab facility. It was nice to see him smile back at her. "Show them what you got, tiger."

He winked at her. "Keep the beer cold for our victory celebration."

She laughed. "Still cocky, I see."

"Not cocky—confident. I always love it when people underestimate me."

Like both Mitch and I had when we first met you, Maddy thought.

The game began with a recording of the national anthem. With their right hand over their hearts, everyone in the stands sang along. Then came the traditional "play ball" from the umpire. Vineyard was the home team this year and took their positions on the field.

Let the game begin, Maddy thought. *And please don't let anybody get hurt,* she added.

Mitch struck out the first two batters and walked the third one. Next up was Sullivan, batting clean-up and grinning like a Cheshire cat.

"Pitch to me, fat boy," he hollered.

Mitch ignored the insult and concentrated on the signals from Nick. Sullivan swung and missed his first curveball. The second pitch ended up being a foul ball, followed by two consecutive balls and another strike. With the count full at three balls and two strikes, Mitch's next pitch was a fastball that hit Sullivan squarely in the shoulder. The Cordova cop seemed stunned at first, then charged the pitcher's mound and almost made it there before he was corralled by Goodwin, the Vineyard fire chief, who rushed in from shortstop.

After Sullivan calmed down and walked to first base, Mitch struck out the next batter, leaving the two Cordova players stranded on base. As he passed Sullivan on the way to the dugout, he gave him a head nod, which only infuriated the big guy even more. Everyone held their breath when Mitch walked up to the plate, knowing that Sullivan, no doubt, would extract his measure of revenge. The first pitch was headed directly at Mitch's head, but he anticipated the play and stepped slightly to his left and connected with the ball. The crowd went wild, especially Maddy, when Mitch made it all the way to third base.

The rest of the game progressed like every other inter-city rivalry, competitively and hard fought. At the top of the ninth, Vineyard was up by one run. There was one out with a man on first base and Sullivan on second. Freddy Ponder, a Cordova firefighter, well known for his ability to hit the ball out of the park, swung at the first pitch—a fastball—and missed. Four pitches later, the count was full—three balls and two strikes.

Maddy held her breath, knowing the pressure that Mitch must be feeling right then.

He threw a screw ball, and Ponder connected, hitting it deep into center field, looking like it was going to be a three-run homer. Somehow, in what could only be called an ESPN highlight clip, Danny Landers jumped way off the ground and caught it at the fence moments before it went over. He hurled it to Flanagan, the second baseman, just as Sullivan, who had tagged up after the catch, scrambled to third base. With a stupid grin on his face, he headed for home.

Flanagan threw a perfect ball to Nick who was positioned right over the plate. Sullivan, who outweighed Nick by at least thirty pounds, slammed into him, but not before Nick tagged him with his gloved hand and then rolled several times. There was an anxious silence as both teams waited to see if the catcher had been able to hold onto the ball, despite the brutal hit by Sullivan. The crowd erupted when Nick held up his glove with the ball in it and the ump shouted, "You're out."

Final score: Vineyard 8-Cordova 7. There were enough hugs all around to last a lifetime, and when Nick reached for Maddy their eyes met for a split second before he pulled her close.

"That last play was awesome," she said when he released her. "Glad I wasn't the one behind the plate."

"Thanks. That big lug would have run all over you. I'm sure I won't be able to get out of bed tomorrow without some serious drugs."

She slapped his shoulder gently. "Thank you for letting me live."

For an hour or more, they stayed at the park, celebrating with laughter, pizza, and a lot of cold beer. One by one they began to head to their cars, all of them with designated drivers, except Nick.

Mitch approached him. "Ride with us, Ryan. We're meeting Sara's sister for more drinks at the Stallion." He grinned. "Hell, I may even get my lady on the dance floor for the Cotton Eye Joe."

"Now, that's a visual I could have done without," Nick said, his eyes filled with mischief. "Thanks, but I'm ready to call it a day and grab an Uber. I'll pick up my car tomorrow."

"You'll do no such thing. I only had two beers and never even finished the second one," Maddy said. "After all, you were the hero out there today and slammed that old goat Sullivan's big mouth shut for a long time. At least until next year's game." She giggled. "How will he ever live down being beaten by—what was it that he called you—oh yeah, the skinny guy from Fort Worth?"

"It felt good playing ball again, and winning was the icing on the cake." He couldn't hide his smile. "I will take you up on that offer, Maddy. Maybe you could put on a pot of coffee to sober me up and then drive me back here to pick up my car. It will save me having to find a motel nearby."

"Sounds good. We could both use some coffee."

After two cups each, the celebratory high they were on was beginning to fade. Maddy stood up and carried her cup to the sink, and when she turned around suddenly, she bumped right into Nick, who was behind her waiting to put his cup in the sink. He caught her when she nearly fell, and then looked into her eyes, questioning her.

When she nodded, he brought his lips close to hers, giving her one last-minute opportunity to say no. When she didn't, he dove in, kissing, tasting, moaning. For Maddy, it was like no other kiss she'd ever experienced. Maybe it was because both of them were sweaty and grimy from the dusty ballpark, which seemed like a turn-on, or maybe because it was simply meant to happen. Right when Maddy thought she might end up next to him in the morning, her phone rang.

She answered it just as Nick's phone rang. "Castillo."

"Maddy, this is Sergeant Johnson. We got a call from Carl Linden's neighbor. He found Carl's dog wandering around in the front yard and went over to tell him. The front door was unlocked, so when Carl didn't respond, he walked in and found him dead on the living room couch."

"Dead? From what?"

"Not sure. I was the first officer on the scene and found an empty prescription bottle by a laptop on the desk, so I'm guessing that drugs had something to do with his death."

"Secure the scene, Johnson, and call the ME. I'm with Nick Ryan right now, and we'll both be there in about twenty minutes."

"Will do. And Maddy, there's something else. Linden left a suicide note on the computer, admitting that he was the one who killed his ex-wife and David Foster."

STILL DRESSED in their grimy baseball clothes, Maddy and Nick climbed back into her car and headed across town. When they arrived at Carl Linden's house, they were met by Doug Johnson, Vineyard Police evening supervisor.

"Hey, Doug, thanks for the call." When Maddy noticed the police officer giving Nick the stink eye, she realized that he probably didn't recognize him since he hadn't worked with him. "Doug, this is Nick Ryan, the NCIS officer in charge of Pamela Linden's murder."

Doug's disapproving expression turned into a huge smile, and he shook hands with Nick. "Everybody's talking about that last play of the game today. I would have loved to have been there to see the look on Sullivan's face when he realized that you still had the ball in your glove after his vicious hit." He laughed. "I heard from a buddy of mine over in Cordova that Sullivan is still crying about it and trying to figure out a way to make Vineyard forfeit the game. He claims you're not really one of us, and that disqualifies you."

"Not a chance in hell of that happening," Maddy said. "Mitch was smart enough to get Sullivan, as head of the rules committee, to sign a permit allowing Ryan to play. Mitch made sure Sullivan faxed it over to us himself." She looked around. "Speaking of Mitch, is he on the way?"

Johnson opened the door and made a swooping motion with his hand before stepping aside to allow them to enter. "He's in there waiting for the ME to finish." He chuckled. "Probably driving Rory crazy."

"No doubt. Thanks, Doug. Good job."

After donning shoe covers and gloves, she and Ryan stepped into the house and walked directly to the living room where Rory Daniels was on the floor completing his initial exam of the deceased. Mitch was crouched next to him, nearly on top of him.

Rory sat back and bumped into Mitch. "For pity's sake, Mitch, can you give a guy a little room?" When Mitch moved back a step, the ME said, "Thank you. I don't know how much more of your garlicky breath I can take."

"Oh, sorry, doc. You know how I like to drown everything in garlic. Supposed to be good for my blood pressure." Mitch spotted Maddy and pointed to the empty prescription bottle on the end table. "Looks like this might be our culprit," he said, walking over and picking it up. "Belongs to Linden." He squinted to read it. "Triptothyazide. No idea what that's for."

"Migraines," Daniels replied. "That stuff is potent. Two of these would have put him to sleep. If he swallowed the entire bottle, that, my friends, would be our cause of death. We'll have to wait on the toxicology report to verify that." He bent over the dead body and sniffed. "And my guess is that the empty bottle of scotch next to him will be responsible for a high blood alcoholic level. Couple that with the Triptothyazide, and this man was probably dead in less than an hour."

"Where's the suicide note?" Ryan asked.

Mitch bobbed his head toward the desk behind the couch. "On the laptop over here." He followed Ryan and looked over his shoulder as he opened the computer.

After putting in the password from the sticky note on the front of the laptop, Ryan pulled up a file. The suicide note flashed on the screen.

"Read it out loud," Mitch prompted.

Ryan nodded, then began speaking, "I never meant to kill Pamela, but I'd had too much to drink, and I lost it when I saw her kissing that other man. God forgive me for killing them both, but I can't bear the thought of living without her."

"That's it?" Maddy asked when Ryan stopped talking.

He nodded, then wrinkled his brow in deep thought. "Do either of you ever remember Linden ever calling his ex-wife Pamela?"

Maddy shook her head. "It was always Pammie, and usually

my Pammie. And I don't remember him ever mentioning that he'd seen them kissing, either."

"Me, neither. And I definitely recall Linden telling us on that first day we questioned him in this house that the laptop belonged to his ex, that she'd bought a new one and left the old one so he could look at all the pictures from their marriage. He'd joked, and I quote, 'She never told me how to turn the damn thing on,'" Mitch said.

"That's right. And one more thing that's bugging me. Linden loved that stupid dog of his. Said he never left him out of his sight because he was worried about the kids who sometimes drag-raced down the road." Ryan spun around to face Johnson, who had wandered into the room. "And the guy next door found his dog wandering the neighborhood?"

"Yes. So, what is everyone thinking?"

"The same thing you are," Mitch said before turning to the crime scene guys. "Print everything in the house then bag it. This place is now a possible crime scene."

"I'll get my team to canvas the neighborhood to see if they saw anything out of the ordinary." Johnson shrugged. "I'm not very hopeful that any of these run-down houses in the neighborhood have outdoor security cameras, but we'll check that out as well. We might get lucky."

"Good thinking," Maddy said. "Now, let's tear this place apart to see if we can find any evidence that this might not be a suicide."

19

———

It was after dark when they wrapped things up at Linden's house, the two-hour search unsuccessful in finding anything that might help them determine whether his death was a homicide or a suicide. Maddy took one last look at the body before leaving to drive Ryan to the ballpark. Carl Linden had looked peaceful, almost as if his soul was now reunited with the love of his life. The question was, knowing how much he'd loved her, could he really have tied her up and shot her in the head?

When Maddy pulled up beside Ryan's car in the parking lot, she turned to him. "Do we need to talk about what almost happened at my house earlier?"

A slight smile crossed Nick's face. "One day we will. For now, let's just chalk it up to an overindulgence of beer and euphoria over today's victory."

"That's all it was? An overindulgence? Because I could swear it felt like more."

He lowered his eyes. "I think the world of you, Maddy. You have to know that. But my life is so unpredictable right now. Maybe if we had met at a different time in our lives..." He paused. "And no, it wasn't just an overindulgence. I could have been persuaded to wake up beside you in the morning. My gut tells me that we would both have regretted that. We still have to work together, and I would hate to ruin the trust we've built since it was not easy to come by."

She sighed. "You're probably right. I'm just coming off a serious relationship that didn't end well, and I know you're probably still grieving for your wife."

He jerked around to face her. "And how do you know about my wife? Did you check me out?"

Maddy laughed. "Of course, I did. I'm a cop. But as much as I hate to admit it, rushing into a relationship when there is so much going on might prove disastrous for both of us. First and foremost with me is finding my sister." She unlocked his door. "I'll see you in the morning—" She paused, remembering her trip to Grand Fork to see her old neighbor. "I forgot that I have an errand to run tomorrow. I'll be in the office after lunch, and we can talk about this case then."

He held her gaze for a few seconds. "Spending the night with you might have been fun. If nothing else, it would have solved the mystery of how much you really weigh."

"Get out, you wannabe comedian. If you're smart, you won't give up your day job. Now, hit the road and drive safely. I'll see you tomorrow." She drove away, smiling the entire way home, thinking how much she would have loved to wake up next to him.

MADDY WOKE up the next morning with a slight headache. After swallowing two ibuprofens, she hopped into the shower, wondering if Nick would have been in there with her right now if he'd spent the night.

Her head told her his decision to drive back to Fort Worth

had been the right one, but her heart was still undecided. She remembered something that her mother had always said to her daughters about office romances. "Never dip your pen into the company inkwell," she'd preached, saying those things never ended well. It was a great piece of advice which Maddy had always followed faithfully—until last night. Reason told her that if she and Ryan were meant to have a relationship, it would have to wait until they were both in a better place.

She dried off and walked to her closet, choosing a nice outfit in case Mrs. Williams talked her into hanging around for the ceremony. Although she'd told Colt she'd be back at the station after lunch, she could be persuaded to stay in Grand Fork a little longer, especially if it included a trip to Darby's Homemade Ice Cream Parlor afterwards. That's if Darby's was still in the town square.

The drive to Grand Fork brought back a lot of old memories with the many cornfields and the awesome display of wild-flowers all along the sides of the road, truly a gift to Texas from the Man above every fall. Unfortunately, there were no bluebon-nets, her favorites, this time of year, but the bright yellow Maxi-milian sunflowers, the beautiful lilac fall asters mixed in with the pink-purple spikes of gay feathers were a site like only Mother Nature and the good Lord could create.

Maddy remembered her mother packing her and her sisters in the car every fall and spring and taking them on a drive down this very road, stopping frequently to take pictures of the girls frolicking in the flowers. Maddy still had two of those photos hanging on her wall.

Before she knew it, she was driving through the town square, which housed some of the most unique stores in the area—at least it used to. It saddened her to see that most of them were no longer there, probably closed because of the popular new trend of online shopping.

She turned down the road where she and her sisters had spent many hours playing hopscotch and tin can alley with their friends. As she pulled up to the Williams house, she glanced across the street to the home where she and her siblings had grown up. Other than new shingles, it still looked the same—still had the old swing on the front porch that her dad had crafted himself.

She parked the car in front and took a deep breath, a wave of nostalgia overwhelming her. After getting out of the car, nervous for some unknown reason, she noticed a slight movement in the front curtains when she walked up the steps to the porch. The minute she knocked, the door swung open, and Mrs. Williams grabbed her in a bear hug and pulled her inside.

"Oh, my, you've certainly grown into a stunning woman, Maddy," the older woman said before adding, "Not that you weren't adorable way back when."

She led her to the kitchen, which looked to Maddy like it hadn't been touched since she'd last been in it, getting a boo-boo doctored with Mercurochrome and a Wonder Woman band-aid.

"Mrs. Williams, I have to ask—"

"You're no longer a little girl, Maddy. You can call me Pearlie now."

Maddy grinned. "Seeing this kitchen makes me feel like a little girl again."

"You and your sisters will always be little girls in my mind." Pearlie set a cup of steaming coffee in front of Maddy. "What do you take with it?"

"A sweetener if you have one. If not, regular sugar will do."

After bringing her the sweetener, Pearlie went to the window and peered out. "You weren't followed here, were you, dear?"

Maddy stared at her as if she had two heads. What a strange question. "No, but why would you ask me that?" As she waited for the answer, she said a little prayer that her friend hadn't become paranoid in her old age, like many elderly people sometimes do when dementia creeps in.

"No reason," the woman said, walking back to the counter to get her own coffee, giving Maddy a few minutes to size her up.

Pearlie Williams had always been short and stocky, but she looked even shorter now, and she'd gained some weight. Wearing black pants that probably had an elastic waist and a bright colored blouse, she wore her mostly gray hair pulled back in a bun. Maddy guessed her age to be nearing eighty. She wasn't sure if she'd recognize her if she saw her on the street, but she'd know that smile anywhere. Pearlie could light up a room with it and make everything better for the Garcia sisters, even when they were fighting amongst themselves, which was frequently.

"You haven't changed a bit," she lied.

"Of all your sisters, you were always the best liar, next to Tessa, that is. The truth is, getting old isn't for sissies." She sat down at the table with her own coffee and took a sip.

Maddy glanced down at her watch. As nice as this was, she needed to get the hutch loaded into the back of her SUV and head home. "Will I get to meet the lucky guy who's going to whisk you away to Colorado?"

Pearly took a deep breath and let it out slowly, keeping her eyes trained on Maddy. "There is no lucky guy from Colorado."

Maddy looked puzzled. "You're not getting married?"

Pearlie shook her head. "No, dear, I just told you that to get you to drive down here."

"And no hutch, either?"

Again, Pearlie shook her head.

"Then why am I here?"

"There's a good reason." The woman looked over at the curtains. "And you're absolutely sure you weren't followed?"

"I wasn't," Maddy said, trying not to let the older woman see her growing annoyance. "Actually, I'm getting a little nervous about why you called me?"

"Because of me," Deena said, as she emerged from the bedroom.

"Oh my God! Deena!" Maddy jumped up and ran to her sister. After a long embrace, she pulled away. "Part of me wants to never let you go and part of me wants to kill you. We were all so worried about you. Why didn't you call to let us know you were okay?"

Deenna sat down at the table and motioned for her sister to do the same. "Sit. I know you have to get back to Vineyard, and I have a long story to tell you."

Pearlie stood up. "I'll leave you two alone to catch up. I've got a few errands to run, but I'll be back soon."

After she left, Maddy turned to her sister. "Please tell me that you had nothing to do with the double murders at David Foster's house. I know you were there, and although my heart tells me there's no way you were involved, the cop in me needs to hear it from you."

Deena shook her head. "I think I'd better start at the beginning." She took a sip of the hot coffee before speaking. "If you remember, I'd been dating David for several weeks. It started when I began working to renovate the offices at Warner Chemicals. I knew that he could be arrogant at times, but he always made me laugh. I am at a time in my life where I worry about growing old in my boring lifestyle and decided to grab as much fun out of life as I could get." She paused. "And I need to mention that David was very good under the sheets."

Maddy laughed. "Maybe I should have gone out with him. Mitch is always harping on me about my lack of a social life. According to him, getting laid solves most of the problems in the world."

Deena shook her head. "Sounds like something he'd say. But

back to David, even with those two things going for him, it wasn't enough. I'd already made up my mind to call it off and told him so two weeks earlier. Anyway, the night before the murders, I went to the Stallion to meet with a woman I'd met there several weeks before. She seemed anxious about something and was drinking like a fish."

"Pamela Linden?"

"Yes. When I first met her, I had mentioned that I was just ending a relationship with an exec from Warner Chemicals. We hit it off and exchanged phone numbers. That's why she called and asked me to meet her at the bar that night. That's when she told me a story that blew me away." Deena stopped to take another drink of her coffee.

"Deena, you're killing me. What did Pamela tell you?"

"She was a helicopter pilot and flew over most of the bigger ranches in the area, herding cattle, spotting broken fences, and a bunch of other things."

"I know. She made a ton of money doing that, plus, she inherited a huge ranch with close to 500 acres from her parents."

"Funny, she never let on she was rich," Deena commented. "Anyway, about three weeks before the murders, she flew over the ranch directly behind hers and noticed several dead cows on the ground. She looked into the county public records and discovered the owner was Jeffrey Donovan, the chief lawyer at Warner—"

"I know him. Actually, I had dinner with him one night to see if he knew anything about you."

Deena shook her head. "He is so not your type. He changes women like the rest of us change lipstick shades."

Maddy laughed. "Tell me about it. Tessa said he was what Mom would call a rotten egg."

"Tessa?"

"She showed up right after we realized you were missing," Maddy said. "And get this. All of us can see and hear her."

"That's weird."

Maddy glanced down at her watch. "I know. So, get back to your story. I told Colt I'd be back at my desk after lunch."

"Okay. A week later, Pamela called Donovan to tell him about the dead cows, even though he wasn't a client of the helicopter company. He told her that his aunt had left the ranch to him when she died the year before. Said it was vacant, but he intended to move into the place after he retired. In the meantime, he leased out some of the land to other ranchers to rotate their herds. Said it was an extra income source to help pay the property taxes. He told Pamela that he'd get in touch with the ranchers to let them know about the dead cows."

Deena stood up, walked over to the counter, and returned with the coffee pot. "We're gonna need more of this," she said as she refilled both cups. When she sat back down, she continued with the story. "About a week before the murders, Pamela did another fly-by in her chopper to see if the dead cows had been disposed of. To her surprise, not only were the previously dead ones still there, but there were five or six more scattered on the ground. She said she took tons of pictures and then flew around the ranch to see if there were even more. She was shocked to discover a massive, triangular-shaped crater near the edge of the property, about two-hundred yards from the dead animals."

"A crater? From what?"

"Here's where it gets dicey. The large hole in the ground was filled with huge metal barrels. It didn't take her long to figure out that whatever was in those barrels might be toxic enough to have killed the cows. Knowing that Warner Chemicals was the only industrial plant in the area and that Donovan worked there, she wondered if somehow, it was connected. She took more pictures and then left."

The story was getting bizarre at this point, and Maddy leaned in so as not to miss a word. "Did she send those pictures to you or tell anyone else about what she discovered?"

"No, she didn't have her laptop with her at the club and said she would get them to me at our meeting with Foster the next day. And she didn't tell anyone because she had no idea what was in those barrels and didn't want to make false accusations until she had proof of wrongdoing, mainly because of Warner's onsite legal team, headed by none other than Donovan himself. When I met her the night before the murders, she said she'd called me because she didn't know who else to call. After she told me her story, I immediately called David, and he recommended that the three of us meet at his house the next morning. He said he would investigate and when he had all the details, he'd go to Martin Warner with whatever he discovered. He seemed to think that it was not something that his company would be involved in."

"And that's why Pamela Linden was at the house with you and Foster on Friday, correct?"

"Yes, I hadn't planned on spending the night with David, but he was not happy that I was going to end things and persuaded me to come over for one last night. Said he needed to hear the story from me before Pamela arrived the next morning. He insisted on picking me up because I'd had two or three drinks over my usual one margarita, and I was feeling pretty mellow. Long story short, I ended up spending the night with him. He was going to drive me back to the Stallion to pick up my car after Pamela left the next day because I had an important meeting at Warner Chemicals and needed to run home first."

"I know. Your boss called me to see if I knew where you were. That's when I began to realize that you were missing."

"He must have been furious."

"Not furious. More like concerned," Maddy said.

"Well, the good thing is that no one knows I was even at David's house."

"Wrong, little sis. The entire Vineyard Police Department knows."

"How could they know that Maddy? I left with the only two things that belonged to me, my phone and my laptop."

"You forgot the used condom." Maddy said, dryly. "DNA doesn't lie."

"Damn! So, does everyone think I had something to do with the murders?"

"Of course not, although we did want to question you." Maddy's voice broke. "I was so worried that something had happened—" She couldn't finish that thought.

"Does Mom know I'm missing?"

Maddy nodded. "She was supposed to fly here from Florida last week when Lainey told her, but she and Chuck were in an accident on the way to the airport." When Deena caught her breath, Maddy explained. "They're both fine, and they're coming for Thanksgiving." Maddy chugged the rest of her coffee, then set the cup down. "What did Foster say when Pamela told him what she'd discovered?"

"He never got the chance to hear her tell it. Shortly after she arrived, there was a knock at the door. I had gone back into the master bathroom to put on my makeup so that we could leave right after they finished talking."

"Who was at the door?"

"I don't know., but now that I think about it, I don't remember hearing the doorbell, so it was probably the back door. Anyway, all I heard was what sounded like furniture crashing, and Pamela screaming. The man kept asking them where I was. I'm not sure if they told him, but I couldn't wait around to find out. So, I grabbed my stuff and went out the bedroom window. Before I ran away, I heard several gunshots."

"Oh, my God!"

Deena sighed. "I know. I ran like my hair was on fire. When I thought I was far enough away, I called for an Uber, went to the Stallion, and picked up my car."

"That's when you got out of Dodge?"

"Yes. I had no idea why that man was looking for me, but I didn't want to stick around to find out." She stopped and swiped at a tear that had escaped down her cheek. "I should have called you or 911, Maddy, but I was so scared. I lay awake at night worrying that I may have been able to save them."

"You couldn't have. The medical examiner said that both of them had mortal wounds and were probably dead before they hit the floor."

Deena looked up. "Thank you, Jesus. I don't know if I could've lived with myself, knowing that they might still be alive had I not let my own fear cloud my judgment."

"So, did you run into anyone when you picked up your car? Josh, maybe?"

She shook her head again. "I was afraid that whoever was looking for me might follow you or one of our sisters. Might even bug your phones. I didn't want to put any of you in danger, so I headed west and found myself on the highway to Grand Fork."

"Why'd you ditch your Jeep?"

"I was desperate thinking whoever had fired the gun at David's house might be looking for my car. I pulled over on the side of the road and cried. I had nowhere to go and very little cash on me, and I was afraid to use my credit card. I thought about Pearlie—didn't know if she still lived in Grand Fork or even if she was still alive."

"And she still lived in Grand Fork?"

"Yes, I called her, and without asking questions, she met me on the highway and drove me to her house after she ran over my phone several times. Once I felt safe inside her house, I fell into her arms. She never once asked why I was there. When I was ready, I told her everything. That's when we concocted the ridiculous story about her wedding and the hutch."

"It was definitely genius," Maddy said. "Not too many things would have convinced me to drive down here with you missing, but I kept thinking how much Mom would have loved the hutch."

Deena laughed. "Pearlie offered it to her before we moved. Mom politely declined, then told me later that if she wanted old things in her new house, she'd go down to the Salvation Army resale store."

"Our mom, the sentimental one," Maddy joked. "Not to change the subject, but why did you decide to come clean now? Aren't you still worried about the killer finding you?"

"Pearlie and I have been reading the Vineyard Daily online, so we knew that Pamela's ex-husband had been booked for the murders. I wanted to make sure that he was safely behind bars before I showed up with this crazy story. For all I knew, he was still looking for me."

"He's dead," Maddy said. "An apparent suicide, although we're working it as a possible homicide."

"Who'd want to kill him?"

"Maybe the guy who killed his ex-wife and Foster. We had proof that Carl Linden had been stalking his ex and followed her to Foster's house that morning. He even admitted peeking into the window and seeing her on the couch with Foster."

"Was he the voice that I heard?"

"Not sure, but I doubt it. What makes more sense to me is that the killer saw him and got a good look at his car. Maybe even got the plates. Since I'm not convinced that Linden is—was —our shooter, we have to assume that someone may still be looking for you. Stay out of sight, and I'll call you the minute I have news."

As Deena nodded, they heard a car pull into the garage, and a few minutes later, Pearlie walked in with several packages. She laid one on the table. "I bought you both a phone in case someone is tracking your calls. These are called burner phones." When they stared at her, she added, "What? I watch television."

Maddy smiled. "These phones are really a good idea, Pearlie. Thank you." Then she turned to Deena, "I have to get back before Colt gets suspicious. He's already read me the riot act because I had a secret meeting with our sisters about this case."

"He does hate it when he thinks we're interfering."

"I thought he was going to fire me, but being family counts for something, I guess." She reached for the burners and programmed them, then remembered about the blonde in the video with Deena. She pulled out her phone and scrolled to the image and handed it to Deena. "One last thing. Do you know this woman?"

Deena studied the picture before responding. "Not really. She came up to me at the bar one night and asked if I was having an affair with Roger Kennedy. When I told her that I wasn't and had no intention of ever doing so, she was relieved. Said she was pregnant with Roger's child, and they were going to get married." She paused. "I knew he was a loser, but I didn't realize how big of a scumbag he was. I pity his poor wife, having to put up with all his extramarital affairs—and now he's gone and knocked up that young girl."

"Nancy Kennedy is also dead," Maddy said. "Roger's behind bars, as we speak."

"Good. He deserves whatever punishment the law hands out to him." She walked Maddy to the door. "Where'd you get that photo of me?"

"Josh, the bouncer at the Stallion, gave us the video from the camera behind the bar."

She smiled. "I love that guy. We need to hook you up with him."

"No thanks. I'm anti-men right now," Maddy said. "And don't ask." She turned back to her sister before exiting, "One more thing. Do you happen to know the pregnant girl's name?"

Deena squinted. "Hmm! Not sure about her last name, but she introduced herself as Monica something or other. She said she worked with Kennedy at his clinic."

20

———

Maddy's mind was racing as she drove back to Vineyard. Not only had Deena given them a possible motive for the double homicides, but she may have solved Nancy Kennedy's murder, as well. If Monica Townsend, the administrative assistant at the Kennedy Orthodontics Clinic, was the blonde in the picture with Deena, that could be huge.

A jealous woman might stop at nothing to get her man. A *pregnant* jealous woman could be even further motivated to take things into her own hands. But even if Monica wasn't the killer, her pregnancy had just elevated Roger Kennedy from being a person of interest to a prime suspect with a clear motive for getting rid of his wife. It could also explain why he lied to them about the name of the woman he'd had a one-nighter with—the blonde who had been captured on film by the private investigator hired by his wife.

When she was out of the city traffic and on the open road back home, Maddy called Mitch on the burner phone, just in case Deena's suspicion that the phones between the two sisters were being bugged.

After several rings, Mitch finally picked up. "Mitchell. Who's this?"

"It's Maddy. I'm using a burner phone."

"Something wrong with your other phone?"

"Long story. I'll get to that in a minute. I just left Grand Fork, and I'm on my way back to Vineyard."

"Do you want me and the guys to meet you at your house to unload the hutch?"

"There is no hutch."

"Obviously, it didn't work out. At least you got to have that ice cream you're always yammering about."

"Nope. No ice cream, either."

"Geez, Maddy, so you drove all the way there for nothing?"

"Not exactly. Although I got to visit my old neighbor, she lied to me about getting married and moving to Colorado. She—"

"Why would she do that? Is she a looney tunes or what?"

"No, as a matter of fact, she's actually very clever. She had a huge surprise waiting for me."

"And what might that have been? A rich grandson who was looking for a beautiful girl like you? Maybe—"

"Deena was there," Maddy blurted.

"Good God, Maddy. You saved that part for last?"

"Yes, but there's way more." Over the next ten minutes, she repeated Deena's story. When she finished, Mitch was silent for several minutes, apparently trying to absorb it all.

"Holy cow! Is your sister with you now?"

"No. Since we're not convinced that Carl Linden was actually the killer and was more than likely murdered himself, I thought it best if she stayed hidden until we can make sure that the person looking for her isn't still out there, watching and waiting. Thus, the burner phone."

"Good thinking. So, when you get back to Vineyard, we'll sit down with Nick and figure out what our next move will be."

"I already know what needs to come next. As soon as you hang up, call the Fort Worth Police Headquarters and request a flyover at Jeffrey Donovan's ranch. You can get the coordinates from public records. If Pamela Linden was correct, they should find a huge crater in the ground filled with large metal barrels that probably contain hazardous material, toxic enough to kill multiple cows grazing nearby."

"On it." He paused. "I'll see you here in about an hour?"

"No. Call Monica Townsend and set up a meeting with her. She's probably home since it's Labor Day. Text me her address, and I'll meet you there in forty-five minutes."

"Will do. I'm curious, Maddy. What does your gut tell you? Do you think she had anything to do with Nancy Kennedy's murder?"

"Possibly, but like your gut told you the first time we talked to her, she's definitely hiding something. We need to find out what that something is."

"Okay. Are we ready to go to Colt with this information?"

"Yes. Actually, I think you should have a meeting with Colt, Landers, and Flanagan. And don't forget to include Nick Ry—"

Mitch cut her off. "For sure. He's my new best friend."

She laughed. "You are such a dork. Last week you were happy when you thought he would stay in Leroy with his mother. Now, you're kissing his you-know-what?"

"What can I say? He wiped the smile off Sullivan's ugly face. And with that, I'll let you go so that you don't get a ticket for speeding or erratic driving."

She started to hang up, then quickly said, "Oh, and another thing, tell Colt and Danny not to share this information with my sisters. I want to be the one to tell them later tonight."

"Okay. I'll send that text as soon as I get the information, and unless you hear back from me, I'll meet you at Monica's house."

She hung up and took a deep breath. Things were going to

start moving at a fast pace, and she needed to be ready. Other than the arrest of a drug dealer who had murdered a prisoner on her watch when she was a rookie cop, this was her first homicide investigation since she and Mitch became partners.

Thinking back to Deena's story, she concluded that they could rule out the sports betting place as the guilty party since whoever pulled the trigger at Foster's house had asked about Deena—unless Foster had mentioned that he was getting the money he owed them from her.

She shook her head. *It was possible*, she thought, *but not probable*. The more compelling story was that after Jeffrey Donovan was tipped off that Pamela Linden had discovered the illegal dump site on his ranch, he'd decided to kill two birds with one stone—and maybe even three birds if Deena hadn't escaped.

She shuddered, thinking how close her sister had come to dying that day. She said a quick prayer of thanks as she pulled into the drive-thru at a hamburger joint on the outskirts of Fort Worth. Usually, she had no appetite when she was excited or upset about something, but for some reason, she was starving. She ordered a burger and fries, knowing that she would not get another chance to eat until late that night. She scarfed them down before she got on the road again, hoping that she didn't get indigestion.

Thirty minutes later, she turned into the parking lot at Monica Townsend's apartment building and pulled up beside Mitch's cruiser.

"This may be a dead end, you know," he said as they walked into the building together.

"I know, but then again, it might not."

Monica answered the door after several knocks. She was dressed in a pair of blue jeans and a large white shirt that would have concealed a baby bump if she had one. Once inside, Maddy noticed a picture of Roger Kennedy and his employees on the end table. She walked over and stared at the photo and the girl in the front row with long blonde hair. It was definitely the same girl as the one in the picture with Deena.

"What can I do for you, officers," Monica asked when she greeted them. "I've told you everything I know."

Maddy pointed to the picture. "I have to say, Monica, that I like your hair so much better with the shorter style and the new color."

"Thank you. I decided it was time for a change." She mindlessly twirled a strawberry blonde curl between her fingers before glancing at Mitch, who had walked over to look at the picture. "You said you had new questions for me?"

He nodded. "We wondered why you didn't tell us you were the blonde in the photo that my partner showed you the last time we spoke to you."

Her face turned a touch of gray. "I guess I didn't want to get involved," she said before making eye contact with Maddy. "I met your sister that night, and we talked about—I can't even remember what."

"Let me refresh your memory. You told my sister that you were pregnant with Roger Kennedy's baby."

Monica's face drained of all color now. "How could you possibly know that? You said your sister was missing."

"We have our ways," Maddy said. "What we need to know now is whether or not you told Roger that you were pregnant. Were you hoping that he would divorce his wife and marry you now that you were carrying his baby?"

She lowered her head. "He said that although he loved me, he couldn't divorce Nancy for financial reasons."

"So, you decided to take things into your own hands?" Mitch held her hostage with his eyes.

She shook her head, vehemently. "What exactly are you implying?"

"That you saw the situation as hopeless, that you couldn't count on Roger to take care of the problem. Did you go to his wife then and tell her you were pregnant?" Maddy interjected.

Monica nodded and sniffed back a tear. "She laughed at me. Said Roger wouldn't ever leave her for a whore like me."

"Is that why you plunged the knife into her chest?" Maddy questioned.

"No. Nancy was my friend."

"The friend, who in your mind, was the only thing standing between you and the father of your unborn child." Maddy held her eyes. "We know that either you or Roger killed Nancy, so which one was it?"

"I don't know about Roger, but it wasn't me."

Maddy pulled up a picture on her phone of the knife beside Nancy's body and shoved it toward Monica. "Does this look familiar? Take a minute before you answer. You should know that the lab found DNA from Roger and two females on the knife. One was Nancy's. When we take a sample of your DNA, are we going to find out that the other one is yours?"

"Don't you need a warrant for that?"

Mitch laughed. "You've watched too many cop shows, Monica. Did you think I would come unprepared?" He placed two warrants on the coffee table. "One is for your DNA, and the other is a search warrant."

"And you should also know that Roger said he didn't kill his wife—that he found her dying and pulled out the knife to try to save her. Was he lying?" Maddy asked.

Monica began to cry, softly. "It was an accident. I swear. I only went there to talk to her, friend to friend. When she called me a whore, I lost it and slapped her across the face. She grabbed the knife and ran to her bedroom. I followed her to try to talk some sense into her." She reached for a tissue and swiped at the tears. "She wanted nothing to do with talking and came at me. We struggled, and somehow, Nancy ended up with the knife in her chest. I was only trying to defend myself."

"Why didn't you call 911? They might have been able to save her."

"I knew how that would look. I was—"

"You knew that she would eventually die from her wound without medical help," Mitch said. "She'd already told you that you could never have Roger as long as she was alive."

Monica's eyes grew defiant. "That bitch will never call me a whore again."

Maddy quickly moved behind the desk and placed the young woman in handcuffs. "Monica Townsend, you're under arrest for the murder of Nancy Kennedy. You have the right to remain silent."

Monica sobbed as Maddy read the rest of the Miranda rights to her. Then they both walked out the door, and Maddy loaded her into the back of Mitch's squad car.

Before Mitch got in on the driver's side, Maddy whispered, "The good news is that we've got Nancy's killer. The bad news is that we may have to let her scumbag husband out of jail."

"Not if I can help it."

Monica Townsend sobbed all the way to the precinct and was still sniffling when they printed her and led her to a cell. Wanting to take no chances of her coordinating a story with Roger Kennedy in the next cell, Mitch had called ahead to Paul Rivera, the chief of police at the Cordova Police Department, and asked if they would house Roger in their jail for a few days. To his credit, despite the animosity between the two precincts, Chief Rivera immediately sent out a squad card to pick Kennedy up. Because of that, Roger Kennedy wouldn't know that his baby mama was also in custody. That would play to their advantage when they interrogated him again.

Nick Ryan watched the arrest procedure going on around him without saying a word until Maddy and Mitch were back at their desks.

"Great job, you two. We'll have the results from your suspect's DNA by late tomorrow. Maybe you can use it to get a confession."

"The DNA won't help our case," Mitch said. "Monica claims that Nancy Kennedy came at her with the butcher knife, and she had to fight her off. In the struggle, the knife landed in Kennedy's chest. That would explain her DNA on the murder weapon."

"As for confessions, we already have one—sorta," Maddy said. "Although she is sticking to her self-defense theory, she slipped up when I asked her why she didn't call 911."

"And?" Nick leaned in closer.

"And, I quote, 'That bitch will never call me a whore again.'"

"Even with that, it's not a slam dunk," Mitch said. "We'll let her stew in the cell for a few hours, then take another crack at her. Right now, the only thing we can pin on her is failure to stop and render aid and possibly involuntary manslaughter because she left Nancy dying on the floor."

"So where does that leave Roger Kennedy?" Nick asked.

"For now, we've also got him for failure to stop and render aid, but a good prosecutor can argue that because of his medical knowledge he had to be aware that pulling the knife out of a chest wound would leave a gaping hole causing the patient to bleed to death."

"Why do I feel better because that dirtbag isn't going to be able to walk away from all of this?" Maddy asked.

"Because he is a dirtbag, and in my view, he's just as much to blame as his girlfriend," Nick said.

"I agree one hundred percent. For now, though, we've done our job. We'll let the courts decide what to charge both of them with." She turned to Colt who had just come out of his office and walked over to her desk. "Any word on that flyover at Donovan's ranch?" she asked.

Colt nodded. "You're not going to like it. After searching for several hours on the coordinates that Mitch sent, they just wrapped it up and returned to Fort Worth."

"Tell me they found the crater," Maddy pleaded.

Colt shook his head. "No crater. No dead cows after several passes over the ranch."

"How could that be?" she asked. "Pamela Linden had proof."

"Unfortunately, more than likely, her proof was on her phone or computer, both of which are missing," Mitch said, shaking his head. "And that, ladies and gentlemen, is probably the motive for the double murders."

"You're thinking David Foster was merely collateral damage?" Nick asked.

Maddy narrowed her eyes, deep in thought. "There's got to be more to this story than that. Like how the killers knew that Linden would be at Foster's house that morning?"

Mitch shrugged. "Sounds like you and I need to pay Jeffrey Donovan another visit and see if we can get him to say something he shouldn't."

"Absolutely. He's probably not in the office today because of the holiday. In the meantime, why don't the three of us get a warrant and take a ride out to Donovan's ranch to look for the crater ourselves? I can't believe that the police helicopter missed it."

"Sounds like a plan," Colt said. "Hold off until I can get that warrant. We need everything to be done by the book. I'm not Judge Nelson's favorite person right now, though, since I tore him away from his kid's soccer game earlier to get the warrants for Townsend's apartment."

As they were preparing to leave, Nick's phone rang, and he stopped to answer it.

For the next few minutes, Maddy focused on his expressions, and although she could only hear one side of the conversation, it was obvious that whatever the person on the other end was saying, Nick was not happy about it.

After he hung up, he addressed them. "That was my sister. My mother took a nasty fall at the rehab center and apparently broke the hardware in her hip. She's back at the hospital, and they'll take her into surgery after the swelling goes down somewhat. Julie had an emergency and had to leave. Her youngest was injured in a hockey game and was taken to the ER."

He opened the desk drawer and grabbed his car keys. "Sorry, but I have to go. My mother shouldn't be alone right now."

"Of course, Nick," Colt said. "Call and update us when you can."

"I will." Nick turned to Maddy and Mitch. "None of us are convinced that Carl Linden killed himself, but right now, we have no other suspects in Pamela's death. The three of us have come a long way since our first meeting, so I trust that you'll keep me updated on the case until I can get back here, although I have no clue when that will be."

"Don't worry, man," Mitch said, patting him on the back. "We'll take care of things here. You just take care of your mother. If we're lucky, God gives us a good woman to mother us. It sounds like you've got one of those. She's lucky to have you. A lot of men would not be so caring. Know that we'll all be praying for her quick recovery."

Less than thirty minutes after Nick left, Colt handed Mitch the warrant to search Donovan's house and the entire property. On the way there they stopped at Mitch's house, loaded the golf cart on his trailer, and headed toward Cordova. Mitch called ahead to give the Cordova Police Department a heads-up and to see if they wanted to join in the search. He wasn't surprised when Sullivan answered and was less than friendly when he declined.

Once Mitch and Maddy got out to Donovan's property and were seated in the golf cart, they headed toward the south edge of the property where Pamela had noticed the dead cows. Just like the helicopter pilot had told them, there were no dead cows *or* a crater, although they did find a triangular area that looked like it had recently been covered with squares of sodded grass.

"You think this is what Pamela saw and mistook for hazardous materials?"

Maddy shook her head. "Deena said that Pamela was adamant about seeing large metal barrels."

Mitch bent down and used his hand to dig up the edge of one of the newly sodded squares. "Son of a—"

"What?" Maddy asked, bending down beside him.

"Whoever brought in the sod apparently cemented the hole beforehand. I just touched what I'm assuming is solid concrete."

"That makes me believe that this dump site is definitely the motive for the killings, especially because they went to so much trouble to haul off the dead cows and to bring in cement trucks."

"That's the only thing that makes sense," Mitch said. "Pamela talked to Donovan a couple of weeks before the murders. That must have tipped him off, and he tried to hide the evidence."

"I'll call my sister after we get back to the station and see if she can shed some light on this." Maddy made a 360 turn-around. "Not a snowball's chance in hell of finding a camera out here."

"Which is probably why whoever was responsible for this little sod-covered, toxic hole was confident about not being seen.

With Pamela Linden's house empty and no other ranches visible from here, this was the perfect spot for a hazardous dump."

"What do you want to do now?" Maddy asked as she snapped several pictures of the area.

"There's really nothing we *can* do right now. Like you said, Warner Chemicals is probably closed for the holiday. Tomorrow, I'll get Colt to get EPA down here. They have special equipment and can verify if there's toxic waste underneath this." He pointed at the sodded area. "But before they can do that, they'll have to remove the concrete." He whistled. "That's gonna be one helluva job and may take several days, maybe even a week."

Maddy was silent for a few minutes before she replied, "I think I need to pay another visit to Jeffrey Donovan in the morning."

"Not without me, you won't."

"Okay. We'll both go, but then you'll need to find a way to disappear and leave me alone with him for a few minutes. You said it yourself that the man is trying to get me into the sack. I'll use that to my advantage, but he's more likely to tell me something if you're not around."

"As much as I hate that idea, you've probably got a point. But I'm gonna be right outside his door the entire time."

Maddy nodded. "I'll call him first thing in the morning."

Even as those words left her mouth, her earlier bravado slipped a little. If Jeffrey Donovan was, indeed, responsible for the dumping site as well as the killings, did she really want to be alone with him for even a second? Tessa had called him a rotten egg. It sounded more like he might be a killer.

21

___

The next morning Maddy woke up feeling energized. Although she was looking forward to confronting Jeffrey Donovan about the possible toxic dump site on his property, she was still a little nervous about being alone in the same room with him. Knowing that Mitch would be right outside the door only went so far to dispel her fears.

After grabbing a breakfast burrito from the freezer, she put it in the microwave, brewed a cup of coffee, and sat down to call her sister Deena on the burner phone that Pearlie had bought for them.

Deena answered after the first ring. "I've been carrying this stupid phone around ever since you left. Tell me that you have some good news, that I can head back to Vineyard and live my normal, boring life."

"Wish I could, but it's still too risky. I do have some news, though. Today, Mitch and I are going to Warner Chemicals to question Jeffrey Donovan."

"I don't know, Maddy. Jeff doesn't really seem like the type to kill two people in cold blood. Besides, I would have recognized his voice when I heard the killer asking for me in Foster's living room. Trust me when I tell you that I will never forget that voice."

"People can be deceiving, Deena. Although Donovan has an alibi for the day of the murders, he could have hired someone to do the deed."

"Still doesn't sound like him."

Maddy caried the burrito from the microwave to the table and sat down to eat it. In between bites, she told her sister what they'd found at Donovan's ranch.

"What? The crater was cemented over?"

"Yes, and someone even took the time to haul in dirt and sod the entire area." Maddy paused. "Someone who was tipped off."

"Other than being a womanizer, Jeff's really one of the good guys. I can't believe he has it in him to hurt a flea."

"Money makes even the gentlest of men do crazy things. And speaking of money, did he ever mention having problems with it? Maybe he had a gambling debt like Foster?"

"If he did, he never told me about it. As much as I'm convinced Jeff's not your killer, I still need you to promise me that Mitch will be attached at your hip when you go to his office."

"That's a given," Maddy said, taking the last bite of her burrito and swallowing it with a big gulp of coffee. "I gotta run, Sis. Call me if you think of anything that might help when we talk to Donovan."

"Okay, I will. Stay safe."

Maddy hung up, placed her dishes in the sink, and headed out the door. It took nearly fifteen minutes longer than normal to get to the station because traffic was held up by a fender bender in the middle of the square. Apparently, the woman in the car that was hit from behind claimed she had a neck injury and demanded that she go to the hospital by ambulance.

That reeked of a lawsuit waiting to happen. *Not my circus, not my monkeys*, Maddy thought, as she was finally able to pass by the wrecked cars without a second glance. Besides, it looked like a cruiser was already on the scene.

When she arrived at the station, Mitch ran up to her as soon as she walked in.

"I called Warner Chemicals. Donovan's not there yet. The operator said he usually comes in around ten."

"Must be nice to be him," Maddy said, sarcastically. "Actually, I'm kind of glad about that as it will give us some time to run over to Cordova and question Roger Kennedy again before we bring him back here. Right now, he doesn't know that we have Monica in a jail cell. Let's see if he continues to spew lies about her."

"Sounds like a plan. Let me tell Colt first, and then I'll meet you by the car. I'll drive."

She nodded, glancing over at Nick's empty desk, wondering how things were going with his mother. She'd said a prayer for her last night and hoped she was doing all right.

It didn't take Mitch long to get to the car and slide into the driver's side.

"Good cop, bad cop, Maddy?"

She laughed. "Don't even go there. Like I told you before, your imitation of a good cop is like the big bad wolf in grandma's bed waiting for Little Red Riding Hood."

"Is it really that bad?"

"Gramma, what big eyes you have," Maddy joked. When she saw the hurt look that flashed across his face, she added, "Hey, intimidating people plays to your advantage most of the time. And guess what? Right after we leave Warner Chemicals, we can check out that truck stop right across the Oklahoma border. I heard they have awesome home-cooked meals."

His eyes lit up. "As good as that sounds, I'll pass. Let's just stop at Wendy's, and I'll get one of those Apple Pecan Salads with low-fat dressing."

Maddy stared at him. "Who are you, and what happened to my partner?"

He laughed. "I promised my little lady that I'd lose fifteen pounds by the end of the year. She got a little frisky after hearing that and last night—"

"Stop! The last thing I need is to have the visual of you and your sex stuff stuck in my head all day. No more talking till after we question Kennedy."

When they walked into the Cordova Police Station, the air was so frosty that Maddy blew out a breath to see if it came out as an icy mist and was surprised that it didn't. They walked over to Sullivan's desk and stood for several seconds before he looked up.

"Are you two here to take your prisoner?"

Mitch nodded. "We'd like to use your interrogation room first, though. We need to question him before he finds out that his mistress is in custody."

"Nobody's using it right now." Sullivan pointed to the room in the corner. "Go sit down, and I'll have an officer bring Kennedy to you."

"Thanks," Maddy said, shoving Mitch toward the interrogation room before he said something to Sullivan about the ballgame. She was surprised when Sullivan brought it up himself.

"As much as I hate saying this, you played me well, Mitchell. That NCIS guy has some major skills."

"We really pulled the wool—" he stopped talking when Maddy kicked him, "pulled off one of the best games that both teams have ever played," he said, instead.

Sullivan bit his lower lip to keep from smiling. "Hope you don't get a nasty bruise on your shin, Mitchell." He walked away, chuckling at his own joke.

When they were seated in the interrogation room, Maddy punched Mitch's shoulder, playfully. "Now, that was what a good cop would say. No use rubbing it in, especially since this house has accommodated us with Kennedy," she said just as the young officer brought the prisoner into the room.

After the officer closed the door behind him, Maddy faced Kennedy and began. "We just have a few more questions before we take you back to Vineyard."

"Do I need a lawyer?"

"That's up to you, but we're only going to ask what we probably already know."

He nodded. "I've admitted that I found Nancy on the bedroom floor. What else do you need to hear from me?"

"We wondered if you knew that your girlfriend had told your wife that she was pregnant with your baby the day Nancy was murdered."

He narrowed his eyes and swallowed hard. "What girlfriend?"

"Oh, you know, the blonde in the picture that the PI your wife hired took of you and her. Where is that picture, anyway?"

He shrugged. "Guess Nancy destroyed it."

"More likely scenario is that you took it when you pulled the knife out of her chest and left her there to bleed to death."

"You can't prove that," he said, defiantly.

"That remains to be seen," Maddy said. "But back to your girlfriend. What was her name—Christine, if I recall correctly."

His head bobbed up and down. "Like I told you, I don't know her last name."

"You got a girl pregnant, and you don't even know her last name?" Mitch slammed his hand on the desk hard enough that the Cordova officer opened the door and looked in to make sure that everything was okay. After Mitch nodded to him, he closed the door, and Mitch turned back to Kennedy. "Lucky for us, we do know her name, and I need you to know that Monica Townsend is in the Vineyard jail as we speak. Right now, she's singing like a bird."

Kennedy's eyes widened. "Number one, she doesn't know anything, and number two, she would never say anything that might hurt me."

"Probably not, but after we explain to her what happens to babies born in prison cells, she just might have a change of heart."

Kennedy cupped his head into his hands and took a noisy, deep breath. After a minute, he looked up. "She would only be trying to save her own skin if she blamed me for Nancy's death."

"We know," Maddy said. "She's already admitted killing your wife."

"Then you know that I didn't do it. Monica and Nancy fought over the knife, and it was an accident." When both Maddy and Mitch nodded, he continued, "So, why am I still in cuffs?"

Mitch got up and walked around to lift him off the chair. "Because you're not the sharpest knife in the drawer, pardon the pun. You've just admitted to knowing that your girlfriend killed your wife, and that, sir, makes you an accessory after the fact and gets you three years in Huntsville along with whatever other sentence the judge will tack on for failure to stop and render aid."

"Don't forget the possibility of charging him with involuntary manslaughter because, by his own admission, he did leave his wife to die," Maddy added, raising her eyebrows at Kennedy. "What do you have to say now, big guy?"

"I want a lawyer."

"Smartest thing you've said all day." Mitch shoved him toward the door. "Let's get him out of here."

As SOON AS they walked into the Vineyard Police Station, Landers rushed up to them. "I'll take it from here. You two need to get on the road to Warner Chemicals before Donovan decides to take a long lunch."

"Thanks, Danny," Maddy said, grabbing Mitch's arm. "Come on. Let's see if we can bat a hundred and catch another killer today."

Mitch laughed. "Stick to girly things, Maddy. The correct phrase is batting a thousand."

"Whatever!" She shrugged and then picked up her phone. "I'm gonna call Martin Warner to give him a heads up that we'll be coming over there to talk to Jeffrey Donovan again."

"Good idea." Mitch grabbed the keys to the cruiser and pushed Maddy toward the door. "Come on, my little baseball expert, let's go to Oklahoma," he teased.

"Shut up! I may not know all the stuff about baseball, but if you'll remember, I'm the one who got Ryan to catch for the team."

"And for that I am eternally grateful. For now, let's talk about things you do know—like PMS."

She glared at him. "When did you get so misogynistic? If I were you I wouldn't say another word to me the rest of the trip, or I might have to tell the guys how you humbled yourself in front of Ryan." She lowered her voice. "'*I don't hate you, Ryan. I just had to act like I was in charge.*'"

"You wouldn't."

I definitely would, so keep your mouth shut and your eyes on the road."

"Wow! I never knew you had such a mean streak, kiddo."

"Well, now you do."

During the forty-five-minute drive to Rosemont, they devised a plan on how to handle Donovan. At the gate, they were instructed to go directly to Martin Warner's office. Seems he wanted to talk to them before they saw Donovan.

"Wonder what that's all about," Maddy said.

"Probably wants to cross his t's and dot his i's," Mitch responded. "I'm sure he's curious about why we're returning to talk to his lawyer again."

After entering the main office building, they were directed to the elevator and told that the CEO was waiting for them. Before they exited on the third floor, Mitch turned to Maddy. "Let's be really vague to keep him from picking up the phone and warning Donovan, if he hasn't already done that. We both know that first impressions can be very telling when the person hasn't had time to think about the answers to our questions."

"Okay," Maddy said. "I'll let you do the talking."

They exited the elevator, walked up to the desk, and flashed their badges.

"He's expecting you," the redheaded receptionist said as she directed them to his office.

Martin Warner stood up and greeted them when they entered. "Officers, I have to ask why you've come all this way to have another chat with Jeff. I believe he's already told you that he was out of town on the day of the murders and that the missing woman never told him anything that might help with your investigation."

"That's true," Mitch said. "It's just that there are a few more questions that he might be able to help us with."

"Like what?" Warner motioned for them to sit down in the two chairs across from his desk.

Mitch shook his head. "We're kind of in a time crunch here. Our plan is to speak to Donovan and then be on our way," he said, effectively avoiding Warner's question.

The CEO stared first at Mitch, then shifted his focus to Maddy. "Have you found your sister, yet?"

"Unfortunately, no. We're hoping that Mr. Donovan can shed a little light on that."

"Like I've already said, Jeff insists that he told you all he knows."

"Understood," Maddy said. "We'll just ask him a couple of questions and then be out of your hair in short order." She glanced down at her watch. "So, with your permission, we'd like to head to his office now."

Again, Warner stared before hitting his intercom and instructing the receptionist to call Donovan to let him know that the police were on their way to speak to him.

On the elevator down to the second floor, Maddy said, "Is it just me, or did you get a weird vibe from him?"

"It wasn't just you. Wanna bet that he called Donovan himself the second we left his office?"

"To warn him?"

"We're about to find out," Mitch said as they exited the elevator and headed to Donovan's office. "Oh, and I've changed my mind. I am not letting you alone with that weasel."

"I was hoping you'd say that."

Jeffrey Donovan stood and motioned for them to come in, his eyes trained on Maddy. "It's good to see you again, but I was hoping that it would be more social than official. You were going to call me when you found time to meet up again."

"Sorry. I've been really busy," Maddy said, pointing to the chairs. "May we sit?"

He nodded. "Since Martin said you had more questions about your sister, I take it that you haven't found her yet." He turned to Mitch. "Is that what this is about?"

Mitch shook his head, then sat down, facing Donovan. "We understand that you inherited a ranch in Cordova. Is that correct?"

Again, Donovan nodded. "Yes, but why is that of interest to you?"

"We were told that you rented out parts of that land to local ranch owners to house some of their herds. Is that also correct?"

"Yes. But I have to tell you, I'm still trying to figure out why any of this interests you. So, unless you get to the point, I have work piled on my desk that needs my attention."

Maddy leaned forward. "We need a list of those ranchers."

He pursed his lips. "Do you have a warrant?"

Mitch handed him the envelope he'd been holding. After studying the contents for a few minutes, Donovan opened his desk, pulled out several folders, and shoved them across the desk.

Mitch reached for them, then slid his chair closer to Maddy's so they could both read what was in the files.

"There are three local ranchers renting space, but what's this Texas Livestock, Inc.? Do they house cattle on your land as well?"

"They do, although they pay a much higher price since they needed more space than the others."

"And who pays the monthly bills for them?" Mitch asked.

Donovan grabbed another folder from his desk drawer and opened it. Finally, he shoved a piece of paper across the desk to Mitch. "Looks like it's paid by an LLC out of Tulsa."

"So, you have no idea who writes the checks?" Mitch asked.

Donovan laughed. "This is the twenty-first century, Officer. Everything is paid by bank transfers nowadays."

Mitch bristled, but to his credit, his voice remained calm. "I guess my next question is how does Warner Chemicals dispose of the waste products from the manufacture of your—" he glanced down at his phone—"fluoropolymers?"

Donovan shifted on his chair. "Where are you going with this?"

"Humor us a little longer, Jeff. I promise that we'll be out of your hair soon." Maddy smiled, hoping the use of his first name might make him a little less defensive.

Donovan took a deep breath and opened the file in front of him. "They are transported to a hazardous waste facility north of Tulsa."

"May I see that invoice?" After reading it, Mitch looked up. "Who's Arnold Thacker?"

"He's our chief of security. He takes care of all the billings for waste product removal."

"Do you think you could ask him to come up here to speak with us? I promise we'll be on our merry way right after that." Maddy said.

He hesitated for a few seconds, then pushed the intercom and asked his secretary to call the head of security. They made small talk until the man arrived. Maddy took a few seconds to size him up.

Arnold Thacker stood about five-eight and was built like a football player, leaving no doubt that most of his stocky build was muscles.

"What can I do for you?" Thacker asked.

"We're looking into how Warner Chemicals deals with the waste products of your manufacturing," Mitch said. "We were told you handled that. Is that correct?"

Thatcher glanced toward Donovan before he spoke. "It is. What's this all about?"

"We have it on good authority that someone is dumping toxic waste on Donovan's ranch, and since Warner Chemicals is the only big industry in the area, we came to you first."

"What?" Donovan stood up. "What evidence do you have for that crazy accusation?"

"We're not at liberty to say right now," Maddy answered before turning back to Thacker. "Would it be possible to get a look at the process involved in transferring your chemical waste products?"

His eyes hardened before he repeated what Donovan had asked earlier. "Do you have a warrant?"

Mitch pointed to the paper in Donovan's hand. "We do."

Thacker glanced toward the company lawyer who nodded. "Well, then, if I could get you to follow me, we'll head over to the factory. I've got a meeting in thirty minutes, though, so we'll have to make this quick."

They followed him out the door and rode with him in a golf cart to the manufacturing facility down the road. At the door, Thacker nodded to a man who was obviously the supervisor. A quick look revealed that there were more than a hundred employees in hard hats, all working on various production lines.

"The waste products are stored in the basement," Thacker said as he led them to the elevator.

Once there, they got their first look at forty or fifty barrels in the corner of the large room, all labeled as hazardous. Thacker pointed to them. "They're kept here until they're transported on an eighteen-wheeler to the facility in Tulsa twice a month."

Maddy's burner phone rang at that moment, and she said, "Excuse me. I have to take this call." She turned her back to the two men and whispered into the phone. "Deena, I can't talk right now."

"I just wanted to let you—" She stopped. "Maddy, who's in the room with you?"

"Mitch and the security chief at Warner Chemicals. Why?" Maddy turned slightly and caught Thacker watching her.

"Move closer to them and be quiet."

Maddy had no idea why her sister wanted her to do that, but she did just as she requested and took several steps closer to the two men as Thacker was describing the mechanics of moving hazardous material to Mitch.

"Oh my God!"

Maddy's eyes widened. "What?"

"That voice. That's the man I heard asking David where I was before I heard the gunshots."

Maddy's eyes widened even more. "You're sure?"

"One-hundred percent sure. I hear that voice in my dreams." Deena paused. "Maddy, get away from him as soon as you can."

Maddy cupped her hand over her mouth and whispered, "Call Colt and tell him what you just told me. Tell him to have one of the guys start the paperwork for a broader warrant, and then to bring the rest of the guys over here ASAP. I'll get Mitch and leave as soon as we can get away." When she hung up, she made eye contact with Thacker.

"Why were you whispering?" he asked, suspiciously.

"I didn't want to disturb you two. It was just my daughter. She's stranded at the library, so I'll have to leave now to pick her up." She turned to Mitch "Let's allow Mr. Thacker to get back to his job. I think we're done here."

Mitch looked at her, confusion clouding his eyes. Before he could respond, Thacker walked up behind him and hit him in the back of the head with the butt of a gun. Even before Mitch hit the floor, Maddy had her own weapon out and pointed it at the man who she now was certain was a ruthless killer.

"Drop your gun on the floor and kick it over to me," Thacker instructed as he pulled Mitch's gun from the shoulder holster, never taking his eyes off Maddy.

When she hesitated, he bent down and put his gun to Mitch's head.

22

———————

"Wait," Maddy screamed as she dropped her weapon then kicked it over to Thacker before he pulled the trigger and killed her partner.

His face crinkled in an evil smile. "Good choice. Now do the same with your phone." He waited until he had the phone in his hand before he instructed her to walk over to the wall and sit down against it. "Keep your hands out in front of you where I can see them at all times."

Do what he says, Maddy, Tessa said, suddenly appearing next to her. **I've met a lot of crazy men in my life, and believe me when I tell you, this dude is the real deal.**

Maddy walked slowly to the wall and sat down, keeping her eye on Mitch. Despite the fact that he was unconscious, his chest rose and fell with every breath he took. She breathed a sigh of relief.

She watched her dead sister walk over to stand next to Thacker, and, although she knew that Tessa really couldn't do anything to help her, just seeing her there gave her a sliver of hope that she and Mitch might make it out of the basement alive.

"I repeat myself. Who were you whispering to on the phone?" Thacker asked, placing her phone with her gun on the table behind him.

"I've already told you. It was my daughter."

Tessa shouted. **Tell him the truth. If he knows that Deena is alive and well and can finger him for the murders, it might keep you and your partner alive a little longer. At least until I can figure out if there's anything I can do to help you.**

"You're right," Maddy said. "It wasn't my daughter. It was my sister Deena, and she recognized your voice. We know that you killed David Foster and Pamela Linden."

"Do you have any proof of that other than the fact that some woman thinks she recognized my voice?" He smirked. "Not even a dumbass like Donovan would embarrass himself with that so-called evidence in front of a judge."

"See, that's where you're wrong," Maddy said, watching as Tessa inched closer to the security guard. She decided to lie to the man. "Pamela Linden sent the pictures that she took from her helicopter to Deena."

His eyes hardened. "She swore the only copies of those pictures were on her laptop, which I have."

"And you believed her? If so, that would put you in that same category as your friend, Donovan." Maddy paused. "Is that why you killed her?"

"Are you sure you should be questioning me about that? What little time you have left on this earth might be better spent telling me where your sister is. If you do that, I'll let her live once she gives me the pictures."

Maddy stared at him. "You must think I'm as stupid as you and Donovan. We all know why you killed Pamela, but why you killed David Foster is another question. Was he not a colleague of yours? Or was he your partner in the dump site fiasco with you and Donovan?"

"Donovan? He couldn't find his ass with a map and a flash-light. He had no idea that when he was transferring the money for the waste disposal to the LLC account that it was going directly into my offshore account." Thacker threw back his head and laughed out loud. "The same goes for David Foster. He was a loser and should never have been hired here in the first place. I tried to talk Martin out of hiring him, but he didn't listen. I always wondered if Foster had something on the Warners that they didn't want made public."

"If Foster wasn't in cahoots with you, why kill him? Surely, you must have known that he had gambling debts and goons in the wings waiting either for a money exchange or to rough him up. He would have jumped at a cash payout for his silence."

Good job, Maddy. Keep him talking. I'm trying to figure out how to somehow tip the table over and get your gun closer to you.

"Okay."

Thacker narrowed his eyes. "Who are you talking to?"

She gave him a sly grin. "I'm going to tell you, but you won't believe me. I'm talking to my dead sister, who, by the way, is standing right behind you."

Slowly, he turned in a circle. With his attention off her for a few seconds, Maddy pulled the burner phone from her back pocket, hit video, and then shoved it under her shirt.

He glared at her. "Nice try. I'm beginning to think that you're as batty as Foster. The idiot thought he could blackmail us."

"Us?"

"I meant me. He called me late Thursday night to tell me about the meeting with that woman the next morning. He said he'd confiscate all the evidence she had, and for a little more money, he'd get her out of the way permanently."

"How did you know my sister was there too?"

"Foster told me. I knew what I had to do—and I did it." He

pointed the gun directly at her. "No more talking. Where's your sister?"

Maddy shrugged. "I have no idea. We only communicate by phone. She's a smart girl, so I assume that wherever she is, you won't find her."

Just then, the door opened, and Martin Warner walked in. He stared at Thacker for a few minutes, then walked to the table. "Is this her gun?"

Thacker nodded. "She knows."

Warner pulled a pair of rubber gloves from his pocket and slowly put them on. "Knows what?"

Before Thacker had time to respond, the CEO fired two shots into the security chief's chest.

Thank the Lord, Tessa said.

But Maddy wasn't so sure about that. Why had the man put on gloves before he killed his own security chief? In her mind, there was only one reason. He didn't want his prints on the gun. But why?

"So, Detective Castillo, by now you're probably thinking that you should have let this go when you discovered there was no evidence that Warner Chemicals had anything to do with the deaths."

How could he know that?

A light bulb went off in Maddy's head. "The only way you could know that is if you were the one who tried to destroy the evidence by covering up the crater on Donovan's property. You knew that Thacker had killed Foster and that other woman."

"Beautiful and smart, I see. And yes, but unfortunately for you, the world will never know all that. Thacker was the one who came up with what we now know was an ill-advised plan to save thousands of dollars by burying our own hazardous waste. Too bad you found out and confronted him." He walked over and bent down to feel for the security chief's pulse. "He had no choice but to kill you and your partner. When I walked in and discovered what he'd done, he came at me, but I was able to wrestle his gun from him and kill him before he killed me." He pulled off his gloves, picked up Thacker's weapon, and pretended to fire it so that his fingerprints were on it.

"Nobody's going to believe you were able to manhandle your security guy. Soaking wet, you probably don't weigh more than a hundred and seventy pounds." She pointed to the dead man. "Now, take a good look at him. I'll bet he played tackle for some Big Ten school."

"Add smart mouth to your resume." He grinned at her. "But who will dare question me when I'm the only one alive to talk about it?"

"How will you explain a bullet from my gun in Thacker's chest if you shot him with his own gun?" she fired back, then grinned. "And there's still the issue of the crater on Donovan's ranch."

"I'll figure it out. With Thacker gone and you two also out of the picture, I'll just say he was a lone wolf. I was smart enough to make sure everything was in his name and nothing leads back to me."

"What did Foster have on you?" Maddy asked.

"What do you mean?"

"Your security chief told us that the only reason you hired Foster in the first place was because he had something on your family."

Warner laughed. "Thacker always did talk too much, but it doesn't matter if you know as you'll take that knowledge to your grave. It might even make you a little sympathetic as to why I did what I had to do."

Keep him talking, Maddy. I have an idea, Tessa said, slowly pushing the table towards Warner's back.

"Tell me. It's the least you can do before you kill me," she said.

He stared at her for a moment with a look that could almost be mistaken for sadness. "I was the oldest son and my father's pride and joy until my sister, Janet, came along. After that, she was the only thing my dad ever noticed, and even when my younger brother, Josh, was born, it was always only his beautiful red-haired daughter."

He paused and turned away from her for a minute before continuing, "One day, Janet and I were swimming, and my father got an important phone call. He told me to keep an eye on my sister while he went to his office to finish the call. I was trying to make the swim team at school and was concentrating on how long I could hold my breath underwater. When my father returned, I heard him scream, a sound I will never forget as long as I live."

"What happened?"

He swallowed hard. "Janet was floating on top of the water. He tried to revive her, but she'd been under too long." Martin sniffed back a tear. "He never forgave me. The only reason he had the Board appoint me as CEO when his bad heart forced him to retire was because Josh had two more years of college left."

"Is that what Foster had on you?"

He nodded. "Got drunk one night and told him the story. He never let me forget that he knew."

"A sad story, no doubt, but what does that have to do with you illegally dumping the hazardous waste?" Maddy knew if there was even the slightest chance of a miracle for her and Mitch, she needed to keep this man talking.

"I spent my entire adult life trying to prove myself to him. I knew my time here was limited, that my father would demote me as soon as my younger brother graduated from college, so I tried to do something that I thought would make him realize that I did have the goods to run the company."

"What did you do?" Maddy asked, wondering what Tessa had in mind as she had nearly reached Warner with the table.

"I invested most of the company's cash in the crypto market. At the time, people were making a fortune going that route." He paused. "At first, we were also pulling in the big bucks, but then...Well, you know what happened. We lost everything. There was no way I could go to my father and tell him. One day I was talking to Arnold about our hazardous waste disposal. We spent a fortune sending it to Tulsa. So, we—"

Just then, Tessa slammed the table into Warner's backside, causing him to fall forward and jarring the gun out of his hand. As it clattered to the floor Maddy jumped up and got to it seconds before Warner did.

"Don't move or I swear, you'll see the devil," she said. She retrieved her cell phone from the floor and called 911. "This is Detective Madelyn Castillo of the Vineyard Police Department. I'm in the basement of the manufacturing building at Warner Chemicals, and I need an ambulance now. I have an officer down. I also need you to notify Chief Winslow of my location." She pulled the burner phone out from under her uniform and held it in front of Warner. "Just in case you try to talk your way out of all this and act like you're Mr. Innocence Personified, know that I recorded your every word."

He glared at her before he charged. She fired a single shot, hitting him in the abdomen, causing him to fall backwards.

"Come at me again, and you're a dead man," she warned, just as the paramedics arrived and rushed over to Mitch. She pointed at Warner, who had closed his eyes and was moaning in pain. "We'll need another ambulance."

"Yes, Ma'am," the younger of the two said. He phoned it in

while the other medic continued to work on Mitch, taking his vital signs. Then, he moved over to evaluate Warner's condition.

Mitch opened his eyes and began to fight with them.

"Whoa, Mitch," Maddy said, bending down next to him. "You took a pretty good hit to the head. Let these guys do their job."

"You okay?"

She nodded. "Better than okay, and the next words out of my mouth are gonna make that big bump on the back of your head hurt a lot less."

"What?"

"As of right now, partner, you and I are batting a thousand."

MADDY GLANCED around the table as they finished their dinner. These were her people. People she loved. Nick Ryan, who was sitting directly across from her, caught her looking and smiled. It had been two and a half months since they'd put Kennedy, Monica Townsend, and Martin Warner behind bars. All three were at Huntsville serving out long sentences for their crimes. Towsend pleaded self-defense for her part in Nancy Kennedy's death, but both she and Roger Kennedy got twenty-five years for failure to render aid and the more serious charge of involuntary manslaughter.

Warner didn't get away so easily and was serving life without parole for the first-degree murder of Arnold Thacker and accessory to the murders of Pamela Linden and David Foster. In her heart, Maddy knew that he and Thacker were also responsible for the pseudo-suicide of Carl Linden, despite Carl's note that claimed he'd killed his wife and her boyfriend in a jealous rage. But they had no evidence to prove that theory, not even when they'd scoured the email exchanges between the two killers.

The EPA had spent almost the entire two months cleaning up the toxic mess on Jeffrey Donovan's ranch. But because one of the barrels had tipped over and leaked into the soil, they'd quarantined the ranch for a year and possibly longer if it still tested positive for the poisons after that. The price of the clean-up to Warner Chemicals was north of two million dollars, not including the hefty fine that was also imposed. Martin Warner Sr., who was forced out of retirement, was now facing a court battle with Jeffrey Donovan, who, after leaving the company, had filed a multimillion-dollar civil suit against them.

All this because one very stupid man, filled with insecurity and low self-esteem, had tried to impress his daddy.

Maddy smiled back at Nick, who had brought his mother with him, then continued her scan of the rest of the people at the table. With their bellies full, they were just relaxing with a cup of coffee and making small talk. Besides her sisters, Colt and Danny Landers were there, along with Mitch, Sara, and Sara's sister, Kelly. The two teens, Colt and Lainey's daughter, Gracie, and Maddy's own daughter, Jessie, were gigging at something on Jess's phone. Maddy hated that they were growing up so fast and soon would be into boys and whatever else teenage girls gravitated toward these days.

Who was she kidding? Jess already had boys calling her at all hours, and Maddy couldn't help but notice the way her face lit up when she was talking to one boy in particular.

She wasn't ready for that phase of her daughter's life yet. She needed at least ten more years. But she knew that she couldn't stop the process. Jessie was already talking about playing in the band at the University of Texas.

Oh, Lord. Maddy wasn't sure she could handle it with her being so far away—and no parental control. She and Robbie Castillo had been sweethearts all through high school and college, so she really hadn't been much of a party animal.

Watching the way the young boys reacted to Jessie and her obvious delight in their attention, she suspected that her daughter would blossom in that party scene.

Maddy looked away from Jess and caught Nick staring at her again. She couldn't help herself and smiled back. He'd left town right before all the drama with Roger Kennedy and Martin Warner had played out. And as he'd promised his sister, he'd made the permanent move to Leroy within two weeks to care for his mother, who was now in a wheelchair.

He surprised them last month and showed up at the station. Everyone had welcomed him with open arms, including Mitch, who hadn't stopped singing his praise since that miraculous play at home plate at the Labor Day ballgame. Somehow, Nick had managed to get Maddy alone for a few minutes and confessed that he hadn't stopped thinking about her since he'd moved away. He made it clear that although the timing wasn't perfect, he was ready to see if she would ever consider a romantic relationship with him, now that he was no longer her colleague.

Although Maddy felt the same way about him, she'd tried to play hard to get, but in the end, she remembered how close she'd come to permanently checking out of this world—how she'd thought she and Mitch would never leave that basement alive.

And damn! The guy made her tingle all over when he looked at her.

She'd agreed to meet him at a quaint bed and breakfast in a small town outside of Wichita Falls. They'd spent the entire weekend, getting to know each other...among other more fun things.

A shame they'd wasted money on the extra room.

Maddy was aware that he was still grieving for his wife, and several times, she'd given him the option of just being friends with benefits. Without saying the L word, he'd answered that it was not what he was looking for—that he wanted more. They'd started their long-distance romance, talking every night on the phone. She had no idea if this relationship would last, but if she'd only learned one thing from her sister, Deena, it was to grab life by the horns and to live every day like it was your last.

Meeting his mom for the first time had been a little scary, but the two of them hit it off almost instantly. What's more, her own mother hadn't stopped chatting with Nick's mom since they'd sat down at the table.

Maybe that was a good sign.

Carolyn and Maddy's stepdad had arrived from Florida the week before, despite the fact that Chuck was still recovering from broken ribs.

Tessa had disappeared right after she'd shoved the table into Martin Warner. Maddy knew that sooner or later, they'd have to tell their mother about her dead daughter, but she decided that the Thanksgiving dinner table was not the right place to do it.

"I've got an idea," Carolyn said, interrupting Maddy's thoughts. "We all have busy lives and so much to be thankful for. Why don't we go around the table and tell each other what one of them is?"

"Good idea, Mom," Lainey said. "You go first."

"Okay. I'm thankful that God gave me five wonderful daughters, even though he took one back. I know Tessa's in heaven waiting to see all of us again."

Maddy heard Kate gasp and gave her a don't-you-dare-tell-her look.

"And I'm also thankful to have been loved by two God-fearing men in my life," Carolyn added.

The others took turns verbalizing how blessed their lives were, and when it came to Kate, Danny stood up and faced the matriarch of the family.

"I'm thankful that this family has adopted me like one of

their own, but I want more. If your daughter will have me, I'd like to spend the rest of my life with her—with your blessing, of course."

Carolyn's eyes brimmed with tears. "Kate couldn't have picked a better man. I know her father would have loved you. Welcome to the family, Danny."

With a big smile on his face, he bent down on one knee in front of Kate. "I don't know what I did to deserve someone like you, but what I do know is that I can't live without you. Will you marry me, Kate Garcia?"

"Yes," she whispered, fighting back tears of her own.

After everyone congratulated the couple, Lainey stood up. "Colt, Gracie, and I have an announcement of our own—something we're especially thankful for." She paused and looked at her daughter. "This young lady will be a big sister to a baby brother in five months."

"Oh my," Carolyn exclaimed. "This has been the best day of my life."

When everyone had taken a turn giving thanks, Mitch growled, "Yeah, yeah, we're all feeling pretty good about our lives. My only question is where's the dessert?"

Maddy looked at Sara, who nodded. "He's doing so well on his new diet and has already lost ten pounds. I told him today was reward day."

Mitch nailed Maddy with his eyes. "Is dessert your mother's Pumpkin Pie Crunch?"

"It is."

He raised his hands up in the air. "Hallelujah! Bring me a big piece with lots of whipped cream."

Maddy looked again at Sara.

Before Sara had a chance to respond, Mitch said, "My little lady made homemade whipped cream. She used sweetener, so it has no carbs."

Maddy laughed. "So, now, you're a carbs expert?"

"I am, Maddy, thanks to both you and Sara."

"Good for you, partner," Maddy turned to Sara. "One question. Do you have a hidden coffee can?"

"What woman doesn't?" the petite woman replied with a wink.

"Crap!" Mitch said, pulling out his wallet.

"I'll get my fifty bucks later," Maddy said as she summoned her sisters to the kitchen. "Come on. Let's go dish up Mom's special dessert." She stood up and headed for the kitchen, followed by her sisters.

As soon as they were all there, Maddy closed the door. "Kate, I was gonna tell Mom about Tessa, but she was so happy seeing all of us together that I couldn't bring myself to do it."

I'm glad you didn't, Tessa said, suddenly appearing and leaning up against the stove. **Every night, she asks the Good Lord to take care of me. It would break her heart to think that I'm still hanging around, haunting my sisters.**

"I agree," Lainey said. "We'll just keep it our little secret for now."

You won't have to do that, anymore.

Maddy raised her eyebrows. "One of us will probably always find ourselves in a jam, Tessa. I honestly don't even want to think about what would have happened if you hadn't literally saved my life."

Tessa smiled. **I'm curious. How did you explain that to people?**

Maddy laughed. "I lied. Said that Warner backed up into the table and lost his balance."

You always were a great liar. Tessa smiled, then her face turned serious. **I'm here to say goodbye.** She teared up. **I love you all so much.**

"Tessa, please don't say that. We need you," Kate begged.

You really don't, Katie. You all have come together in every crisis and can take care of each other now better than I ever could. She pointed up. **The Big Guy has other plans for me.** She walked over to the door and said over her shoulder, **Goodbye, my sweet sisters. We'll meet again someday.**

And then she disappeared.

"Did she have—"

"She did, Katie. Our girl has finally gotten her wings." Maddy sighed. "Goodbye, Tessa. Rest in peace."

ACKNOWLEDGMENTS

This past year has been hard for me. I lost my high school sweetheart after 55 years of marriage, but I know he's in heaven watching over me, encouraging me, still protecting me.

I also lost my brother Don and my sister Dotzie last year. I know they are in heaven with the rest of my siblings and our mom and dad. Had I not grown up with these people, I might never have known how to love unconditionally. Thankfully, I still have my baby sister, Lilly, who has always been my best friend. I don't know what I'd do without her.

Next comes my kids and grandkids who make every day worth getting out of bed for. Thanks, Nicole and Dennis, Brody and Abby, Grayson, Caden, Ellie, and Alice. I love you all so much.

And thanks to the Bunko Babes, my sisters from other mothers. For over 30 years, you've kept me supplied with humorous wisecracks, all of which go directly into my books.

I can never give enough thanks to my biggest supporter, my agent, Christine Witthohn, who has made this journey way easier than it should have been, both as my voice to the editors as well as my friend. I love this woman.

And to my fabulous critique partner, Joni Sauer-Folger, who always makes me laugh with her WTF comments. (Check out her books.) Also, to my wonderful beta readers, who kept me honest —Christine Keniston, Abby Lipperman, and Ronda Pollack.

And last but not least, thanks goes to my awesome publisher, Tanya Ann Crosby at Oliver Heber Books as well as to all her talented, exceptional staff, who go out of their way to make this process so painless. I am so grateful to have found them.

ALSO BY LIZBETH LIPPERMAN

As Liz Lipperman

Jordan McAllister Mysteries

Liver Let Die

Beef Stolen-Off

Murder for the Halibut

Chicken Caccia-Killer

Smothered, Covered & Dead

Enchi Lotta Bodies

Steak Through the Heart

Shorts

Can't Buy Me Love

As Lizbeth Lipperman

Garcia girls Mysteries

Heard it Through the Grapevine

Jailhouse Glock

Mission to Kill

Rock Around the Corpse

Deadly Triangle

Romance

Mortal Deception (a Romantic Mystery)

Shattered (a Romantic Thriller)

SWEEPERS: A Kiss to Die For (a Prequel to Die Once More)

SWEEPERS: Die Once More (an International Romantic Thriller)

ABOUT THE AUTHOR

Liz Lipperman started writing many years ago, even before she retired from the medical field. Wasting many years thinking she was a romance writer but always having to deal with the pesky villains who kept popping up in her stories, she finally gave up and decided since she read mysteries and obviously wrote them, why fight it? She has two mystery series: the Jordan McAllister Mysteries (formerly the Clueless Cook Mysteries) and the Garcia Girls Mysteries (formally the Dead Sister Talking Mysteries, which are available in all formats.) You might also want to check out her Romantic Thrillers, Mortal Deception and Shattered Dreams as well as a military thriller titled Die Once More with the prequel to that book titled, A Kiss to Die For.

She wants readers to know that her G rated cozies are written as Liz Lipperman and her PG rated, grittier mysteries as Lizbeth Lipperman. Check out her web page for more detailed listings and description of her books along with reviews and trailers. www.lizlipperman.com

Lipperman lives north of Dallas with her family close by. When she's not writing she spends her time spoiling her four wonderful grandchildren.

OLIVERHEBERBOOKS

A small press bound by the belief that every voice matters.

Sign up for our newsletter to learn about new releases and more.
https://oliver-heberbooks.com/subscribe/

Follow us on social media:

facebook.com/oliverheberbooks
instagram.com/oliverheberbooks
amazon.com/oliverheberbooks
youtube.com/@OliverHeberBooksPublisher

www.ingramcontent.com/pod-product-compliance
Lightning Source LLC
Chambersburg PA
CBHW021344150726
47989CB00005B/2088